TRUSTING TANNER
By
Nicky James

Trusting Tanner
Copyright © 2016 by Nicky James
Re-edited 2017

This is a work of fiction. Names, characters, businesses, places, events, and incidents are either the products of the author's imagination or used in a fictitious manner. Any resemblance to actual persons, living or dead, or actual events is purely coincidental.

Cover Artist:
Nicky James

All rights reserved.
No part of this book may be reproduced or transmitted in any form or by any means without the written permission of the author.

Acknowledgments

Books don't write themselves, and it's for that reason I'd like to spend a second and thank some of the people who've helped make this happen.

Top of my list, I'd like to recognize my husband, Jamie, who puts up with me day in and day out when all I can talk about are the people inside my head. You supported me every step of the way. Thank you. I love you with all my heart.

My readers! Without you, I am nothing. Thank you for picking up my books and giving them love.

Lastly, this book required some creativity in the swearing department, and I reached out to some lovely fans to help get those creative juices flowing. Mia Sciberras, you are the queen of fake swear words. Thank you for giving Zander one of my favorite lines. You rock!

Chapter One

Zander-End of April

    When I started noticing other men, the beauty that encompassed them—their lines, curves, and individual characteristic—I knew I'd slipped down that road again. I knew the lie I was living was breaking through the cushioned front I portrayed to the world and was seeping back up to the surface for everyone to see. It meant the loneliness that I always seemed able to manage was becoming too great to hold onto and my subconscious mind was screaming for a way out—screaming to be saved.
    But damn if I could ignore the gorgeous man who, quite apparently, was wandering lost on the other side of the glass wall separating my kinder-room from the main foyer of the preschool center. His jet-black hair fell, sweeping down in front of his right eye where he blew it once again out of his face as he spun around, reading the signs on the walls and above the doors.
    His arms were full with an over-packed, zoo animal diaper bag in one hand, booster seat under the same arm, and a wide-eyed toddler with bouncing blonde curls clamped to his other, sucking her thumb.
    His seriously sculpted arms, peeking out of his fitted black t-shirt, were covered in tattoos to the wrist, and his denims, hanging low on his hips, were faded and full of holes. My eyes trailed over his biceps, pecks, and perfect six-pack abs that he was not hiding well under his tight shirt and I knew, just from my initial reaction alone, that my prison walls had retracted to the point of suffocation again.
    When the world outside my window of life looked as refreshing as that man, and I couldn't help but notice, I knew the oxygen I breathed was stale, and the window had been closed for too long—nearly seven years too long.
    A tugging on my pant leg pulled my attention off the mysterious bad boy, and I redirected it to the pint-sized tot beside me. Squatting down, I smiled at little Andy's exaggerated sad face as he rubbed a fist in his eye, brushing away tears that weren't really there.
    "What do you need, Andy?"

"Lexi taked my blocks." His lip quivered as he batted his big brown eyes with practiced innocence.

"That's no good. Let's see if we can sort this out. Do you want me to help you talk to Lexi?"

Andy nodded his head dramatically, sending his auburn hair to flop around his head.

Taking Andy's hand in my own, we headed over to sort out what would be the first of many preschool dilemmas I dealt with that day.

I snuck a glance back into the foyer and noticed my supervisor, Maureen Langley, engaged with the lost hottie, cheerily holding open an introduction package and flipping through pages as she talked excitedly with her hands flailing.

Damn, wouldn't it be nice if he was registering his kid with us? I could feast my eyes on him regularly and not get tired of the view.

Stop it! That's the last thing you need.

Giving my head a shake, I reluctantly turned my attention to the group of preschoolers lying on the floor, building block castles. Lexi was among them, head down, and deeply engaged in the structure she was erecting. I plopped down beside her and drew Andy into my lap.

"Lexi Lu, did you take my friend Andy's blocks?"

Lexi's baby blue eyes grew wide behind her overgrown, blonde bangs as she shook her head with a look of guilt she was too young to hide.

"Yes she did," Andy admonished from my lap.

Lexi was about to argue, and I could see the downward spiral beginning. Having worked with children since graduating college a few years back, I was skilled at picking up when a situation was about to turn sour.

"You know what?" I quickly interrupted. "I think maybe we don't have enough blocks out to share. Andy, would you like to help me find some more and then maybe everyone can have their fair share of blocks, and no one will be unhappy?"

Andy jumped from my lap, clapped his hands excitedly and cheered.

"And disaster averted as usual." My room partner, Angie Rogers, smiled from where she was cleaning up spilled paint by the easel. "I really need to take that class and learn your secrets, Zander."

"Which one? Preventing war in a preschool classroom 101? You'll never get in. It was only offered once. To me. All information about said class has been burned to avoid having it fall into underprivileged hands.

You. Sorry about your luck." I winked as I took Andy's hand and guided him to the toy cupboard where we stored the excess rotation of toys and games.

"You are an A-S-S," she spelled.

"I don't deny it. Got an A in that class too." I tossed her a cheeky grin over my shoulder.

Angie and I had been running the preschool room together at Maureen's Munchkins for the last year and a half. We couldn't be more suited to each other. She was the yin to my yang. Where I seemed naturally gifted at smoothing out fights, killing it with songs and stories at circle time, and wearing off all the excess energy three-year-olds brought with them every day to the playground, Angie was the creative mind. She would bring in the best arts and crafts and dealt with the endless messes that were inevitable when you put sixteen kids in one room with a ridiculous amount of toys and glitter. Angie was also the compassionate one and the person the children went to when a friend broke their heart or newest creation.

Having pulled down two bins of different kinds of blocks from a higher shelf, I popped the lids and held them low for Andy to look inside. "What do you think? Do one of these look like something you could use?"

Without a second thought, Andy snagged the container with the smaller, interlocking blocks and bounced back over to the carpet to play. I looked up in time to see Angie's shoulders slump and her face drop when she saw what blocks Andy had picked. Knowing what was coming, I couldn't hide the smirk from my face. So, when her head whipped around, sending her bone-straight, blonde ponytail to swing in a high arc and smack her opposite shoulder, I laughed. Her pale blue eyes seared into me, and I slapped a hand over my mouth to try and contain my outburst. It was too late.

"Zander! You did that on purpose. You know those blocks are the death of me."

"I let him choose. It's what we are supposed to do. Provide choices. I can hardly be held responsible." Clearing my smile the best I could, I shrugged, feeling the guilty look on my face was a direct reflection of Lexi's earlier. You'd have thought at twenty-five I could have hidden it better.

"Oh yeah? What choice did you give him?"

I held up the other bin of blocks I was still holding in my hands, and Angie's hands flew up in a huff as she rolled her eyes. "I hate you, Zander."

"I hate you more." And to prove it, I blew her a kiss.

Cramming the lid back on the box, I then stuffed it back in the overfilled cupboard. It was cruel, I knew it. The other option for Andy was a sad array of handmade cardboard boxes that had been decorated with floral sticky tack paper and were left behind by a student we'd had a few months back. Not a single child in our room would ever choose to play with them, and I knew it.

Stealing a glance at the clock, I noticed it was almost time for tidy up and outdoor play. I danced around multiple messes as I headed to the light switch by the door.

"I'm calling it, Ange."

"Roger Dodger."

We had a system, and it worked like a well-oiled machine. As I was about to flick the switch to indicate tidy up time, my supervisor swung the door open, halting me with her beaming smile as she escorted the tattooed hottie and little blonde girl into the room.

"Ah, perfect." She grabbed my shoulder, spinning me from the light switch to face them. "This is Zander Baker. He's one of our preschool room staff and our best-kept secret here at the center. Don't go telling anyone he's here," she said, leaning into Mr. Hottie as she patted my chest, "we don't want to lose him."

My cheeks flushed at the compliment, and I set my jaw to fight it off—because apparently, I can fight off a blush, right?

Kill me now, this is so humiliating.

Mrs. Langley had always gone overboard with her praise of me, and I was never sure if she really thought I was that great of a worker or if she was just thrilled to have snagged one of the few men who'd chosen to put themselves in that field. Either way, it was always a little more than embarrassing listening to her praise, and with her current tour being all muscles and oozing sex, I just wanted to crawl in a hole and die.

"Tanner," Hottie said, offering me his hand with a lopsided grin, which told me immediately, the embarrassing burn in my cheeks did not go unnoticed.

Shaking it, ignoring the warmth flooding through his fingers into my hand, I tried to compose myself, feeling awkward that I'd become so flustered in the first place. "Nice to meet you. And who's this little princess?" Diverting the attention, I squatted down to address the child clinging to and hiding behind his leg.

"This is Anna, and she's no princess I assure you. Don't be fooled."

"Pleased to meet you, Princess Anna. You are a princess, aren't you?" I winked at her. "He's just pulling my leg, isn't he?"

A smile curled the girl's lips, and she nodded while still holding a death grip to Tanner's leg.

"Your secret is safe with me." I displayed zipping my mouth closed and gave her another wink before standing to speak with the adults.

"Anna here is going to start with us on Monday," Mrs. Langley explained with a grin. "They are going to have a little visit today so Anna can get used to the room. Zander here can answer any questions you might have," she said to Tanner.

Mrs. Langley handed the registration package she was still holding over to Tanner, who tucked it under the same arm that was balancing a booster seat and bag. Then she was gone.

Taking note of his overburdened arms, I quirked a brow. "You came armed to the teeth. Did you plan for her to move in or something?"

Tanner let out a laugh and glanced to his fully loaded arms. "Yeah, I didn't realize she couldn't just start today. This is all new for me. I figured I could just drop her off, you know? Then split."

"Common misconception about preschool centers. Turns out we have to know who you are and ensure you'll be returning for your kid at the end of the day."

"Makes sense." He gave me an abashed smile and shrugged his shoulders.

"Anyhow. Come on in. You can unload over there if you'd like." I nodded to the newly cleaned craft table by the door. "We are just about to tidy up and do a little circle time before heading outside. Do you have any questions before I start this ball rolling? It's gonna go from zero to chaos in about ten seconds in here."

Tanner placed the booster seat and diaper bag on the table and took hold of Anna's hand again. "Honestly, I have about a hundred questions, but I feel kinda stupid already for assuming she could start today. I didn't want to risk looking like a complete doofus in front of that lady, so I didn't ask them." He blew the hair from his eyes once again and rewarded me with yet another winning smile that left my insides hot.

Don't blush dammit.

"No problem. Give me a few minutes, and I'll see what all I can answer."

Before killing the lights, I dodged around a few running children and made my way over to Angie who was supervising a few kids over the half-wall separating our room from the preschool-sized washroom.

"Wash your hands, Bree," Angie said as she watched me approach. She sent lingering looks back to Tanner and Anna behind me, and when I was beside her, she lowered her voice.

"Ah…Yum."

"I know, right? You could maybe try being less obvious and suck the drool back into your face."

"But he's magnetic, I can't pull my eyes away. Damn the force, it's too much. Save me, Zander."

I pinched her arm and laughed as she shoved me playfully.

"Moe asked me to show this guy around and answer his questions. He's pretty lost by the look of him. Do you mind taking the reins on circle time today?"

Angie's wandering, ogling gaze was instantly drawn back to me with a look of exaggerated disgust and a turned nose. "I suck at circle," she whined. "You just want me to look bad in front of the hottie."

"That was not my goal. However, it should have been. The guy's here with his kid, in case that piece of information passed you by. Probably married or at least has a girlfriend, so stop drooling. Besides, might I point out, you have a Brad at home. Remember, Brad? Your boyfriend? Does this ring any bells?" That time, I reached up and helped her close her mouth.

Batting my hand away, she laughed. "I'll stop drooling when you stop."

"I'm not—"

"Knock it off, Zander. You're not fooling me. I saw you checking out the goods."

That was the point where my hyper-acute senses over having noticed the sexy Tanner came up and slapped me in the face. Internally reeling, realizing what I'd done, a shiver cumulated in my gut and ran unbidden over my skin. As much as I tried to hide it, Angie picked up on my inner panic and placed a hand on my arm.

"Zander, don't. I was kidding—"

"Just do circle, Angie," I snapped.

Shoving her arm off, I headed back to the light switch and flicked it off before she could catch up and stop me. The teasing, joking fun was no longer funny, and I felt sick to my stomach. How did I let that happen? I was only asking for trouble.

When the room fell dark, it sent the children into automatic mode. Children learned best with a solid routine, and that was something which happened at least three times daily in our classroom.

The busy room fell silent as I waited with my hands on my head, while the sixteen preschoolers that had been scattered about stopped what they were doing and mimicked me. Including Angie, who was pinning me with a scowl.

Once everyone was frozen in spot, and all eyes were glued to me, I started into our tidy up song. Some of the older children sang along as the room came alive again in a bustle of what was supposed to be cleaning. It never quite worked out that way. No matter how rigid the routine, children just didn't like tidying up toys.

With lots of encouraging words, and hand over hand help from Angie and me, the room looked put together again in no time, and the children gathered on the large rug for the anticipated circle time. At that point, I left Angie to it and made my way over to Tanner and Anna who'd been watching us with matching wide-eyed azure stares. The shocking contrast of Tanner's eyes to his dark hair and stubble made it hard for me to realign my thoughts. But I inhaled a deep breath, scolding myself, before re-engaging him in conversation.

"That was seriously impressive. You just got all those kids to clean up what amounted to a practical atomic disaster, and I didn't hear one of them cry or stamp their feet." Gaping, he shook his head. "Are you a God?"

I chuckled. "Maureen would tell you yes, but no. I'm just a regular guy with a knack for wrangling wild animals."

"You know it took me over an hour to get her dressed and in shoes so we could come over here this morning, and I'm pretty sure I'm going to have scars from the claws she's growing on those fingers."

I glanced down at the accused and got a familiar look of innocence in return, one I'd seen a million times before. "Not you, right, princess?"

She shook her head, bouncing her curls.

"Would you like to go sit for circle with the other kids?"

Again, I was rewarded with a bouncing nod.

Anna shifted her eyes to Tanner, hesitantly seeking permission, and he smiled. "Go ahead."

She bounced over to the carpet and sat, giving herself a wide berth from the other kids she didn't know.

"I swear to you, screaming banshee this morning."

I laughed as I sat on a low table to watch them, indicating for Tanner to join me. "I don't doubt you. Kids are always a thousand times worse for their parents. You're not the first, don't feel defeated."

"Oh, she's not mine." He jumped so fast to correct me, you'd have thought I insulted the guy. "I'm just the uncle. My sister's husband left her and the kid high and dry last month, and she was struggling, so I jumped ship and moved out here to help her out. Her job was cool giving her time off to sort things out for the first while, but she had to go back. She fired the nanny. Jerk husband was having a thing with her and got busted. So anyhow, I relocated here, and I've had the kid with me at her place over the last week, but I'm not a stay at home uncle or housekeeper. I need to set up shop or find work at least if I'm gonna stick around and help her out. So, I told my sister I'd look into daycares in the area."

"Oh, sorry. I just assumed—"

"It's cool."

"So, where's home?"

"Thunder Bay."

With raised eyebrows, I stole a sideways glance at Tanner. "You're a ways from home then."

"Yeah, but I grew up in Toronto, so it's not unfamiliar. It's just been a few years since I've been here."

"Well, welcome home I guess."

Tanner's left cheek and lip rose into a crooked half-smile, bringing out tiny crinkles around his eyes and mouth; remnants of having laughed a lot in life. "Thanks." His eyes lingered a little too long, so I refocused on the circle of children surrounding Angie and the puppet on her hand, bouncing along to the song she was singing about a kangaroo.

"So," Tanner said after a few moments. He was still watching me, but I didn't turn back. The attention was nice—not gonna lie—but it was an illusion, and I wouldn't allow myself to be fooled. "You're a hot commodity in the preschool world then I take it."

I gave a short laugh and lowered my eyes to the ground, shaking my head before chancing a glance to the still smiling face beside me. "No.

Maureen just likes to flaunt that she hired one of the few qualified men out there. I'm not anything special, I assure you."

Tanner bumped me with his shoulder, wiping the smile clean off my face and replacing it with wide-eyed discomfort. I shuffled over in a panic, giving myself more space. "And modest to boot. Did you go to school around here?"

I didn't say anything; I couldn't. The physical contact, the smile that had yet to slide off his face, and those blue eyes that seemed permanently glue to me, were all working together to throw me off and choke me up. And damn if I didn't register how incredible he smelled; cologne, leather, and all man. It was enough to cause me an all-out panic attack.

And is he flirting with me?

Without thinking on it further, I jumped up and put distance between us, clearing my throat. Angie had started into a variation of *Head and Shoulders* that had the kids standing and doing actions. I focused on the group of children and indicated to his blonde niece with a nod of my head. She had moved in to join the other kids and was bouncing along with them as she tried to keep up with the rapidly changing movements.

"She looks like she'll fit in just fine."

Tanner had stood and joined me, keeping a few feet between us, with his decorated arms crossed in front of him. "She's a social butterfly. I wasn't too worried." A long pause ensued. "So, is there anything I should bring for her when she starts?"

The conversation returned to a more professional give and take about what to expect when a child started daycare for the first time; social anxieties, routines, naptime, and toilet training among many more random questions.

Once Angie finished up circle, and the children moved to their cubbies to find their jackets for outdoor play, Anna bounced into Tanner's arms.

"You ready to go, pea?" he asked. "You get to come back Monday and stay all day."

Tanner pulled Anna's coat out from where he'd threaded it through the strap of the diaper bag and helped her fit her arms in the holes. Zipping her coat to her chin, he kissed her nose then stood, offering his hand forward to me to shake. "Thanks for your time, Zander. It was nice to meet you."

Shaking the proffered hand, I tried to ignore that same warm tingle it sent up my arm as the first time we'd shook. Retracting my hand, I gave him a smile. "See you Monday."

I couldn't help but watch him go. My brain liked to do those funny things sometimes, where it showed me snippets and half-pictures of what life could be like if things were different. That was one of those times, and despite the bustle of children running around my ankles, preparing for some outdoor playtime, I lingered on Tanner's receding perfection as he walked with overloaded arms through the foyer and out the front doors, Anna in tow.

I'd been fooled by kind words and soft smiles seven years before. Fooled into a place where I didn't see any means of escaping and had succumb to what I'd been given. The fairy tale, relationship ideal I clung to from all those romantic comedies I'd watched and books I'd read were somebody else's truths, not mine. For all I knew, that guy was no different than Paul.

"Tell me he's a single dad." Angie had sidled up beside me unnoticed.

"Not his kid. His niece."

"There is a God."

"Again. You have a Brad at home."

She smacked me on the shoulder good-naturedly. "Don't kill my fantasy." She moved to the door leading out to our playground. "You ready, Zander?"

I nodded and gave myself a mental shaking, trying to break free of my gloomy thoughts. I probably should have told her I suspected he was gay and was hitting on me, but I figured if that was the case, she'd know soon enough. Besides, as much as I wanted to enjoy the idea of being hit on, it was only making me more aware of my messed-up existence.

God, I'm in a bad place right now.

Chapter Two

Tanner

"So, you're telling me you researched all of *one* daycare centers in the area?"

"Yeah, but it's perfect. Anna already loves it there."

"One?" My sister, Stacey, glared from across the table, a forkful of spaghetti halfway to her face.

"Yes. She sat for circle and warmed right up to the staff. Did you know male daycare workers are a rare commodity and Anna will probably have the only one in the whole city as her teacher?"

Stacey quirked a brow. "Really, and was he good looking?"

"Oh. My. God. You should have seen him. Blond hair, hazel eyes, and so painfully shy—"

"Tanner Vincent Mathews, you shopped for daycare centers for *my* daughter with your dick?"

We both shot a glance over at Anna, who was thankfully oblivious to our conversation as she hummed a tune and shoveled her 'psghetti' into her mouth.

"I… But—"

"You should be ashamed." Stacey dropped her fork and crossed her arms over her chest, scowling. Her eyes were as blue as my own, but hers were flaming at the moment.

Yeah, I probably should. I hated being flayed by my sister. The truth was, I really had looked up the best daycare centers in town, and Maureen's Munchkins was the top of the list. However, I'd forgone the rest of the possibilities after our visit, because I knew I wanted to see Zander again, so I knew it was the daycare center for us.

"Come on, Stacey, it has the top rating in the area. It's not like I didn't do *any* research before heading out. It's just a happy coincidence that her classroom is run by a seriously, drop dead gorgeous male teacher. She loved it there. Ask her."

Her glower never wavered. "Look," I said holding my hands up in defense. "Do research online. Read the package I brought home. If you aren't happy with it, I'll keep looking on Monday. I'm sorry."

"Anna?" Stacey's death glare never left me. "Did you like the new school Uncle Tanner brought you to today?"

"Yeah! I wanna play on the climber. I can go back, Mama?"

"You're lucky I don't have time for this shit, Tanner. If she has even a smidgen of a problem there, it's on you."

"Understood." I fought off the grin that so badly wanted to creep onto my face at her submission, but I knew it was not the right time.

"You'll need to take her Monday for her first day too because I have an early meeting. Do me a favor and try not to hump her teacher's leg. I'd like to avoid acquiring a reputation before I even meet these people."

Scraping up the last bite of spaghetti from my plate, I gave her a teasing grin. "I can't make any promises. Did I mention he's—"

"Gorgeous, yeah, I got it. Behave." She pointed her finger and fixed me with her best, "I'm not above tackling you to the ground and issuing nipple twisters and wedgies" look. All those years later and my big sister was still a little witch determined to own my ass if I got out of line.

"I'll behave."

* * *

Saturday was not an ideal day to go job searching, but I was feeling antsy at not having work and thought I'd scope out some of the local tattoo shops to see if they needed or wanted another artist on their team. With my portfolio under my arm and a light jacket over my shoulders to protect myself against the cool, end of April breeze, I headed out at a brisk walk to a shop I'd read about around the corner.

I'd left Thunder Bay after selling my half of the tattoo parlor I'd opened with my ex-boyfriend two years back. It was a dream for both of us to have our own shop, but that dream shattered when we realized working side by side every day was more than either of us could take.

I hadn't wanted to sell. I'd dumped most of the inheritance my grandparents left me into opening it and walking away meant leaving my dream behind. Life just hadn't been on my side though. Between the constant arguing with Greg and having it spill into our workdays, tainting our reputation and then my sister's sudden falling out with her husband, and crying every night on the phone to me that she couldn't do it alone, I figured it was a sign I should walk away and start fresh.

I arrived at Crazy Eye Tattoos just before noon—somebody was on some serious drugs when they named the place. A chime sounded when I sauntered in, alerting the staff to my presence. The place was bigger on the inside than it appeared from the street. One wall was covered in flash prints while another was a photographic collage of real people and the work they'd had done in the shop; everything from tiny ankle tattoos to full sleeve and body covers. A counter was set up to the left with a glass display case holding hundreds of body jewelry; decorations people could purchase for every kind of hole you could put in your body. It looked like every other tattoo shop I'd been in over the years.

A big, heavier set guy, covered in art all the way up his neck to his bald head, peeked up from where he worked on a woman's ankle at a station farther in. He smiled through a thick, reddish-brown beard and called over his shoulder to the back to someone I couldn't see.

"Hey, T.J., get your ass up here, man. Customer." He nodded at me. "How's it going?"

"Good thanks." I approached where he worked and glimpsed the Japanese, cherry blossom tree he was detailing. "That's great work. I'm Tanner. Are you the owner?"

Shaking my hand, the man scoffed. "Ricky. Nah, it's my brother's shop. The guy who's obviously not listening to me right now." Turning his head, he yelled even louder than before into the back reaches of the large room. "T.J."

A slightly smaller man appeared from behind a partition. I could see the family resemblance in the skin tone and facial structure, but that was where the similarities ended. The other guy had a full head of long dark hair the color of a copper penny which he had pulled back into a ponytail at the base of his neck. He was clean-shaven, and his muscle to tattoo ratio under his tank top was about even, only his art stopped below the neckline.

When he met my gaze, I had to consciously make an effort not to flinch. His left eye was slightly askew from the center and had a filmy haze over it, washing out the green iris to a more milky hue.

Crazy eye; I understand now.

He dipped his head in greeting and extended a hand for me to shake. "T.J., what can I do for you today?"

"Nice to meet you. I'm Tanner. I'm actually returning to the city after being away for six years, and I was looking for work. I've been tattooing since high school, but more professionally in the last five years. Was wondering if you were interested in a new artist."

"I don't generally take on new peeps." His eyes moved to the big binder I had crammed under my arm. "What's your style preference? What are you good at, kid?"

Well, at least it wasn't a resounding no and a boot out the door. "Fantasy, surrealism, graffiti, script. I prefer working in color, but I've done more black and white than I can count."

His stern scrutiny was unnerving—*or is it the eye?* Either way, I inadvertently shifted my gaze away in my failed attempt at maintaining eye contact.

"Photorealism?"

"No, not my thing."

"Oriental?"

"I've done some, not my favorite."

I forced myself to look back again and saw his gaze had shifted to my book. He nodded to it. "You have a portfolio there?"

"Yeah. Have a gander." I handed it over and followed him as he walked the two feet to the jewelry counter where he put it down. He flipped through, squinting at the photographs filling the pages.

"You have a good eye for detail." He turned another page. "You a gamer?"

He'd reached a page where I had displayed many tattoos I'd done on people relating to popular video games. They were my personal favorite and the thing I liked tattooing the most.

"Yeah. Hardcore. Console and online. Love drawing the stuff. People used to seek me out for that kinda shit."

I pulled my jacket off and held out my arms. "I designed these too. Made my ex put them on my arms."

He studied my designs and nodded. "She's good too your ex."

"He," I corrected.

His eyebrow raised slightly, and he gave me a once over before turning back to the book, seemingly unaffected by my bold declaration of my sexuality. It was a good sign too, I wouldn't have wanted to work for some homophobic ass if he offered me a job. I'd been out and proud since I was sixteen and had no desire to be anyone but myself. I didn't care how comfy someone made the closet look, I wasn't going back in there for anything.

"Where'd you work before?"

"Owned a shop with the ex in Thunder Bay for two years. We split, I sold my half and came back home to help my sister out. She left her husband, needed a hand with the kid. Before that, I worked in a little shop doing my apprenticeship." Okay, that was probably too much information, but whatever.

T.J continued to flip through pages while I let my eyes drift around the room again. "You have a piercer I take it?" I motioned an arm to the display case we were leaned against.

"Yeah, Elvira. She's only in the shop on Tuesdays and Thursdays. You have good techniques, kid. You have any schooling?"

"Two semesters of an Art major at Lakehead, but I dropped out to open shop."

T.J nodded and closed the binder, patting the cover. "Good stuff in here."

"Thank you."

"You mind if I hold on to it for a couple of days and talk to my brother. He's been pushing me for more help around here. Me, I won't lie, I'm sketchy on the idea still. Not sure how I feel about bringing in new people."

"Sure, I understand." Although I wanted to go other places, I was excited that the guy seemed genuinely interested in giving me a chance.

He slid a pad of paper and pen over. "Leave me a number. I'll give you a call."

I jotted down my name and cell on his paper and shook his hand again. "Thanks a lot. I appreciate you even considering me."

Seeing as my weekend job hunt was pretty much concluded when I'd had to give up my portfolio, I headed home with high hopes for having work soon. The shop was close to my sister's house so it would be the ideal place to work. I crossed my fingers and hoped that crazy-eyed T.J would see potential in hiring me.

Chapter Three

Zander

It was nearing the lunch hour on Monday, and Angie and I had already been outside with the kids for over forty-five minutes when a white, beat up Toyota Tacoma pulled into our parking lot. The thing looked rough and sounded even worse.

"Heads up, Zander. Hottie's back."

As the words left Angie's mouth, I watched Tanner climb out of the driver's side door and walk around to the passenger side where the little blonde—what the heck was her name again? —was strapped into her booster seat.

Figured I would remember his name and forget hers. I'd spent all weekend lecturing myself on our possible encounter that day. Seeing as it was almost noon, I'd assumed it wasn't going to happen, and they'd found alternate care arrangements. I refused to admit that seeing him pull up made me pleased beyond belief.

Good, God, knock it off!

Tanner seemed more organized that day; less frantic and lost than he'd been during our initial meeting. The diaper bag with Goldie Locks' belongings—*I really do hate myself right now*—was packed within reason and it no longer looked like the poor toddler was moving in. Clearly, he'd read the packages we'd sent home.

Tanner sauntered up to the playground with a wide grin beaming across his face. His gaze trailed up and down my body, coming to rest on my lips a moment before finding my eyes again.

Bad sign. I'm not available, buddy. So. Not. Available.

"There's the little princess." I went with something safe since I still couldn't remember her name. It worked wonders, and I was rewarded with a matching grin from the bouncing girl on the other side of the chain-linked fence.

"I can play too?" Her blonde curls bounced up and down in response to her energetic jumping as she stretched her arms up to me.

Reaching over the fence, I secured a grip under her arms and heaved her over, getting all kinds of giggles as I set her down to run with the other kids.

"Okay, let's get something straight. Not a princess. Demon. Hellion. Gremlin. A rabid angry animal with fangs and a taste for blood. These things I can work with, but this," Tanner trailed a finger after her, "is no princess. I swear it took two hours just to get her dressed and another to get her fed. Then, we needed to get her dressed again because her Fruit Loops ended up all over her. The whole ordeal was done while her head spun and I almost called a minister to perform an exorcism."

"Aww, sweetie, she is running all over you." Angie joined us at the fence and leaned in, smiling her most adoring, charming girl smile directly at Tanner. I couldn't help the eye roll. She was so obvious in her flirtations it was sickening.

"Yeah well, she's all yours now. I need a nap. I'd considered going job hunting again, but I don't think I have anything left in me." He heaved a deep sigh. "Where can I put her things?"

"Come on, I'll take you in and show you her cubby. We have it all set up for her." Angie went out the gate and took Tanner by the arm to lead him inside.

"Hey, Angie."

She turned back, glaring.

"One word. Brad."

"Hey, Zander. One word—" And she proceeded to stick out her tongue over her shoulder as she escorted Tanner inside.

Brat.

All I could do was laugh. She was all innocent fun. She and Brad were really close, and she'd no doubt gone home Friday and told him all about the hot new parent at the daycare.

When Tanner and Angie returned, Angie seemed to lose interest in Tanner and reengaged with the children running and playing in the yard. Tanner came over to lean against the fence beside where I stood, crossed his arms over the top, and rested his chin over them. He didn't seem to be in a hurry to leave, so I stayed close—in case he had more questions.

I'd spent enough time trying not to stare at the man before that I hadn't paid close attention to what exactly the art was all over his arms. I'd thought in passing that they'd looked tribal, but upon closer inspection, I saw what they really were.

"Holy crap, is that a Horde symbol?" My hands flew out without thinking and grabbed his wrist, turning his arm so I could see it better. Tanner's knowing grin spread across his face, lighting up his every feature.

"For the Horde, my friend."

"You're a nerd hiding behind tattoos and a bad boy persona."

"Busted. You play?"

"Are you kidding? Since the launch, man. Ten years. Horde to the core." I kept hold of his arm and turned it around, noticing his other tattoos and tracing my fingers over the top of them. "I can't believe I didn't notice these before."

Tanner's full sleeve tats were devoted entirely to my favorite massive, multiplayer, online role-playing game, World of Warcraft. They consisted of every Horde race found in the fictitious world of Azeroth; Blood Elves, Orcs, Trolls, Goblins, Undead. Each was drawn with explicit detail, sporting recognizable in-game armor and weapons. They were absolutely incredible.

World of Warcraft was my escape. It was the only online game I played, and I'd been Horde faction dedicated since the game's birth ten years before. When I felt cut off from the world around me, Warcraft gave me a means of socialization that was acceptable and didn't get me in trouble.

"They are a depiction of my own characters. This one," Tanner held out his other arm, pointing, "is my main character. Undead Rogue; Krul. I've had that baby since day one."

"These are incredible." It was a full two or three minutes before I realized I'd practically been groping the man's arms, running my fingers over each picture and reveling in their beauty, depth, and color.

Tanner's eyes were on me, and the quirk in the corner of his lips was that of a controlled smirk. When I looked up and saw him watching, it dawned on me what I'd been doing. I yanked my hands back in alarm and shoved them in my pockets. He didn't make it awkward, for which I was grateful, and instead turned his attention back to his niece where she climbed up the ladder to slide down the slide again.

"What server do you play on?" he asked with a huge grin. Thankfully he seemed to be ignoring my little inappropriate fondling session.

"Kul'Tiras."

"Main Character?"

"Zulsori." I spelled it out for him and then wondered why I had. Was I inviting the guy to look me up?

"I might have to start a baby toon and come find you."

I guess I was. I didn't answer but instead thought how it might be nice to have someone I knew to game with. Apart from Paul, I didn't have friends, even online. And playing Warcraft with Paul had lost its appeal years before.

"So, do you live around here?"

"I... Umm. Yeah, not far. Kinda."

Smooth.

"Do you game with close friends or just randoms you hook up with in-game? It's really cool running into people who play in real life."

"Well, I used to... Sometimes. Mostly randoms now." I ducked my head, feeling awkward. Paul used to game all the time, but he never played anymore, and as for friends... Yeah, well that was a story in itself—one I wasn't getting into. Tanner must have picked up on my discomfort because he changed the subject.

"So, how does this work exactly? Do I just leave and hope she doesn't cry her face off? My sister will kick my ass if she has a bad day. I've been warned."

"She looks like she's doing well. I'm not concerned. Generally, the worst is when a parent leaves, but she doesn't seem too worried about you going."

"After this morning, she's probably glad to be rid of me." Tanner laughed and pulled back from the fence looking ready to depart.

"Will you be picking her up?" I asked.

"No. My sister is coming. She wants to check this place out and make sure I did okay. She works crazy hours and has meetings and such all the time. Paralegal. I'm just going to help her out if she needs it."

"Right. I guess you'll be starting work soon yourself?"

"Here's hoping. Talked to a guy on the weekend about a job, just waiting to hear back. But with my line of work, we don't generally get started until later mornings so I could be stuck with drop-off duties more times than I'd like." Tanner rolled his eyes to the heavens and shook his head.

"It'll get easier as it becomes routine. So, what do you do?"

Stop talking and let the guy leave.

"Tattoo artist. I had my own tattoo shop back in Thunder Bay with the ex, but I sold him my share when I came here. I'm hoping to eventually open a shop again, but I'd be happy to just work for someone else for now while I get settled."

Ex? Him? I knew you were gay. Angie's going to be so sad.

"Wow. Cool. So this isn't temporary you moving here? You're not planning to head back up north?"

"Nah. To be fair, I hated it. I've been looking for an excuse to come home for a while. Just got stuck there after college and then the mess with Greg—" Stopping himself short, he shrugged. "Anyhow, Stacey called and begged me to come home and help her out. I had no reason to stay, so here I am."

"Huh."

"Well, I should split. I did plan on checking out a few other shops in my neighborhood today. In case this one I went to on the weekend doesn't pan out."

"So no nap then."

"No. Sadly, I probably should try to be the responsible adult. I'll see ya around, Z." Tanner gave me a wink as he headed to his truck.

"Yeah. See you around. Good luck."

Chapter Four

Tanner

I stretched my arms out above my head and yawned, jaw creakingly huge. Readjusting my laptop on my lap, I then fit another pillow behind my back for comfort as I leaned against the wall, sitting up in bed. I'd been up to my eyebrows for the past hour in a failing Warcraft dungeon run and finally made the decision to bail on the group, seeing as it was long past midnight and there was no light at the end of that tunnel.

I knew I should call it a night since I had a job interview with crazy-eyed T.J in the morning after I dropped Anna off at daycare. It had only taken three days for him to get back to me. I was excited and nervous at the same time. Apart from my portfolio, I didn't have much else to share, so the purpose of an interview was a little boggling and lost on me.

As I was about to shut down my game, a thought crossed my mind. I hovered the cursor over the "exit game" tab for a moment while I considered what I was doing.

Shuffling up to sit straighter, I then crossed my legs and moved the laptop to rest on my bed. I logged off my server and searched through a list of about fifty alternate servers in search of the one Zander said he played on. Kul'Tiras. There it was. I clicked it and moved with practiced speed through the create character screen.

The process of character creation would ordinarily be a much longer, more articulated process, but for my purpose, I just needed to get online again, and I couldn't have cared less what race or class I made, nor what my toon looked like.

Speeding through the setup, I clicked on "random name generator" — again, ordinarily a much more thought-provoking task—and entered the world as Ceronys.

The purpose was not for leveling or questing, but simply to see if Zander was online. There was something about that reserved, shy guy from my niece's preschool that intrigued me; apart from the fact that he was incredibly good looking. He seemed comfortable enough when talking about his work or gaming, but the minute the conversation steered to something even slightly more personal, he shut down and got distant, stumbling over even the easiest of questions. Not that he'd known me for more than ten minutes, but there was something there that screamed high alert and made me step back and respect his discomfort. I just hadn't figured out what it was.

The way he'd lit up when he'd noticed my tattoos, and the smile that radiated over his face when he'd talked about gaming was the first personal thing he'd shared that didn't send him diving behind thick walls.

I did a "/who" search for the name of his main toon, typing it exactly how he'd spelled it out and hit enter. A smile spread through my whole body when I came up with a successful find and saw he was indeed online. I quickly typed out a private message and hit send.

Ceronys: Thought I might find you here.

I waited a few minutes, and when I didn't get a response, I wondered if he was away from his keyboard, or as we say in the gaming world, AFK.

Ceronys: It's Tanner btw :)

I waited. Still nothing. Leaned back against my headboard, I stared at the blinking cursor as it pulsed in front of me and wondered if maybe he couldn't talk because he was in a dungeon or battleground or something. I was about to give up and log off when a chime indicated I had received a private message.

Zulsori: Hey stranger. Was just in a BG, sorry.

Ceronys: Ahh, PvP'er. I see how it is. You like to slaughter real people in the game. I'm more of a PVE'er myself. Love the dungeon and raid grind.

Zulsori: Yeah, me too normally. Just dive into PVP when I have some immediate stress to let go of and need to slaughter the innocent.

Ceronys: I'm sure you'd own my ass in PVP if we ended up out there against each other. It's a good thing we are on the same faction.

Zulsori: So are you saying you suck?

My mind dipped right into the gutter, and I grinned at his choice of words. I figured I'd play along to see what he'd do.

Ceronys: Suck like a boss. Never had any complaints.

Silence.

Zulsori: Maybe you just need some help.

That a boy, play along. Now let's get some questions answered just to be clear.

Licking my lips, I thought for a second before typing my next message.

Ceronys: Good thing we play for the "same team" then, am I right? *You are gay, right?*

I waited for what seemed a long time before another message finally popped up.

Zulsori: Indeed?

Hmm...Was that a yes?

Ceronys: Not sure that was a confirming answer to my question.

Figuring I might have to go in bold soon if he didn't catch on, I hoped the "once removed, being online" thing helped with his nerves some and I wouldn't scare him off.

Zulsori: Umm... For the Horde? Sorry, I didn't see a question, I'm confused.

Is he avoiding it on purpose or is he really just that innocent? Bah...Fine, here goes nothing. Bold it is.

Ceronys: Okay, how about this. Are you gay?

I stared for so long at the blinking cursor, I wondered if I was still connected or if I'd dropped offline. It wasn't a hard question, and I wouldn't have asked point blank if I wasn't already fairly certain of the answer. My gaydar was generally spot on, and I knew I hadn't imagined it when shy guy Zander had checked me out, nor had I imagined the guilty look and flushed cheeks when he so obviously manhandled my arms the previous day. When no message came after a full two minutes of sitting, I let out a sigh and started typing out an apology for having put him on the spot. When the chime sounded again, my fingers froze as his three-little-letter response stared back at me.

Zulsori: Yes.

I grinned. Huge.

Was that so hard?

Backspacing through what I was about to send, I thought a moment before retyping a new message.

Ceronys: I'm sorry if I made you uncomfortable. I just thought I should be sure so I didn't proceed to make a fool of myself.

Zulsori: I'm involved.

And bam! Hopes dashed.

Damn.

It shouldn't have come as a surprise. The man was gorgeous, even though I got the feeling he had no idea just how gorgeous he was. To think someone hadn't already scooped him up was just fool's thinking.

I hovered my hands over the keyboard as I formulated a response. There were two avenues I could choose from. I didn't really want to be a dickhead and turn away, just because he was off the market, but I had strict rules to never get involved with people who were in relationships. It was low, and I was not a douchebag, nor did I condone cheating under any circumstance. So, I could be strictly his friend, or I could cut all ties and walk away. The answer was obvious.

I was starting to get the sense I'd figured out the root cause behind Zander's reservation. It explained a lot. Making my decision, I typed out a quick response, aiming for lighthearted and then added a second message soon after to steer us away from any awkwardness.

Ceronys: I shouldn't be surprised with a sexy guy like you being off the market, but I respect that, and this is me backing off with my dignity. Trust me. I will not be a problem for you. I promise. I hope we can be friends.

Ceronys: Wanna help a brother power level a baby toon?

Zander jumped all over the change of subject and agreed to meet me in the newbie starting area in a few minutes. We grouped up, and I sent him a quick message letting him know I was going AFK while I grabbed a beer and waited for him.

The rest of the night flew by while Zander brought in what he called, "The Big Guns" to help me plow through all low-end areas and get my character leveled up. "The Big Guns" referred to his top level, undead shadow priest, Wormz, with not a gun to be had. Wielder of magic and death—as Zander so elegantly put it—took the reins and slaughtered everything in sight. Zulsori had been around since the birth of Warcraft, Zander explained, but Wormz had taken over as his main character one expansion before.

We chatted as we gamed and Zander ran my new character—which I should have spent more than five seconds creating—through numerous quests and low-level dungeons. A more relaxed Zander started to show for the first time while in a place that was clearly his comfort zone.

It wasn't until the morning light crept through around my blinds that I realized we'd been at it all night.

Ceronys: Fuck man! Did you know it's morning?

Wormz: Crap! Lol! I'm going to be a train wreck at work today. I can't believe we played all night.

Ceronys: IKR. I'll be a mess for my interview.

Wormz: We should probably call it, huh?

Ceronys: Yeah. I guess I'll see you in a bit when I drop off Anna.

Wormz: Yeah, I'll be the guy sleeping in the book nook when you get there.

Ceronys: Lol. Had fun, man. Thanks for the help.

Wormz: Np. See ya.

Chapter Five

Zander*-End of May*

"I can't believe I got denied. I never get denied. Paul is going to be pissed. What am I going to do? We are supposed to be going to another one of his stupid conferences in Chicago and having a *romantic weekend*."

Regularly, about four times a year, Paul had to attend those kinds of things. His work as a pharmacist meant he needed to be constantly up to date with new drugs, and therefore, he attended any number of workshops and conferences all over North America to stay fresh. I crumpled up my request form and tossed it into the trash.

It was the end of the day on a Tuesday and Angie and I had been trying to put our room back into some semblance of order since most of the kids had gone home. Maureen had just returned my vacation request form as she walked out the door. Kind of her to leave before I could read it through and protest her decision.

I rarely asked for extended amounts of time off, and all I was looking for were a simple Friday and Monday so I could attend a work thing with Paul. Apparently, that time, it was too much to ask.

I didn't really want to go to Chicago. I was much happier with the prospect of being home for a weekend by myself, but it was breaking the news to Paul that I was not looking forward to. He was not exactly the understanding type.

"It's not your fault, Zander. He can't blame you. Anyhow, think about it, now you'll have a weekend free and clear to do whatever you want. We should go out. We never get to do that."

I rinsed out a paint covered rag in the sink and thought about it. We rarely did go out, even though Angie was one of the only friends Paul seemed to approve of. Maybe it wouldn't be such a bad idea, once I got past telling him that I couldn't go to Chicago.

"Yeah, maybe," I said halfheartedly. "Or we can stay in and watch movies. I can go to yours or something."

"Forget it." Angie stacked the chairs from around the craft table up out of the way, giving the cleaners better access to the grimy floor. "You never go out and party. You're twenty-five, and you act like you're eighty-nine. We should go clubbing. Maybe hit the Fritz."

"That's a gay bar. You know that, right?"

"Yes, ya dork, I know that. It's why I suggested it. You need some fun."

"I don't know." Taking the wet rag back to the paint easel, I did a final wipe down. "I'll think about it."

"God, you think too much. You're gonna end up home all weekend playing that stupid World of Whatever, I just know it."

"Whoa, whoa, whoa, don't you be knocking the Warcraft," Tanner said as he sauntered into the room. "I heard that and it sacrilege."

"Hey, T-man," Angie said, placing her hands on her hips. "Help me out here, would you?"

"Don't, Angie," I interrupted.

"No, you don't get a say." She pointed her finger at me, daring me to interrupt again. "Your brain is all muddled from spending too many years as a homebody. Tanner is going to weigh in here." She turned her attention back to Tanner. "Zander has the weekend to himself now because Paul's going to Chicago and I suggested we go out and have some fun. You know, clubbing, drinking, dancing, partying type of fun. Thought we could hit the Fritz. But he thinks he's an old man and might break a hip or something. Help me convince him to go."

Cutting in, I gave her a saucy grin. "You know you're pleading your case to one of my fellow gamers who would see the pros to my staying home for an uninterrupted weekend of raiding, right?"

"Oh. My. God. Seriously, T-man? Say it's not so."

"Guilty, baby doll. Hence the offense to the sacrilegious comment about World of Whatever. However," he said turning to me, "it could be fun to get out and live a little too. I have nothing going on Friday night, maybe I can join you."

Angie's pleading eyes were more than I could take. Added to the mix was Tanner's bad version of a puppy dog face, and I was done. I let out a defeated sigh. "Fine."

Angie jumped up and down clapping. "Yay! This will be so much fun."

All I could manage was a groan while I redirected the attention to Anna as she gathered her things to head home for the day.

A weekend of freedom. I made it sound like I lived in jail and only got a few days off a year to go out and enjoy fresh air and sunshine and truly be myself. When I looked at my situation, I guessed it wasn't too far off the truth. But to think that other people saw inside my prison cell was unsettling.

"It won't be so bad." Tanner leaned in and whispered as he slung Anna's backpack over his shoulder and scooped her up onto his hip. "A couple hours shaking your stuff on the dance floor, mixed with a handful of beers and you'll feel like a new person."

"I don't dance."

"I'll teach you." Tanner bumped his shoulder with mine. "Don't look so devastated, it will be okay. You gonna be online tonight?"

We'd been playing together regularly over the past month whenever we happened to be online at the same time—which turned out to be fairly frequently. His baby toon was coming along nicely.

"Yeah, hopefully around nine. You wanna level your baby up some more?"

"I'm game." Tanner held out his hand expectantly. "Phone," he responded to my quizzical stare.

"Huh?"

"Give me your phone."

I handed my phone over, confused as I watched Tanner punch at it before handing it back.

"There, I put my number in. Text me when you log on. I'll flip servers, and we can play."

"Oh." I stared at my phone, and the confusion must have still been written all over my face.

"That okay?" Tanner asked. "Or did I cross some line?"

"No. That's cool." I found his contact info in the list and shot him a smiley-faced text. His phone buzzed in his pocket. "There you have mine too."

"Perfect." Tanner's smile took over his whole face, making a discrete dimple appear on his left cheek, hidden in his scruffy, unshaven face. He winked. "I'll see ya online."

"Ya. See ya," I said as he walked out the door.

I watched him go with Anna through the lobby and out the front doors. He bounced her on his hip, and they laughed together and chatted, even though I could no longer hear what they said. She giggled and clung to his neck with such love and trust it did funny things to my insides to see it.

"It's okay to have friends you know," Angie said beside me. I hadn't heard her approach, and she ruffled my hair before leaning her head on my shoulder. "He's a nice guy."

"I know. We've played a few times online together over the last month. He plays Warcraft too."

"I caught that. Nerds unite." She raised a fist in a cheering motion.

"Shut it," I said, shoving her off my shoulder as I laughed.

"You just looked freaked out by the fact that he wants to come out with us and hang out. It's a good thing, Zander. You need to get out more." Angie turned back to the few remaining kids who were playing on the rug. She sat down and joined them.

I knew it was okay to have friends—or that it should be okay to have friends. Paul didn't always see it that way though, and Tanner was not only a guy, but a gay guy—a downright gorgeous gay guy—and I knew for a fact that being friends with him would only bring on a whole shitstorm of problems that I wasn't prepared to face.

***

The week flew by and our weekend plans stayed solid. Sitting at a table in a dark corner of the Fritz on Friday night, I waited as Angie grabbed us a few drinks from the bar. Tanner was supposed to be meeting us there, and I scanned the room again looking for him. He'd got his job at Crazy Eye Tattoos and worked late most Fridays.

The deep thumping base of the dance music pounded through my head and radiated through my body, making me wonder again why I'd agreed to go. The strobing lights, pulsing random colors, the gyrating bodies, rubbing against each other on the dance floor, the drunks, and the crushing crowd just wasn't my scene, as much as Angie thought it should be.

She was convinced I lived the life of a hermit, held ransom and smothered under Paul's thumb against my will. She was not entirely wrong. I didn't get out much anymore. It was just easier. I did what I could to keep the peace, and if staying home and junking out on video games every night kept the storm from raging, then it was a small price to pay in my opinion. Besides, I liked gaming.

Angie thought Paul was controlling, but I could go out if I wanted to. *Liar.* I did go out. My routine consisted of running every morning at five o'clock before work. Didn't that count? It was peaceful and quiet, and it was my own time, free and away from everyone. That was going out. Wasn't it? Maybe I was just not social because I didn't want to be. Didn't anyone ever think of that? *You're pathetic, that's what you are.*

Angie returned to the table with two drinks in her hands—my vodka and cranberry and her Strawberry Daiquiri—and put them down. She leaned in and talked into my ear so she could be heard over the music.

"Tanner's here." She pointed to the doors and waved her hand over her head to get his attention. "I'm just saying, if that man wasn't gay, I'd be all over him. Damn, he's fine."

I shoved her in the arm and laughed. She hadn't let up since we'd met him and I was starting to think she was just doing it to get a rise out of me.

"Umm... Brad? Remember?"

"Honey, Brad's got nothing on him. Brad can move over." She laughed as she looked to me. Ruffling my hair, she plopped down in her seat. "I'm kidding, Z. Don't look so horrified. Tanner's a good-looking guy, I'm just pointing out the obvious. It's okay to notice these things you know. You cannot tell me you haven't checked out that fine figure. I've seen your eyes wander."

"Shut it," I hissed, "he's coming."

Of course, I'd noticed him. I'd noticed him the first time I laid eyes on him. And how could I not notice him right then? He was wearing black jeans which were so tight I had to question how on Earth he'd put them on. It was taking everything I had not to stare at the bubble of his ass, formed so damn perfect in them. His gray t-shirt, under his leather jacket, hugged to his body and muscles just right. As he approached the table, he pulled off his jacket and slung it over the back of the free chair, leaving all those amazing tattoos running down his arms exposed. I'd have had to have been blind to not see what was in front of me and I was not blind.

He's your friend, stop checking him out.

"Gonna grab a drink. Be right back." He headed to the bar and Angie jabbed me in the ribs with her elbow.

"It's a nice ass. Take it all in, Z, don't be ashamed."

Efforts to control my eyes failed, and I shot a death glare Angie's way.

"I hate you."

She laughed into her drink.

"Live a little. You can look. Brad knows I look. Brad looks. It's human nature. There is nothing wrong with noticing a gorgeous body. You know who you're going home to at the end of the day, so relax. It's innocent."

Yeah and if Paul ever catches my eyes wandering, I'll be in so much shit. He'll fail to see the 'innocence' involved.

As the night moved on and the drinks kept flowing, Angie made her way to the dance floor all drunk and bouncy after having spent enough time unsuccessfully trying to coax me to join her. The idea of all those bodies squished together, bumping and grinding, and the free flow of hands in places I didn't want them, just made me more interested in sitting back to watch as I sipped my drink. Tanner, the unlucky fool, agreed to join her and I knew Angie wasn't too upset to grind up against him on the dance floor. Gay or not, she looked downright thrilled.

After watching them dance through a few songs and seeing the sweat pouring off them, I decided to head to the bar to get us another round of drinks. Tanner and Angie would probably be needing a break soon so I figured it would be a good time.

Squeezing through the congestion of bodies, I found an open section of the bar and leaned against it, waiting for the bartender to take my order. The crowd had thickened since we'd arrived, and people were pressed into every available inch of bar space there was, looking to place their own orders.

Anticipating a long wait, I pulled out my phone to check for messages while I leaned against the bar. After a few minutes, a large body came up behind me and pressed alongside my length, engulfing me in sweaty heat. A wet mouth licked its way up my neck to my ear before I could process what was happening and turned around. The large man behind me grabbed my waist, spun me, and pulled me toward him, grinding his already rigid length into me.

"Those lips would look amazing wrapped around my cock, blondie. Let's say we head to the bathrooms and see if I'm right."

My whole body stiffened, and as hard as I tried to pull away from the wet mouth lapping back down my neck, I had nowhere to go. He was much bigger and stronger than me and was on a mission. Pinned with my back against the bar, I couldn't move and was in borderline, panic attack mode.

"No thanks," I said, trying to nudge him off. The alcohol wafting off his breath told me he was probably half in the bag, if not all the way in.

"Don't be a pussy. You suck my cock, I'll return the favor."

I shoved a little harder, but the man was like a brick wall and didn't move. My heart raced uncontrollably. Between being stuck and having some stranger's mouth sucking hickeys on my neck, I found myself nearly crawling up onto the bar to get away from him, before his weight was suddenly gone.

"Hey, dickhead. Get your fucking hands off him."

Freed of the weight, I looked up with wide eyes to see my rescuer. Tanner. He was in the guy's face, hand balled around his shirt, a look of venom in his blue eyes. The stranger scanned Tanner up and down before his face broke into a greasy smile.

"Relax, man. We can share the little fucker. What do you say?"

Tanner got within an inch of his face. "I don't share."

"Who are you? The boyfriend or something?"

"Or something, now fuck off."

I watched the man stumble away through the crowd before turning to Tanner, who was scanning me with concern.

"You okay?"

My heart thumped in my throat, and I was no longer in the mood for loud music and drinking. None of it was remotely fun anymore. I wasn't sure if it had been fun to begin with. I couldn't slow the shaking in my hands and body, and nausea sickened my stomach.

"I think I'm gonna take off. You and Angie have fun, I'll find my way home. Umm…Thanks for that."

Shoving past Tanner, I fought my way to the front doors as a prickling sweat made the hairs on my arms stand up. The crush of bodies was almost impenetrable and more suffocating than they had been when we'd arrived. I needed to fight off the sense of panic smoldering to life in my gut.

Outside in the cool night, I stopped for a minute while I tried to refocus and slow the spinning that had started to alter my world.

"Z? Are you okay?" Tanner had followed me outside and placed a gentle hand on my arm where I was hunched over, hands on my knees, gasping in great mouthfuls of air.

"Yeah. It's just...this really isn't my scene. I don't do this kinda thing." I stood up, trying for nonchalance, but I knew I wasn't pulling it off. "This was Angie's idea of a good time, and I know she's just trying to help, but it's too much. I'm gonna go."

"Okay. Fair enough. How are you getting home?"

"I'll walk. I need air."

"Give me two minutes, and I'll walk with you, okay? I just want to run in and let Angie know what's going on."

"You should probably stay with her."

"Her boyfriend, Brad I think his name is, called about ten minutes ago, right before that dick approached you. He's coming to pick her up so they can head out elsewhere. Two minutes, Z, wait for me?"

"Okay."

After a silent ten minutes of walking, with neither of us saying anything, it occurred to me I had no idea where Tanner lived. For all I knew, he was walking farther away from his place just to walk me home.

Why was he walking me home anyway?

"So, you gonna be online later or are you hitting the sack once you're home?" he asked, breaking me out of my thoughts.

Pulling my phone out of my pocket to check the time, I saw that it was only just short of midnight. I laughed to myself and shook my head.

"I really am eighty-nine years old. Angie's right. Look at me, heading home before midnight, thinking about tea and a warm bed. God, I'm messed up."

Tanner smiled sidelong at me. "You and me both. Clubbing isn't really my thing either. Next time, I say we pull out our rocking chairs, suck our gums, and tell stories about the good old days instead. It'll save us some money at least. Damn, I didn't realize how expensive it is to drink at a bar. I can't afford that shit."

"Now you're just being patronizing. You don't do bars? Why did you come if you hate clubbing?"

"Because I could tell you were going to be dragged there against your will, and I thought maybe you could use a friend to escape with when it got to be too much. Turns out I was right." He winked. "So, you going to be online? I could seriously go home and kill stuff right now."

"I don't know, I thought I might pop in a movie actually. It's not often I get full rein on the TV. Paul and I don't really agree on movies." *Understatement of the year.*

"Want company?"

"Umm…" Panic stirred in my belly again, and I chewed my lip a second, watching my feet while I contemplated.

Paul didn't like it when I had friends over either. In fact, Angie had only been over twice in the year or so we'd been friends, and both times, Paul had grumbled about it for days afterward. I didn't really understand his thought process, nor did I even try anymore. I just did my best to keep him happy, so I wouldn't see his ugly side.

Paul was gone until Monday though, and for once, I didn't have to answer to him and could have a friend over without feeling wrong about it. "Sure. That would be cool. I think I might have a couple of beers in the fridge too."

"What? No tea?" He laughed and bumped my shoulder with his. "I'm teasing."

Back at my apartment, we rode the elevator to the eighth floor in silence, and I let us into my place. I tossed my keys on the table by the door and flicked on the lights, bathing the living room in a warm, yellow glow.

"Make yourself comfortable." I waved an arm around the small living space. "It's not much, but it's home I guess."

"You guess?" Tanner hung his coat on a hook beside the door and wandered into the living room.

It was a tight space, even though the furniture was sparse. The small, beige loveseat had seen better days and had scratch marks down one side. Paul's cat had destroyed it. Eventually, Paul had had enough of her and gave her to the pound.

Two end tables with metal frames and glass surfaces flanked each side of the loveseat, and the only other place to sit was Paul's ancient, brown leather recliner whose springs had long ago lost their bounce. Instead of being the comfortable chair it appeared to be, wires stuck into places they didn't belong. No one ever sat in it for long once they discovered its flaws. It was a useless piece of furniture, but Paul refused to get rid of it.

The coffee table was a mismatched, solid cherry wood that didn't go with anything. The nicest thing we owned was the fifty-inch flat screen which hung on the wall, and the curio cabinet full of hundreds of DVDs. I preferred Netflix, but Paul was set on owning everything he liked, so the collection had grown to overflowing proportions and piles were now stacked on the floor in front of it.

Tanner made himself at home on the loveseat and propped his feet up on the coffee table.

"So what movie did you have in mind?"

I headed to the adjoining kitchen to grab us a couple of beers. "I don't know. Fire up Netflix, and we can pick one together. What kind of movies do you like?"

"Comedies mostly. Sometimes documentaries, superhero stuff. I'm easy."

"I'm cool with anything that is not classified as an action movie so choose away."

After busting a gut through *Spaceballs*—I was still reeling at the fact he'd chosen that classic movie; one of my top favorites—and drinking through a couple more beers, Tanner checked the time on his phone.

"I should probably head out."

He called a cab, and we both headed down to the lobby to wait for it.

"So, Paul's not home until Monday?" Tanner asked.

"Yeah, he flies in Monday morning at eleven."

"Do you have plans for the rest of your weekend?"

"Not really. Laundry. Gaming probably."

"What do you say to a *Lord of the Rings* marathon tomorrow instead? I'll bring the beer and pizza or something? Beats sitting around here by yourself."

Feeling a lot more relaxed, be it the copious amounts of alcohol I'd consumed, or just the general fact that Tanner was fun and easy to hang out with, I felt at ease with the idea of having him back over. Angie was right, it was okay to have friends, and Tanner and I seemed to get along great. We had a lot in common, and it felt really good having a friend again. It'd been a long time since I'd just hung out with anyone who wasn't Paul. My worries went out the window less than ten minutes after we'd got back there that evening, and it was so nice to just be able to relax and be myself.

"Sounds like a plan. How about you swing by about one or two 'ish."

The cab pulled up outside, and Tanner swung his jacket on and headed out into the cool May night. "See you then, Z."

Chapter Six

Tanner

By the time *The Fellowship of the Ring* ended, I was pretty sure I was going to be sick because I'd eaten so much pizza. When I'd showed up at Zander's door with two extra larges, loaded with every topping I could get my hands on, Zander had laughed and asked if I'd invited five other people without telling him. I'd gone overboard, I saw that.

Sitting on the floor with my feet sprawled out under the coffee table, I eyed the pizza box that was wide open, taunting me with its delicious goodness. With my stomach already stretched to unnatural limits, I pulled another slice from the box and took a bite.

"Are you nuts? I thought you were full three slices ago."

"I don't want to see it go to waste. Plus, you gave up after only two pieces. Somebody needs to make the sacrifice."

"Ever heard of leftovers?"

"Leftovers is just another word for failure."

"I stopped eating because I was full. That's what normal people do when they get full. They stop eating." He reached down from where he was laid out on the couch and closed the lid. "There. Maybe if you don't see it, you'll stop eating it."

"Won't work. I can still smell it," I said around a mouthful of food.

Zander laughed and rolled off the couch. "I'm putting it in the kitchen. I doubt you can even manage to roll that far at this point."

"Aww, but what if I want more?"

"Trust me," he called over his shoulder. "I'm saving your life—and maybe my carpets."

"You want me to pop in number two?"

"Sure."

He was right, the act of moving had become more than difficult; it was painful. Groaning as I crawled my way over to the DVD player, I regretted the last two slices I'd eaten. Maybe the last three. How many had I devoured? Six? Seven? Yeesh. I didn't even know.

Once the movie was in and the title screen up, I crawled back to the couch and took Zander's spot, sprawling out over the entire length of the loveseat and dangling my legs over the side.

"Hell no!" Zander returned and planted his feet in front of me, hands on his hips. "Move over, I'm not sitting on the floor."

I pointed at the recliner and grunted something that wasn't English.

"No way that thing sucks, sit up and share or I'll sit on you."

"I'll barf if you do that."

"Then sit up." He slapped my legs aside, and I shuffled to a sitting position, sinking into the couch as I rested my feet on the coffee table.

Zander scooped up the remote and quirked an eyebrow at my anguish. "You ready?"

I managed another caveman grunt and nodded.

At some point during the second movie, I fell into a pizza coma and didn't wake up until the credits rolled up the screen. When I looked around, a little disoriented and embarrassed, I noticed Zander scrutinizing his phone, mashing his fingers in what looked to be aggravated texting.

"Dammit. I missed it all. Now we have to start again," I teased before yawning and pulling myself more upright.

Zander didn't respond, his head was in his phone and his brow furrowed as he typed some more.

"Everything okay?" I nudged his foot with mine.

"Hmm." He glanced over before his phone buzzed again and he swung his head back to read the message. "It's just Paul," he muttered.

He sent one last text and turned his screen off before placing his phone on the table beside him, face down. It wasn't much of an explanation, but it wasn't my business either, so I dropped it.

"I think I'm done with our marathon. I botched it by falling asleep. You should have kicked me or something. Woke me up."

"You looked peaceful, I didn't want to disturb you."

"Did you watch me sleep? Cuz that's kinda weird you know."

"No! I watched the movie," he snapped, jumping on the accusation like I'd accused him of robbing a bank.

Ignoring his obvious discomfort, I threw a finger toward the TV. "You want to watch something else?"

"I don't know. Do you?"

Finger combing my messed-up hair, I squinted at the movies stacked around the room while I thought. "What do you prefer, comedies or actions?"

"Comedies. Hate action movies, remember?"

"Hate? That's pretty definitive."

"Long story. You?"

"Oh, like I said, comedies all the way."

His grin grew to face splitting dimensions. It was beautiful to see, and it was only that it stood out so much that I realized I didn't see him smile often.

"I like action sometimes," I added, "but I'm picky about them. Do you like superhero movies?" I asked, "They're kinda actiony."

Zander seemed to consider. "I'm gonna say mostly no, just for that reason."

"Wow, that's a big aversion. So, does that eliminate a *Star Wars* marathon from our near future?"

"It does."

"Sadness."

He chuckled; an even sweeter sound and right away, I wanted to hear it again. It was like music to my ears.

Oh, music! "Classic Rock or New Age Pop?"

"Definitely rock. Country or Rap?"

"Rap, but only because I hate country music about as much as you hate action flicks. Rap is not a favorite for the record."

"Fair enough. I've got one; Xbox One or PS4." Before I could open my mouth to respond, he added, "If you say PS4 I might ask you to leave, and this friendship will be over."

A laugh rumbled out of my chest at his warning. "Like that is it? Well, you can relax, nerd boy, I'm the proud owner of both Xbox 360 and Xbox One. You?"

"Bought myself an Xbox One the day it came out. Spent way too much money on it too. Got a deluxe edition with all the bells and whistles."

"Nice."

Zander stood from the couch and headed to the kitchen. "Beer?"

"Please. So here's one for you; first-person shooter or RPG?"

Role-playing games were my personal favorite, and call it a hunch, but I already figured I knew his answer.

"RPG. Skyrim is my console Warcraft," he called from the other room, "but I like playing two player shooters sometimes too. I'm good at them."

"And you're cocky too it seems."

Returning and handing me a beer, I was graced with another face-splitting smile. "I'll kick your butt someday, you'll see."

Sipping my beer, I shook my head at his confidence. "Okay, how about this; Mario or Luigi?"

"To screw or to play because their little, pixilated rear ends don't do much for me."

It was fun. That laid-back version of Zander was something I'd not seen before, and I liked it. Ordinarily, he seemed quieter and more reserved, maybe even uptight or nervous. Although, what caused it, I didn't really know. I was beginning to get the sense that his relationship with that Paul guy wasn't all that glamorous. He didn't talk about him much, and whenever his name came up, it brought on an instant frown and sense of discomfiture I didn't like seeing. Hell, the insouciant Zander I was seeing was funny too. I'd work to keep that version of him around.

"If you've even thought about fucking Mario or Luigi, I'm not sure I want to hear about it. That's a little too far into the nerd zone for me. How about to play, dumbass?"

He stuck his tongue out and sipped his beer, slouching back on the couch and looking laid-back and serene. "Luigi. You?"

"Mario." Gnawing my lip, I tried to think of another question to ask, but Zander beat me to it.

"What's something you've always wanted to do, but haven't?"

Readjusting on the couch to face him, I smiled, knowing my answer right away. "Learn to play guitar."

"Really?"

"Yup. Ever since I heard Eddie Van Halen when I was ten years old, it's been a dream."

"No way. I love Van Halen."

And that was pretty much how the rest of our night played out. No one had ever cared much about listening to me gush over my dream of playing guitar, but Zander seemed genuinely interested.

I told him how I'd taken a year of piano lessons when I was a kid but dropped out after not taking it seriously, goofing off, and wasting my parent's money. It wasn't what I'd wanted to learn. Years later, my parents refused to give me guitar lessons because they figured it was just a passing interest that would die off, and they didn't want to flush any more money down the drain on my whims.

An hour or later, we were interrupted when Zander's phone buzzed again on the end table. He hesitated when he looked at it, seeming unsure if he wanted to pick it up.

My eyes shifted from his phone to the perturbed look on his face. "Do you need to check that?"

Chewing the inside of his cheek, he picked it up and glimpsed at the message, failing at nonchalance. "Fargin' Smangle," he said to his phone under his breath, while popping off a quick reply.

What the hell was that?

I couldn't hold back the chuckle at his lame use of made-up curse words. "You really don't swear much, do you?"

His cheeks instantly reddened as he tossed his phone aside again. "Nature of my job I guess. I'm not against it, I've just trained myself otherwise."

"It's cute."

Rolling his eyes, he ignored the next buzz that came from his phone. "I hate being referred to as cute."

"Noted. Sorry." I fought the grin and added, "It's fargin' sexy."

That got me shoved off the couch onto the floor. "You're a butthole."

"Careful! Language, mister, that was harsh." I continued to laugh as he threw a pillow at my head.

"Get more beer, I'm putting on a movie."

Rolling to my stomach, I peeled myself off the ground, laughing. I waited until I was around the corner in the kitchen before calling out, "Make sure it's PG. I wouldn't want to pop the cherry on those virgin ears."

I was sure I heard a groan and couldn't help laughing even harder as I pulled two more beers from the fridge.

Sometime during another failed attempt at watching a movie—I fell asleep even sooner than the previous one; like opening credits sooner—Zander woke me with a nudge.

"I'm going to bed. Do you want a blanket and a pillow?"

Barely opening my eyes, I made a half-assed effort at sitting up. "Nah, I'll take off."

"Forget it. You're out cold, and you've had a half-dozen beers. You're not driving. Lay down, I'll get you a blanket."

Without arguing, I curled back onto the too short loveseat and was out before Zander returned. I vaguely remembered him tucking a fleece throw around my shoulders, and after that, the next I knew, it was morning, and the sun was blazing through the doorway from the kitchen. I didn't know if it was the beer, the pizza, or both, but I'd slept like a rock.

The apartment was quiet. I stumbled my way to the bathroom, took a piss, and wet down the cockeyed pieces of hair that wouldn't stick down with a finger combing.

Zander's door was closed, so I made my way to the kitchen, found the stuff to make coffee, and set it to brew. It was just past nine in the morning, and my stomach rumbled. Fishing through the fridge like I lived there, I found the leftover pizza and pulled the box out, helping myself to a cold slice. Eating through the congealed cheese and chewy bread, I watched out the window at the traffic zooming up and down the street eight stories below.

"You are unbelievable."

Jumping at the noise of someone directly behind me, I spun. With pizza hanging from my mouth, I stared at a sweat-soaked Zander who stood four-feet away, mopping his face with a hand towel. He was dressed in spandex gym shorts—that left nothing to the imagination—a tank top that clung to his muscles, and Nike runners.

"I thought you were asleep," I said around a mouthful of pizza, making a concentrated effort not to stare at his toned body all slicked with sweat.

"Nope. I run every morning, I've been up for two hours, sleepy head. I can't believe you're still eating that stuff. You're disgusting."

"It's good. Wanna bite?" When I offered him the half-eaten piece I was working on, I just got a look of disgust in return.

"No thank you. I'm gonna hop in a shower."

He turned and headed down the hall. I couldn't help ducking my head around the corner and ogling his tight ass in his spandex.

Fuck that's a firm ass.

I shook my head, trying to wipe away my wandering thoughts. Green was not a good color on me, and right then, I hated that Paul guy even more and I didn't even know him.

"Do you want coffee?" I called after him.

"Sure. Milk and sugar please."

Finished with my pizza, I searched for mugs and poured out the coffee.

I was halfway done my first cup when Zander returned, hair damp from his shower and dressed in cargo shorts and a light blue polo. He joined me at the table, and we sat in silence while we sipped our morning brew. An awkwardness hung in the air. One that hadn't been present the previous night, and I wondered where it came from and why it was there.

Did you catch me staring at your ass?

I shuffled uncomfortably in my chair. Neither of us spoke until we'd finished our drinks and I got up to pour us another.

"What's your game plan today?" I was probably pushing my boundaries, but I'd enjoyed hanging out with him that weekend, and I wasn't sure I wanted it to end.

"I really need to get some laundry done before Paul gets home. It's gonna take me all day."

It was a delicate way of saying we needed to part ways and I took the hint. Hiding my disappointment behind another slice of pizza, I agreed, saying something about working on some sketches for a client. A blatant lie.

It had been a good weekend, and I felt like Zander had let me in a little more. There was more to him than what he showed every day at the daycare and online, and the more I knew, the more I liked him. We had tons in common, and even though I had to curb my ridiculous attraction to him, I was okay with it. He had the makings of becoming a good friend.

Chapter Seven

Zander-Early June

    I hated Wednesdays. More so than any other day of the week. Technically, it had the same number of hours in it as any other day, but I would have put money on someone sneaking in extra when I wasn't looking.
    That Wednesday was especially dragging. I had been up late gaming with Tanner the previous night and had cut myself short on sleep again. It was becoming a bad habit. Since getting to know each other better two weekends before, after our failed night out at the club, we had been hanging out regularly on Warcraft and playing way too late into the night. Fine for him who didn't start work until ten in the morning, but when my alarm screamed at me at five a.m. every day, it was making it hard to function.
    Tanner had offered to hang out a few times after work or meet up again on the weekends. He'd even invited Paul to join us, but knowing how that would all play out, I'd made excuses every time. Tanner didn't know much about Paul, and I wanted to keep it that way. Paul was…difficult to explain. Tanner was fun and lighthearted, kind and free-spirited, the complete opposite of Paul. Paul was…a stick in the mud to be nice. Angie knew more than I liked just because we'd been friends for so long, and the truth had a way of slipping out, even when I did my best to hide it.
    After hitching a ride home with Angie, I pulled open the front door to mine and Paul's apartment and was greeted with a delicious whiff of garlic and herbs along with some other kind of mouth-watering food that was cooking.
    "Something smells good," I called out. My backpack landed with a thud by the door as I kicked my shoes off and wandered into the kitchen, shucking my jacket. "What's cooking?" Holding my breath, I waited for a response.
    Paul was standing with his back turned in front of the stove, stirring a big pot. "I was watching this cooking show last night and had to try this

recipe. It looked so damn good. Fucking expensive as shit for ingredients, but whatever."

A quick analysis of his mood told me to relax. That single statement could have included his rather harsh opinion of the government and how they liked to inflate prices on everything, making the average hard-working Joe even poorer; but it hadn't. The evening was going well for him so far, and I could release the tension I always held in my shoulders whenever I walked in the front door.

Shimmying up beside him, I peered into the simmering red sauce as I ran a hand gently down his back to rest at his hip. "Will it be long?"

"Twenty minutes yet."

"Okay." I lifted to my toes and pecked his cheek. "I'm gonna hop in a shower."

Collecting some clean clothes from the bedroom, I reflected on Paul's love for cooking. He really took joy in making new dishes, and he constantly sought exotic and fun recipes to try. I liked how relaxed he could be when he worked in the kitchen. As though all the bad things—all the mood swings and harsh words, all the yelling and spontaneous rage bursts—just disappeared when he was engrossed in cooking. Too bad it never lasted. It was sad because even that small good thing generally had a way of turning ugly. He couldn't seem to just be happy with something from start to finish. It wasn't in his nature.

Our relationship was far from perfect. His love for cooking had a way of smoothing out all our rough patches and helped me forget. But it was always short lived. While so many things in our relationship fell into the gutter, I clung to those small bits of joy when they were rewarded. Like that gleam in his eyes while he cooked. I reminded myself that somewhere deep inside, maybe there was some good. Almost seven years and the things that made me happy were becoming harder and harder to find.

Letting the hot water of the shower run down my body, soothing my muscles as it washed away the grime of my job, I tried to think of the best way to approach the subject of possibly hanging out with Tanner that weekend. Paul was in a decent enough mood. That helped. If I was careful how I brought it up, it might not be that big of a deal. But in the same breath, it could all go to shit in an instant. That was why I'd always avoided making friends. It was just easier not stirring the pot.

Paul was possessive over our time together, and it flattered me in the beginning. Over time, it had become smothering. In just under seven years, I had managed to push away every friend I used to have and had successfully prevented any more from taking shape, all because Paul thought time away from work should be our time and no one else's. The only friend I had was Angie, and I was pretty sure she was beginning to see Paul for who he really was.

Rinsing the shampoo from my hair, it echoed again in my brain just how much of a prison sentence my life had become. Never leaving the house, except for work. Defending myself if I came home too late. Pleading my case if I wanted to spend any time with Angie outside of my job.

With a sigh, I shut off the water and grabbed my towel. Where the heck did I go wrong?

Tanner seeking my friendship shouldn't have caused such confliction. Maybe I should have shut him down like I had all the other attempts people had made over the years. Enough excuses and people eventually took the hint or got tired of trying. But, for some reason, Tanner was different, and I couldn't put my finger on it. His approaches were always kindly made and pressure free. His personality gave the impression of someone who lived life openly and happily. Conversations between us flowed easily and were never uncomfortable or cramped. It helped that we seemed to have a lot in common. We talked and gamed for hours without things ever being weird.

Since his initial inquiry, and learning my relationship status, he'd never made any further advances and had just remained a solid friend. When he came to pick up Anna at preschool, we'd yammer on and on about Warcraft or other games we played. Angie just rolled her eyes at us because the excited exchanges we shared were emulative of teenage boys. I'd forgotten what it felt like to have a friend.

Tanner's invitation that morning to join his work buddies at paintball on the weekend sounded like a lot of fun, and I was surprised at how much I wanted to partake in the activity. Paintball just sounded like my first-person shooter games brought to life, and I'd have killed for the chance to experience it. But, it all came down to convincing Paul.

God, it shouldn't be this hard.

After tossing my dirty clothes into the hamper, I finger combed my hair as I made my way back into the kitchen.

"Can I help with anything?" I always asked, even though Paul never wanted my help.

"Nah, I'm good. Just going to plate it up."

Paul opened the oven and pulled out a baking dish with what looked like chicken all fancied up. I wasn't sure what he was making, but it smelled incredible. His back was turned, and I watched him, chewing my lip as I worked through what I wanted to say.

Paul was ruggedly handsome. A big guy of six foot four with solid muscles and broad shoulders. He dwarfed my five-foot-eleven frame easily, making me feel small. He wore his dark brown hair cropped short, military style, and carried a stern "don't mess with me" attitude wherever he went—and most people didn't mess with him.

I met him at a gay bar on my nineteenth birthday. He was the bouncer—surprise, surprise—and when my sorry-ass self, drank way too much celebratory drinks, it had been him who had literally carried me to the cab and deposited me inside. The following morning, I'd found a note shoved into the pocket of my jeans with his name and number along with a short message; *the next time I throw you over my shoulder, you won't land in a cab. You'll land in my bed, sexy.*

My initial reaction had been: *cocky prick, as if.* I should have taken it as the red flag it so clearly was, but my group of college friends at the time wouldn't stop bugging me about him until we'd wound up back in that bar the following weekend. True to his word, after that night, I'd landed in his bed and had been there ever since. Those college friends; long gone. I often wondered if they regretted pushing me to return to that bar.

I grabbed silverware from a drawer and a couple cans of soda from the fridge. Paul heaped our plates high with chicken, veggies, and some noodle thing with sauce. My saliva glands and stomach reacted instantly as I pulled up a seat at the small table in our kitchen.

"Looks great."

"Yeah. It's okay. The sauce is kinda shit. Fuck Emeril Lagasse."

Careful not to roll my eyes, I gave a quick smile. "You are too hard on yourself. You make amazing stuff."

Ignoring me, Paul sat at the opposite end of the table and shoveled his food in his mouth without enthusiasm. He was his own worst critic, which I knew was normal for people, but with Paul, it generally was always the tipping point.

We ate in silence, and I refrained from making any more comments about our meal. It really was delicious, and I couldn't find a flaw in it, but if Paul saw something wrong with it, there was no point in arguing. I'd be wrong, and it would only escalate things until, God knows, we'd have broken dishes and food on the walls.

The tension in my shoulders was back. That wasn't how I'd pictured my life to be ten years back, but it was what it was, and there was nothing I could do about it.

Paul wasn't a fan of cleaning up dishes, and I thought it was always a good compromise for me to take over kitchen tidy up duties on the nights he cooked. It was only fair, and he never complained.

"I'm going for a smoke, then I'll find us a movie to watch. Grab a couple more sodas and join me when you're done."

It wasn't a question, so I didn't protest that maybe I was too tired for a movie after such a long day.

"Sure."

Paul headed to the living room after his smoke, while I began rinsing the plates under the tap.

Movies were not a compromise. Years before I'd made my aversion to car chase, blow everything up action films known, but either he didn't hear me, or he didn't care because that was what we watched. All. The. Time. Another battle that wasn't worth fighting. I simply endured and tried to find something enjoyable about them. More times than not, I lost track of what was going on when my mind wandered, and by the end, I was so lost I'd just be grateful it was over.

Dishwasher loaded, I wiped down the counters and the table and washed my hands in the sink. I grabbed two more sodas from the fridge and joined Paul in the living room.

Settling in on the far side of the loveseat, I sank deep into the cushions. It was the coziest thing we owned, and I loved curling up there with a good book on quiet evenings. Paul was not a snuggler, so there was a vast expanse of space open between us, despite it being a loveseat. He pressed himself to the opposite end and rested his feet on the coffee table. I curled my feet under me and laid my head back. Paul was already waiting and had the remote at the ready.

"What are we watching?" I asked.

Please don't say Die Hard.

"Die Hard."

Oh my God! Seriously?! Again?!

"Cool."

Of all the available movies we could have watched on Netflix, he picked *Die Hard*. We owned *Die Hard,* and I swear to God we watched it at least once a week. I hated that movie. Not a little hate, but a great freaking big one. I might, quite possibly, have been the only man on the planet who despised it, and maybe there was something seriously wrong with me, but I *loathed* that movie.

Ugh!

About halfway through the flick, I fell asleep. It wasn't like I meant to. I'd had a late night and long day, and the movie was barely holding my interest.

A sudden loud noise blast me awake, and I bolted upright, confused and blurry-eyed. It took me a minute to figure out that the noise had been Paul, slamming the remote on the coffee table as hard as he could, purposefully to get my attention. A shot of adrenaline released inside me, seeping throughout my body as I came to my senses.

"Shoot. I fell asleep. I-I'm sorry." Normal people wouldn't have to apologize for something like that. Normal people.

"It's nice to see this is how fucking important our time together is for you."

Paul was on his feet, and his anger had gone from zero to about a million and a half in a matter of an instant, and it was all directed at me. I hated when it was directed at me. It was bad enough when it was about someone or something else. During those periods, I generally disappeared into a dark corner and avoided being noticed. But right then, it was all me. Might as well have shone a big spotlight on my head because that was how centered-out I felt.

"I-I didn't m-mean to. I'm sorry," I stammered. It pissed me off when I heard the vulnerability in my tone. Paul always called me out when I acted weak, but he didn't seem to realize, it was him who made me that way.

"If you didn't want to fucking watch a movie, you should have said so."

But that would have made you just as angry.

"I had a long day. I-I guess it's just catching—"

"It's all about you and your fucking long ass day. If you're that fucking tired, put your ass to bed and get the hell out of my face."

Paul had bent down to within an inch of my face, stopping my words short. When he yelled, his spittle sprayed me. Frozen in place, not moving a single muscle, all I could do was shrivel up in terror. I was pretty sure I'd stopped breathing.

He picked up the remote and whipped it at me. It was so sudden and forceful all I could do was bring my arms up to protect my face. He stormed down the hall to the office and slammed the door so hard the walls vibrated, and the hanging pictures rattled. I wouldn't have been surprised if old lady Mildred, mostly deaf in her old age, heard it on the first floor.

"Gladly," I whispered to myself. My heart was in my throat as I picked myself up off the couch on shaky legs. *It could have been a lot worse. Just go to bed, it will be better in the morning.* It was something I told myself on a regular basis; it had become my mantra. I was starting to see it plain as day.

Only who was I kidding, it was never better in the morning.

Chapter Eight

*Tanner-*Mid-June

    I woke up with an abrupt start, arms flying, flailing, and trying to grab hold of an edge that wasn't there. It took a full minute for my mind to realign, eyes searching through the dark shadows of my bedroom for comprehension before I realized my cell phone was buzzing on the nightstand. I snagged it and squinted at the brightly lit display, blinding my light sensitive eyes. Zander's name and number flashed across the screen, and I flicked over to check the time. It was half past three.
    What the hell is he calling for in the middle of the night?
    Sliding my finger across the screen, I flopped back on my pillow while I let out a less than audible grunt hello. Silence hung on the other end of the line, and I pulled the phone away from my ear to ensure I had indeed answered it. Replacing it, I cleared my throat and tried again with a little more clarity.
    "Hello? Z, are you there?"
    I could hear faint, labored breathing on the other end, but still, he said nothing. More awake, I pulled myself to sit, switching ears as my heart raced a little faster. Somewhere in my gut, I knew it wasn't a friendly, "I can't sleep, what are you up to?" kind of call.
    "Zander? Are you ok? Answer me." My tone grew frantic.
    "Can I come over?" His voice was small, and it took a second for me to register what he'd said.
    "Yes. Of course. Z, where are you? Are you okay?"
    "Corner of Wellesley and Yonge. I'm walking. Where do you live?"
    Walking?
    "Stay put. I'm coming to get you." I was out of bed like a shot, yanking my jeans up my legs while balancing the phone against my ear. "Zander, are you okay?"
    Silence followed, but I knew he was still there. I could hear him shuffling the phone as he sighed. Grabbing my jacket, I reached for my keys and shoved them in my pocket before pulling a second helmet from

the high shelf in my closet. I rarely took passengers on my motorcycle but had always kept an extra helmet just in case.

When he still didn't answer, I steeled myself for what I might be up against when I found him. Call it a hunch, a gut instinct, whatever you will, but I knew whatever was up had to do with the boyfriend somehow. The more I learned about that fucker, the less I liked him.

"Listen, Z, I'll be there in less than ten, okay? Stay put, I'll find you."

The roar of my Ducati Diavel echoed loud down the quiet streets as I raced much faster than was the official speed limit toward Zander's location. It was a good six or more blocks from where I knew he lived, and I wondered if he'd been out wandering for hours before he'd called me. I twisted the accelerator a little more, bringing the bike up to dangerously high, city street speeds, but I didn't care.

When I rounded the corner onto Yonge Street and headed toward the intersection Zander had relayed, I took her down to a more appropriate crawl. Then I spotted him, leaned against a wall, arms hugged across his bare chest—*his bare fucking chest*—wearing nothing but a pair of sleep pants. Anger jetted through my veins, and I had to clench my teeth together, forcing it away before I could approach him.

He spotted me as I pulled up to the curb, but he hung his head and wouldn't look up as he peeled himself off the wall and wandered over.

I dropped my helmet over the bars and pulled my jacket off to wrap it around his bare shoulders. It was mid-June, but with the sun down, it was still way too cold to be out like that. When my hand brushed his skin, it was like ice, and that was when I noticed he was covered in goosebumps.

"You can't exactly stand around these streets looking like this you know. Someone is going to think you're a piece of meat to be bought." It was meant as a joke, but I failed in execution, and it came out serious and mothering.

Zander pulled my jacket snug and zipped it up, shuttering. "Thanks." He kept his eyes downcast and shuffled between feet from either nerves or cold, I wasn't sure.

He looked so distraught; I didn't know what to do. I could tell he was freezing and uncomfortable. Instinctively, I wanted to pull him into my arms and hold him until he calmed down. Hug warmth back into his body, but it wasn't my place. Nor did I think it was the place for a friend. There I was wavering on that stupid line again, dancing around right and wrong. Zander *was* a friend. Hugging a friend was perfectly acceptable in a time of need. Wasn't it? He seemed to need it, but why did it feel wrong? Why did the idea bring on feelings of guilt?

Ultimately deciding against it, I handed him the second helmet I'd brought and secured my own back on my head.

"I didn't know you rode." His feet were planted on the spot, and he made no effort to put on the helmet. "I mean, I'm not surprised, I just didn't know. I've never seen you with a bike."

"I had it sent from Thunder Bay. Couldn't drive both the truck and bike down and it's only just becoming warm enough to take her out again. Is this okay?"

Zander hesitated another minute, then fit the helmet over his head. "It's fine."

Zander's grip around my waist on our ride back to my sister's house was nearly suffocating and a dead giveaway to his nerve status. It clearly wasn't fine.

When he got off on shaky legs and handed me back the helmet, I couldn't help smiling inwardly at his discomfort. First timers always looked like they'd just had their lives threatened after their initial ride.

"Come on."

Entering the side door from the garage, I indicated for him to follow. We walked through the open concept living room and formal dining area to the stairs leading to the second floor. Stopping at the bathroom, I turned back. He'd followed silently but was still managing to avoid looking at me. He hadn't been that awkward since our first meeting months before. I figured a hot shower, clean clothes, and a beer were in order before I made any attempts to pry information from him.

"How about you warm up in a hot shower, I'll find you something clean to put on and then meet me downstairs?"

"Sure." He nodded with an attempt at a smile and headed into the bathroom while I wandered further down the hall to my bedroom.

Returning with a clean pair of sleep pants and an old band t-shirt, I found him standing awkwardly, holding my jacket to his bare chest. He offered it out. "Thank you for this. I left too fast to think of grabbing a shirt."

"No problem. Here's something clean for when you're done. Take your time, I'll be downstairs. Are you hungry? Can I make you something to eat?"

"Nah. It's okay."

Leaving him to shower, I headed downstairs and paced a hole in the carpet while I waited. My mind was on overdrive trying to figure out what had happened. That fucktard of a boyfriend was about to have dealings with me if I found out he'd done something to hurt Zander. Something told me not to trust the guy, even though I'd never met him. The idea alone had me so riled up, the adrenaline pumping through my veins was thick and angry, and I wanted to punch something...like the douchebag's face. I couldn't shake the eerie feeling I had about the guy, and the way Zander avoided discussions about him at every turn only made me more suspicious.

It was a full twenty minutes before Zander wandered downstairs. I'd already polished off two beers trying to calm my nerves so I didn't snap. He looked weary and tired. I didn't even ask if he wanted a beer, I just opened him one and shoved it into his hand before steering him to sit on the couch.

"Your sister's place is nice." His eyes trailed around, taking in his surroundings.

I had to agree. My sister really should have considered a job in interior decorating the way she managed to pull together a look. Every room complemented the next, subtly pulled together through color flow or furniture arrangement.

The living room was warm earth tones. The walls a gentle sand color, covered in a perfect array of wooden framed family portraits—minus the ones of the ex-husband/father, which had obviously been taken down. The couch was a corduroy, chocolate brown sectional—far too squishy in my opinion—with a few striped pillows thrown about in various other shades of brown. They tied in nicely with the lighter brown rug centered in the room. The coffee table was square, solid walnut and fit perfectly into the middle of the L-shaped couch. A flat-screen TV hung on the wall with a walnut curio beside it containing DVDs, books, more framed photos, and knick-knacks. There were ferns and other plants spread throughout, giving it a homey, relaxed feel without cluttering it up or making it look like a jungle.

"Yeah, I like it here. Going to miss it when I get my own place. I can't afford anything nearly this nice though. Apartment living for me."

"Yeah. I hear ya." The faraway look in his eyes was concerning.

Silence seeped through the room again as we both sipped our drinks.

"So, wanna tell me why I'm picking you up on the street at three in the morning while you're dressed only in pajama pants?"

Zander stayed quiet as he picked at the label on his beer, peeling up the corner. "It's complicated."

"Z, I'm your friend. You can talk to me. Explain complicated, because I don't like what I'm imagining in my head, and I'd prefer knowing what's wrong."

Zander shifted and passed a worried glance in my direction before turning his attention to the room, avoiding direct eye contact yet again. "Paul was not in a good place tonight. I should have known better than to get in a battle of words with him."

Battle of words was better than a battle of fists.

"Did he kick you out?"

"No, I left. It was getting…" Zander shrugged and shook his head. "He's going to be livid now. I shouldn't have run away."

His lack of detail wasn't helping my presumptuous brain. It took every effort I had to keep my breathing even and my voice gentle as I pressed him for more.

"Z." His trailing eyes came to rest tentatively on mine, and the look behind them utterly broke my heart. There was fear and uncertainty, and I couldn't tell if it was because of the pressure I was putting on him or the situation he'd left at home. "Did he hurt you?" It was blunt, and the flicker of panic that came and went behind his eyes told me all I needed to know before he answered.

"No," he choked.

Liar.

His gaze fell to the drink balanced on his knee. Even he must have heard the uncertainty in his tone, because within seconds, his gaze was back on mine and he backpedaled anxiously, trying to right a wrong. "It's not like that. I-I mean he… He has anger issues. He gets… He breaks things. Yells a lot, you know? Normally I'm more careful, and I can skirt around it and not be in the spotlight. I was just tired because he woke me up, and I spoke before I thought and…"

I wasn't even sure he could hear the words he was saying because if he could, he'd understand my look of sheer horror. He stopped his desperate rambling and just stared blankly, worry etched into so many deep grooves along his forehead I was rendered speechless. He looked on the verge of running, so I slowly moved a hand to his knee while removing his beer with the other, placing it on the coffee table.

Usually, he can skirt the man's anger so it wasn't focused on him? What the ever-loving-fuck did that mean?

"*Has* he hurt you before, Z?" Maybe it was time to be more specific.

Without a beer to hold, Zander fidgeted with his nails, picking at the skin around them as his mouth seemed to work around yet unspoken words. His voice was barely audible when he finally answered. "It was a long time ago. I'm more careful now. I know better how to stay out of his rage path. Tanner, I don't want you to get the wrong idea about him. He's a good guy, truly..." Even he couldn't finish the sentence with conviction.

Mother Fucker!

Heat tendrils grew out of my belly and worked their way over my limbs. The seething anger flowing through my veins was so over the top it took me more than a few minutes before I got myself in control enough to speak. I kept my hand stilled on his leg as I fought the urge to clench my fists. Zander did not need more people flipping out in front of him, no matter how pissed I was at that fucking lowlife boyfriend. Clearly whatever had happened that night was enough to make him run, and I needed to be the friend he was reaching out for and not another problem he needed to escape.

"Why are you with him, Z? You shouldn't have to walk eggshells in a relationship so you don't get the shit beat out of you. What are you doing? You need to get away from him."

Zander sighed and shoved my hand from his leg before standing. "You don't get it. Anyway, I didn't come here for you to fix me or tell me I'm doing something wrong. I know it's messed up, but there's nothing I can do about it. It's complicated. I don't expect you to understand." His cheeks took on a rosy flush and his words, although sharp and pointed, remained soft and hesitant.

Was that what Zander was like angry? Because if so, it was such a controlled, careful anger it almost seemed he was afraid to own it. He laced his fingers through his hair and began to pace, chewing his lip.

I rose to stop him with a carefully placed hand on his upper arm and forced him to look at me. "What's to understand, Z? The guy has rage problems, and if you don't cower in a corner and keep your mouth shut, you get the snot beat out of you? That's what I'm hearing. You see, in my books, that's not okay. So please correct me if I'm wrong here."

"Tanner—"

My phone buzzed on the coffee table interrupting us.

"This conversation isn't over," I said, stooping to grab my phone. Not recognizing the number, I considered dropping it back on the table, but the fact that it was past three in the morning and Zander was standing in my sister's living room looking worse for wear made me think it could somehow be relevant to the situation, so I swiped my finger across to answer.

"Yeah."

"Tanner? It's Angie. Please tell me Zander is with you."

"He is." I glanced at Zander whose face had gone from uncomfortable irritation at my persistent quizzing to ghastly white and all-out panicked.

"It's Angie," I explained, reassuring him.

He visibly relaxed, but his face remained screwed up in question.

"Tanner, Paul came by here looking for Zander."

"Oh shit. What did he say? What did you tell him?"

"I told the asshat to fuck off. I told him Zander was here and was staying with me tonight and I wasn't letting him talk to him, only I had no idea where Zander actually was. He's with you? Is he okay?"

"Shaken. He'll be okay."

"I didn't want that fucker to keep looking for Zander if Zander was out there still. I don't trust that guy. Zander doesn't say much, but I don't get a good vibe from him."

"Me neither. He's safe here, Angie. I'm not letting him leave tonight."

"Thank you, Tanner. Please take care of my boy."

"I will."

"Can I talk to him?"

I held the phone out to Zander. His exhaustion was apparent as he took it and mumbled a few coherent answers to Angie's badgering. I realized it probably wasn't a good time to continue hammering him for answers. He'd sought me out as a friend to lean on, so I owed him that at least. The anger and protectiveness I felt would have to be pushed down, and I'd need to be satisfied that he was safe. *For now.* Maybe I could convince him to talk more the following morning when he was rested.

Zander ended the call with Angie and handed me back my phone.

"Thanks."

We stood in awkward silence for a moment, Zander studying his feet and me studying him.

"Come on, Z. You can stay in my room tonight. I'll hit the couch."

"No, no. I'm fine on the couch, I'm not kicking you out of your bed. It's bad enough I've brought my problems to your doorstep. I'm okay here."

"I insist." Grabbing his hand, I pulled him to the stairs. "Besides, when Stacey wakes up she's less likely to freak out finding me on the couch unannounced than her daughter's daycare teacher."

"Oh." Zander followed with less resistance as I steered him down the hallway to the end door on the right.

"I'll get fresh sheets. Give me a sec."

Zander grabbed my arm, halting me. "Don't. I-it's fine." His eyes were so sad and lost. For the second time that night, I wanted to scoop him into my arms and hold him, but I resisted.

"I'll be downstairs if you need anything."

He nodded, and I gave his hand a reassuring squeeze before leaving.

Laying on the couch in the darkness, staring at the reflection of the streetlights shining through the window and dancing across the ceiling, my brain wouldn't allow me to sleep. Every method to calm my wandering thoughts failed. Just as I would force my mind off of one path, another scooped me up into its tendrils, flinging me around like some jacked up version of the octopus ride at the fair, and I couldn't get off. The fears I'd had about Zander's boyfriend were founded and yet Zander seemed insistent on defending the bastard's actions.

No one should be treated that way, and with the knowledge I carried, I was torn between wanting to give the asshole a taste of his own medicine, while savagely protecting Zander, or just taking him away from the situation. Only, I couldn't do either of those things. I'd had my share of bar fights over the years, but somehow, beating the shit out of someone for being an abuser felt wrong and backward. Zander, on the other hand, had some sort of warped idea that it was okay and would probably see me as being a douchebag friend if I tried to step in, even if it was for his own good.

Rolling onto my side, I sighed. I needed Zander to see that life could be better on the other side and he didn't need that in his life.

I would be so good to you if you were mine, Z. I'd spend every day making sure you were happy. I'd work to see that smile and hear that laugh.

When sleep finally came, it was fitful and full of dreams that were forgotten in the morning but left an imprint nonetheless in the form of drained emotions and a tumultuous, rotting gut.

Chapter Nine

Zander

I woke to the smell of coffee and bacon. Sprawled out on my stomach on silky soft sheets, I peeked my eyes open, blinking against the sun shining through the open blinds. It took my sleep clouded brain a few minutes to figure out where I was and why. The moment it dawned on me, the sinking, nauseating feeling in my gut returned.

The incident from the previous night with Paul had cleared in my mind, as it usually did once I'd slept. A new, prickling blanket of fear and anxiety covered me, and I sat up in Tanner's bed and hugged my knees to my chest. It was one thing for people to think they knew something about you and another for them to hear the truth right from your own lips. What had I done?

Caving in and calling Tanner the previous night, going to his home and allowing him to pull strings of facts out of me one at a time was infallible proof of what he was already thinking in his head. There was no going back. I couldn't un-say the things I'd said. It would have been better if I'd let Paul cool off and then gone home to face his fury. Maybe it wouldn't have been so bad. At least Paul didn't know I was at Tanner's. That would probably be the nail in my own coffin. So long as he believed I was at Angie's, I'd be better off.

A soft rap at the door startled me, and Tanner poked his head in before I could answer.

"You up?"

"Yeah." The discomfort of being in his room—in his bed—was back and I fiddled with the blankets, biting at my lip.

"There's breakfast and coffee made. Stacey and Anna will be leaving soon. Anna has swimming lessons early, and I guess they have a play date after, so we'll have the house to ourselves for a bit."

"Sounds good."

"If you want something to wear, you can help yourself to whatever's in the dresser or closet. We're close to the same size. There are sweats or whatever. You can stay in pajamas all day for all I care. Help yourself."

"Thanks. I'll be down in a minute."

Pajamas all day? That just didn't happen in my world. Paul would have none of that.

When the door closed behind him, I glanced around, taking inventory of the dresser and closet in the room. The dresser was solid wood with the same craftsmanship as the furniture I'd seen downstairs. It made me think a lot of the furniture was custom made. The closet was a large walk-in whose doors stood wide open, displaying a messy array of Tanner's clothes, some on hangers, but most piled on the floor. Apart from the double bed and a couple of wooden end tables, the room was a fairly simple setup; uncluttered with random touches of Tanner, including a TV, Xbox, laptop, iPod dock, games, and movies scattered about.

Am I staying past breakfast?

I'd arrived in sleep pants, I couldn't go home wearing Tanner's clothes. Paul would know I hadn't stayed at Angie's if I did that. Cold fear tickled like icy fingers up my nape at the thought of going home. Was Paul going to be pissed that I'd left or would he have cooled off? He'd probably be all forgiving as was his routine after he exploded on me. Either way, I was not prepared to find out what I was in store for just then. Besides, it was Saturday, so I fished through Tanner's clothes and found something to wear. As much as I didn't want to have to explain things to Tanner about my personal life, going home was the less appealing option.

Breakfast was delicious and the coffee even better. Stacey headed out with Anna after we gave a relatively vague explanation about why I was there. We were alone. Tanner couldn't take his eyes off me the entire time we ate, although he acted discreet. With every bite, I awaited the inquisition, chewing each mouthful like it was a ticking time bomb and the next bite was the one that would set off the barrage of questions.

They never came.

When our plates were empty, Tanner cleared them to the adjoining kitchen where I could hear him rinsing and stacking them in the dishwasher. I couldn't decide the best course of action; hang around and wait to be grilled or go home and face the music. Both options sucked and as I muddled them over, Tanner returned with two fresh mugs of coffee.

"Wanna junk out with some Halo for a bit? You can kick my ass like you said you would. Show me what you're made of."

Accepting the mug, I searched Tanner's face for some understanding. Clearly reading my mind, he squeezed my shoulder and smiled.

"Listen, if you wanna talk about it, I'm all ears, but I'm not going to push you. If you need a place to hang while you sort shit out, I'm here for you. You can stay as long as you want. I'm your friend, Z, lean on me if you need to."

Just like that, Tanner lifted the weight off my shoulders and made everything okay. He didn't pry, and he didn't push for answers to questions he knew I couldn't give. He was just there for me; without strings or conditions. He was a friend. He was everything I needed without even knowing I had been needing it.

We sat on his bed in his room and gamed for hours. The fun scale ramped up even more when Tanner pulled out his old N64 system from deep in the closet, and we had a retro game rodeo all afternoon, playing through endless Mario Kart challenges. By evening, we took a break to order pizza. Tanner found us a couple of beers as we sat around and waited for it to arrive.

I snagged my phone off the end table. The previous evening, I'd turned it off after calling Tanner. When I switched it back on, there were a dozen missed messages and three missed calls. Two of the messages were from Angie, but the rest were all from Paul.

Where the fuck are you?
Are you still with Angie?
Answer me dammit.
I'm sorry I was a dick. Call me.
Are you coming home?

And so on and so on. I set my phone down on the bed between us and took a long drink of my beer.

"Are you okay?" Tanner asked.

He'd been watching me flip through my messages. We still hadn't discussed any more about the issue that had sent me running the night before, but I felt like I owed him, as much as I didn't want to talk about it.

"Yeah. I probably should head home at some point. No sense avoiding the inevitable." I knew it was a poor choice of words when Tanner's jaw tightened. "It will be okay. He's chilled out." My attempt at reassurance fell flat.

"You deserve better than him, Z."

I could hear his words, I'd heard them before from other people, hundreds of times, but it didn't matter whose mouth they came from, it never made it any more possible. Somehow, I'd become locked in a cocked-up situation seven years before, and no matter what direction I turned, I couldn't see a way out. At least not one that would end well. I was pulled under years before and I couldn't even see the surface anymore.

"Z." Tanner rested his hand on my knee, drawing me back to the present. "I'm not telling you what to do, but if you ever decide enough is enough, I've got your back. You're not alone. You can stay here as long as you want. Stacey won't mind, and if I get my apartment soon, you can always crash with me for a while."

His words were an olive branch being offered to a drowning man. I knew I should reach out and take the branch before I drowned, but I was scared.

Nodding, I remained silent. The doorbell rang—thankfully—interrupting the somber mood, and Tanner patted my knee before jumping off the bed.

"Pizza's here. I'm starving."

We gorged ourselves on way too much pizza, and the mood relaxed while we talked about other things completely unrelated to significant others. Tanner told me stories of how he'd developed his tattooing art while living up north. How he and a "buddy" he'd gone to school with opened a shop together—I was pretty sure that buddy was his ex, but he failed to mention that part—and how he'd had to sell his half when he'd decided to move back home.

"Do you have any ink?" Tanner asked around a mouthful of pizza.

I laughed. "No. I always thought it'd be cool, but..." *But Paul is totally against the idea,* I wanted to say. "I-I just haven't." I tried to cover my accidental pause with a drink of beer but knew I'd failed miserably when the look on Tanner's face changed.

"What would you get if you got one?" Of course, he'd push the subject.

"Well, not to be a copycat or anything, but I always thought a Horde representation would be kinda cool. I've been escaping into Warcraft for ten years now. It's become a part of my life."

Tanner's smile split his face. "Hell yeah." He tossed his plate on the end table and brought himself to his knees beside me. "Okay, where?"

"Here," I said pointing to my upper arm, enjoying his excitement and intensity. Paul was always so opinionated about my idea and made me feel bad for even thinking about it, and there was Tanner, getting just as excited as me.

Tanner took hold of my arm and ran his fingers over my shoulder, tracing out a picture he clearly saw in his head. "Like maybe the Horde symbol in the background, and you could get Zulsori or Wormz in the foreground wearing their epic gear. Hell, I could see a zee slashed through it too maybe, you know, to represent Zulsori and you, Zander."

His bubbly enthusiasm was so refreshing, but it came to a slamming halt with the following question.

"Can I tattoo you? We can work together on designing something you want, and I won't charge you. I've been drawing Warcraft stuff for as long as the game has been out, it's some of my best work. I'll show you my portfolio. Please, Z, let me do this for you. It would be so great." He continued to cling to my arm as he pleaded.

Pulling from his grasp, I straighten the sleeve on my—his—t-shirt. "I can't."

Immediately, that look returned to his face. The one that saw the truth without me even having to voice it.

"It's him, isn't it?"

"I should really get home. It's getting late."

I jumped off the bed, but Tanner was faster and blocked my escape. "It's your body, Zander, not his. He has no say in this. If it's what you want to do, then do it."

I huffed and scrubbed a hand over my face. "Can we not do this? Please. It's been a good day, I don't get many of those. Don't wreck it."

Tanner watched me a minute more before shaking his head and stepping out of my path. "Yeah. I'm sorry, you're right, not my business."

I headed to the door, but paused, remembering I couldn't go home wearing Tanner's clothes. Turning around, I spotted my sleep pants folded on the dresser and went to grab them as I tried to figure out my predicament.

"Just wear my clothes, Z." He rolled his eyes. "Tell him they belong to Angie's boyfriend if you're worried. You can get them back to me whenever."

That would work.

"Thanks." I headed to the door with my sleep pants under my arm, but before I could leave, Tanner called out.

"Z."

I turned in time to catch my phone midair when Tanner tossed it my way.

"Thanks again."

"Call me if you need me, okay? I'm here for you, no matter what time."

The worried look in his eyes was too hard to watch, so I dropped my gaze to the carpet and nodded before leaving.

Chapter Ten

Tanner-*Mid-July*

The following month happened much the same as the previous. Zander squirmed and turned down all my invitations to hang out outside of work, but sought me out online constantly. Since the launch of Warcraft ten years before, I swore I'd never played so much, but it was worth it. I could tell he needed someone to lean on, and it was the only acceptable way for him to do it.

After my unexpected rescue mission in the middle of the night, I'd learned from Angie that she'd had enough suspicions about Zander and Paul's relationship to write a book. In respect for Zander's privacy, I didn't share what I already knew to be true, but it seemed I didn't really have to. Angie knew.

So many things ate me up inside, and because I'd promised to just be there for him as a friend and not pry, there was nothing I felt I could do about it.

My impression remained that Zander was allowing someone else to run his life and knock him around. He couldn't do the things he wanted to do unless Paul said it was okay.

The way Zander lit up at the mention of being tattooed had stuck in my mind. The smile that had permeated his face, the sparkle that had come to his hazel eyes, and the enthusiasm when I'd explained what I could create, all warmed me up from the inside. Outside of Warcraft, it was the happiest I'd ever seen him. How dare someone take that joy away? I was crushed when he'd said he couldn't go through with it and allow me to ink him.

The thought ate at me enough that it fueled an idea. His birthday was in a couple of days, and a few weeks back, I'd thought of the perfect idea for a gift. I'd spent a while working on it and had just added the finishing touches that morning. It was finally complete, and I was thrilled with the end result. I just hoped Zander would be as happy when he saw it.

Surprisingly, I'd been invited to join in with Saturday night's festivities at a local Italian restaurant, Antonio's. I planned to pick up

Angie on my way since Brad had to work that night and couldn't attend. It would be my first time meeting the douchebag boyfriend, and I was irritatingly nervous. Maybe it was fear that I might not be able to hold my tongue or maybe I hated the idea of seeing Zander and him together, especially knowing what kind of a jackass he really was. I needed to remind myself it was Zander's night and not to spoil it.

I pulled my truck up in front of Angie's house and parked illegally. It was a quiet street, and I didn't plan to be long. I jumped out and headed to the front door, straightening my white and navy checkered button up that I'd paired with a new pair of cargo shorts. It was the dressiest shirt I owned, and hopefully, suitable enough for the restaurant we were attending. It was a warm evening, so I'd rolled the sleeves up past my elbows, exposing my tats, and wore a white t-shirt underneath so I could leave a few buttons in the front undone without looking slutty. To finish off the look, I'd decided to put on my dark-rimmed glasses, ones I rarely wore since getting contacts. I'd been told they looked stellar with my dark hair and brought out the full-blown nerd in me. I hoped to make Zander smile, or bust a gut, either would be okay with me.

I knocked lightly on Angie's door, and before I could lower my hand, Angie ripped the door open and did a double take.

"Fucking hell. Why are all the gorgeous men gay?" she asked, looking to the heavens as though asking the Almighty God Himself. "You look seriously hot, sweet cakes, but that's no excuse for being late."

Rolling my eyes, I held the door open while she grabbed a light sweater and searched her purse for her keys.

"It takes time to be this beautiful, baby doll. I'm sorry I'm late."

Turning the key in the lock, she laughed. "Brad takes thirty seconds tops to get ready to go out, and I have to toss him back into the bathroom at least a hundred times to fix him up and make him presentable. I wish he had an ounce of your fastidiousness."

We headed to the truck, and I opened the passenger side door for her. When she didn't get in right away, I glanced back to find her hands on her hips and her mouth gaping.

"And he opens the door for me too," she said to the heavens. Turning back, she batted her eyelashes and grinned. "I'll leave Brad in a heartbeat if you change your mind about being gay. I'm serious, think about it. If you gotta stick it up my butt on occasion or whatever it is turns your crank, I'll understand."

I couldn't contain my chuckle. "I'll keep that in mind. Now get in the damn truck, woman, and quit trying to convert me."

With an audible sigh, she complied.

"So, no bike tonight? I'm shocked," Angie asked as we weaved down the street toward Antonio's.

"Didn't figure you'd want to mess up your hair when we're going to a fancy restaurant."

"Aww. You're so sweet. I appreciate it."

When we got to the restaurant, we parked about a block away on a side street. The place looked packed, and it was the closest spot I could find. I grabbed the gift I'd wrapped earlier from the back seat and locked the truck.

Angie quirked a brow. "I thought they said no gifts?"

"I know. It's just a little something I was going to give Z anyway, so I thought tonight was as good a night as any." A flutter of butterflies tickled my belly, and I considered putting it back in the truck. Maybe it wasn't the right time. "Do you think it's okay I give him something?" I was feeling more and more unsure.

"It's sweet, Tanner. Whatever it is, I'm sure he'll love it."

The restaurant was crowded and the waiter, a young girl with curly auburn hair tied back into a messy ponytail and with a bounce in her step, directed us to the back party room where Zander's guests were gathering. I took Angie's arm in my own and walked with her into the crowded room, scanning for the guest of honor.

Apart from Angie, I didn't recognize anybody. In fact, I was surprised Zander had so many friends. There had to be over thirty people in attendance.

"I didn't know Z was such a popular guy," I whispered in Angie's ear.

"He's not. Zander doesn't even have any family, so these are probably a lot of Paul's friends."

"Oh, I see. He can have friends but Z can't."

Angie pinched my arm to shut me up all while keeping an innocent smile on her face.

When I saw the birthday boy himself, I was grateful for the clump of people surrounding Angie and I, preventing us from moving closer. I needed a moment to collect myself because Zander looked stunning.

He wore a pair of burgundy chinos with a short-sleeved, white button up. His hair was gelled to perfection, and the smile on his face as he talked to one of his guests, took my breath away.

There was a man beside him who had his arm wrapped firmly around Zander's waist and held him snug like he might get away. The guy was fucking built, like Incredible Hulk huge and seriously tall as well. He made my six feet look dwarfish. His unsmiling face scanned the room as Zander spoke to the woman, and when his eyes scanned past me, I inadvertently looked the other way feeling unnerved.

That must be Paul. I didn't like to stereotype, but the guy actually looked like an asshole. His entire holier-than-thou attitude and military like sternness rubbed me the wrong way. I wasn't so sure I wanted to meet him anymore.

"Come on, there's Zander. Let's go say hi and wish him a happy birthday."

Angie didn't wait for my protests—probably because they were only being made inside my head and she wasn't a bloody mind reader—as she pulled me through the gathered crowd toward Zander and Paul.

He saw us coming and ended his conversation with the woman quickly before turning an even bigger smile our way.

"Hey, you guys." He pulled out of Paul's hold and grabbed Angie, taking her into a huge bear hug.

My feet stayed planted to the floor. Did I hug him? Did I shake his hand? Did I clap him on the shoulder? What the hell was the appropriate gesture for the circumstances? Paul didn't know who I was. Did I introduce myself as his friend? Would that get him in trouble? Zander made a comment about not having many friends.

Before I could answer any of my own questions and figure out how to proceed, the choice was taken away from me when Zander took me into an equally huge hug, squeezing and holding me longer and possibly with more force than was appropriate.

"I'm so glad you came," he said into my ear before releasing me. "You're working the nerd boy thing tonight I see. Are these new?" He indicated to my glasses.

"Nah, had them for years, just don't wear them much."

His smile warmed my insides, and he gave me an approving once-over. "I like them."

"Thanks."

Turning to the man at his side, he patted the guy's chest. "Tanner, I'd like you to meet Paul."

Paul had been scanning me through our entire hug, but I tried not to let my nerves show as I held out my hand to shake his.

"Nice to meet you finally."

"How do you know Zander?" His gaze could have burned a hole right through me for all the intensity it held, and his words were clipped.

"My niece, Anna, is in his preschool room at the daycare. Started a few months back. I'm in and out of there every day."

"He's Angie's friend," Zander amended quickly.

Mine too and we game together online all the time. Not to mention he uses me as a safe house when your abusive ass is too much to bear.

There were so many things I wanted to add to Zander's minimal statement. Although, I was pretty sure that I'd shared enough and shut my mouth before I was tempted to say more.

"Hmm." Was the only response I received before he took Zander by the hip again and steered him away toward other people.

Rude much?

Zander sent an apologetic glance over his shoulder, and I made my face smile for him, even though I didn't feel it.

"Come on. Let's get a drink." Angie re-hooked her arm in mine, and we wandered to the bar to order.

As we waited for the bartender to get my beer and Angie's wine, I turned Zander's gift over in my hands.

"I should go put this in the truck. Maybe it was a bad idea. No one else brought gifts."

"Don't you dare. Fuck Paul for making you uncomfortable. He doesn't even know you, Tanner. Zander is lucky to have you as a friend. I'm telling you. He needs more friends. He needs to spend some time outside of that apartment and live a little. I just keep hoping that one day he'll wake up and leave that guy. I've never heard him say one nice thing about him and I've known Zander for almost a year and a half."

She was right. Not one goddamn thing. I took the bottle of beer the bartender slid over, and Angie accepted her glass of red wine. "I just don't get it. What the hell does he see in him?"

Angie sipped her drink as her gaze found Zander across the room, still clung to Paul's side. "I don't know. I think whatever he once saw died away years ago. He just can't move on." She turned back to me and stood on her toes to kiss my cheek.

"What was that for?"

"Give him the gift. It's his birthday. He deserves to smile, and I have a feeling whatever you've got in that package was thoughtful and from the heart and will make him do just that."

Everyone gathered for a delicious Italian feast served family style in our private party room, and after a number of toasts of champagne to the birthday boy, the atmosphere relaxed and people mingled again at a much more leisurely pace.

On top of the four beers I'd had before the meal, I managed two glasses of bubbly during. I had a nice buzz and when I saw Paul wander off, leaving Zander alone—finally—I felt brave enough to give him his present.

Zander hovered near the dessert table as he nursed a flute of champagne and people watched. When I approached, I leaned against the wall beside him.

"So, twenty-six now, huh? Careful, the joints are going to start creaking soon. It's the first sign that your body is falling apart. It's all downhill from here." My comment was rewarded with a shy smile that made me buzz.

"You'd know, old man. What are you, thirty?"

"Easy now. I'm twenty-eight and still holding it together."

"So there's hope for me?"

"Maybe. We're not all this lucky."

The gentle laugh that followed made me beam. It was a beautiful sound; open and free. It made me want to work harder to hear it more. Zander carried somberness wherever he went, and I felt like the richest man in the world when I was rewarded with such a simple, rare thing as his joy.

"Here." I held out the gift-wrapped box I'd been clinging to all night. "I know we weren't supposed to bring gifts, but it's your birthday and...Well, I didn't buy it. I...Shit. Never mind, just open it."

Zander watched me speculatively as he accepted the box. Turning it over in his hands, his lip quirk. "Did you wrap it?"

"Shut up. I suck at wrapping. I tried. Just rip it up like a normal person and stop analyzing the outside."

He stole a glance at me and carefully pulled back on the paper, one piece of tape at a time, eliciting a groan from me.

"God, you open presents like my grandma used to."

Once he'd removed the wrapping, Zander held the framed picture in his hands. His mouth fell open as he stared at it. "Did you draw this?" The words were barely audible as he peeked up at me with glassy eyes.

"I did. Based on what we talked about…"

"…That night I was at your place."

"Yeah."

I had drawn a rendition of the tattoo Zander had said he would love to get on his arm. The full Horde symbol, including his two main characters worked around it, both geared in their top end raid gear and his prized, favorite mount out front. I had added color and detail to every part, personalizing it to Zander as much as I could. Slashed into the background was the letter zee, just as we'd discussed. I put everything I had into the drawing, using my best drawing tools and having it custom framed. I held my breath and watched him. As the minutes ticked by and he continued to examine it, I shuffled my feet, staring at my sneakers as I shoved my hands in my pockets.

"So. Do you like it? Is it too much?"

Before I could look up, he flung his arms around my neck, and the picture bounced off my back where it was still clutched in his hand. "It's perfect. I can't believe you drew this for me." My neck was damp where his cheek rested, and I was fairly certain I'd made him cry.

"I can't tattoo you, I get that, but I couldn't let go of what we talked about. So now you have this, and if down the line you ever change your mind, the offer stands."

"Thank you, Tanner." He continued to hold me tight, so I brought my arms up to reciprocate the hug and buried my face into his neck as well, inhaling him. God, he smelled good. I hadn't intended to make him cry, but they were happy tears, and that was enough for me to know I'd done something right.

Chapter Eleven

Zander-End of July

"I'm talking to that piece of shit Maureen on your behalf next time. This is bullshit. She's denied you vacation the last two times you've put in for it." Paul was carefully packing the last few things he needed for his conference into his suitcase while I sat on our bed watching. "I hate going to these things alone. They suck ass."

"It's not her fault really. We have to abide by ratios, and if she can't get a call-in to cover, then I can't go."

"It's bullshit, and you know it. If you were sick, she'd figure it out. It's not like you're asking for a week off, it's a Friday and a Monday. Two fucking days."

All I could do was shrug. There was no point arguing, especially since I hadn't even tried to get the time off that time.

Back in May, I'd enjoyed having the weekend to myself. I'd hung out with Angie and Tanner and luxuriated in me time. It was rare for me to have that kind of independence anymore. I couldn't hang out with friends without having to plead my case to the jury and ultimately failing, and I missed being free to do what I wanted.

Lying was not something I intended on making a habit of, and I hadn't done it to be deceptive, I just needed some breathing room. It was stuffy in my life lately, like I'd climbed into an attic on a hot summer day. I just wanted to open a window and let life blow back in so I could feel human again. It was the only way I thought might work without backing myself into a corner. Every other option left the possibility of me running into trouble.

Paul zipped his suitcase and stood it on the floor as he checked his phone.

"Can I drive you to the airport?"

"Why?" His eyes came up and met mine in an accusatory manner. "You aren't going anywhere but work, take the bus."

"I just thought it'd be nice to be able to drive. It's just going to sit in the airport parking otherwise and cost an arm and a leg. Seems stupid."

"Are you calling my decision stupid?"

"No, I'm just… Never mind."

I jumped off the bed and made my way to the kitchen, quickly changing the subject so he wouldn't get upset.

"Can I make you a sandwich or something for the road?"

Paul came from down the hall, rolling his luggage behind him. "Nah, I gotta split. I'm meeting Chelsea at the airport so we can grab a bite before we take off."

Chelsea was another pharmacist from his team and one he traveled with frequently.

He continued to the door and shoved his phone in his back pocket. I met him as he pulled on his loafers. "Try to have fun I guess."

Rewarded with a grunt, he took me in his arms and held me close. "See you Monday night." Leaning in, he kissed me roughly, face squeezed in his hands. When he thrust his tongue into the back reaches of my mouth, I nearly choked.

There was a time when I'd enjoyed his rough handling, but in the past few years, I constantly fought the urge to pull back or step away. I didn't feel it anymore, I just went with the flow like I'd been doing for longer than I could remember. When had I stopped enjoying kissing? When had it gone from sensual and me needing and wanting more, to a constant struggle of preventing my body from shuddering? I was so messed up.

When he pulled back, oblivious, he grabbed his suitcase and keys and flung the door open. "I'll text you."

"Okay." He closed the door behind him, and I stood there staring at its wooden surface.

The whole world looked like a happier place beyond that door, and I was nothing more than a trapped animal stuck behind it. He was gone. I needed to grab hold of that time and try to enjoy it because four days would pass in a flash and he'd be back and the walls would close in again. I didn't even know what I was going to do with the time I had, but it didn't matter. Even time alone was looking mighty appealing at the moment.

The following day was Friday, and Angie caught wind that I was alone all weekend with no Paul holding me back.

"We so need to do something," she said as she leaned against the fence and watched the kids run around the yard.

"Like what? I was kinda looking forward to just doing nothing. You know, eat in the living room and be a rebel or something."

Angie flicked my ear like I'd said something stupid. Paul hated when I ate in the living room. He bitched so much I quit doing it years before. I didn't know what the big deal was. It sounded like a perfect thing to do while he was away.

"I was thinking more like we should go out."

"I'm not going clubbing. It's not my thing."

"Fine. How about dinner and drinks?"

Noticing a child trying to climb the slide while others were going down it, I moved to the climber to direct traffic. "Will Brad be joining us?"

"Uh yeah, I kinda thought so."

"No thanks then. I don't wanna be a third wheel."

"Invite Tanner. He's fun to hang out with, and you guys are like two nerds in a comic book store when you get together."

"What's that supposed to mean?"

"It means you seem to get along and then there'll be four of us. Not a third wheel."

I considered her offer. A solo night at home, eating takeout in the living room with Netflix or Warcraft sounded great, but maybe hanging out with friends would be good too. I never got the chance often so I planned to cash in on it while I could.

"Maybe. Let me talk to Tanner and see what he thinks first."

"Text him now. We can go tonight if he's free."

I rolled my eyes and plucked my phone from my pocket to send him a message.

"Oh, I have an idea for after dinner." Angie bounced off the fence and joined me on the other side of the slide. "There is this little café in China Town where you can play board games. They are licensed too so we can have some after dinner drinks there and have some fun."

It sounded entertaining enough. Board games, drinks, and dinner already was a lot better than club music and grinding sweaty bodies.

My phone vibrated right away, and I checked it. "He's in."

"Awesome."

We messaged back and forth for a few more minutes and made plans for Tanner to meet me at my place after work. Somehow—I wasn't sure how—he'd also convinced me to ride with him on his motorcycle. That thing freaked me out more than I would admit, but it also felt a little rebellious and was exactly the kind of thing I was going for that weekend, so I'd agreed.

Tanner showed up earlier than I expected. I'd just jumped out of the shower and was deciding what to wear. Answering the door in a pair of joggers and a t-shirt, I invited him to make himself at home while I finished getting ready.

"There's beer in the fridge if you want one," I called down the hall, as I retreated back to my room.

"Not if I'm riding, but thanks."

Sifting through my closet, I couldn't decide what to wear. I had all kinds of outfits reserved strictly for work that were suitable for kid slobber and paint messes, but dressing for a night out almost always set me up for high anxiety. It sounded stupid, but Paul generally always told me what to wear because he hated whatever I picked. In fact, he'd bought most of my nicer clothes, informing me I had no eye for style. Sadly, I'd gotten used to not having an opinion any longer.

I must have been scrutinizing my selection of shirts for too long because Tanner wandered down the hall and knocked lightly on the closed door.

"You okay in there?"

"Yeah. You can come in." He pushed the door open and leaned on the frame. "I just can't decide what to wear. I know I sound like a sixteen-year-old girl whining about clothes, but I kinda suck at putting together outfits."

"Well that's a load of crap. You looked fucking edible at your birthday." Realizing what he'd said, he backtracked. "I mean... You stood out. It was... Fuck, I'm sorry. You looked good, okay. I noticed. Is that wrong?"

I turned him a shy smile. "No... and thank you, but I didn't pick my outfit that night, Paul did."

Silence seeped into the room. Tanner pushed off the wall and came to stand beside me, flicking through my shirts. "You look good in paler colors, pastels, you know? Goes with your blond hair and complexion."

I quirked a brow, surprised by his keen perception. "You watch that show, don't you?"

"What show?"

"What not to Wear."

"Never heard of it." The way he tried to hide the smile tugging at the corners of his mouth told differently. "I like this one. Do you have a pair of tan chinos or something?"

He'd selected a baby blue, cotton button up, with navy and white plaid through it. Paul frequently teased me about that shirt and called it my cowboy getup. He hated it and wouldn't let me leave the house in it, so it stunned me when Tanner pulled it off the hanger.

"Really?"

"Yeah." He held it close to my chest, nodding at his selection and looked pleased. "Tan chinos?"

"Yeah." I took the shirt and dug through a drawer in search of the pants. When I had the outfit laid out on my bed, Tanner left to give me privacy to dress.

When I was ready, I found him relaxed on the couch with his feet up and he rewarded me with an exaggerated whistle. "See, fucking edible."

Rolling my eyes again, I adjusted my collar. "You know, Paul hates this shirt. I can't believe you chose it. He'd never let me put it on, even if it was just to scrub a floor. There would be no way he'd let me go out in it."

It was meant as a joke, but it didn't get the desired effect I was going for, and instead of laughing, Tanner's brow furrowed.

"So you never wear it?"

I shook my head, giving him a half-assed smile, trying to save the moment.

"He's not your fucking mommy, why does he get a say in what you wear?"

"I ask him." Turning and heading toward the kitchen, I tried to get away from the conversation, realizing I'd slipped into territory I didn't want to explore with Tanner. No such luck, he followed.

"And what if you wanted to wear that shirt anyway? Would he *let you*?"

He put air quotes around the last two words, making me irritated. I poured a glass of water from the tap and downed it, giving myself time to answer. "Are you ready to go?" Or yet, I changed the subject, deciding I didn't want to answer his stupid question.

"Why don't you talk about him? Most people gush when they're in a relationship. Look at Angie, she's non-stop Brad talk. Ricky at the shop is always talking about his girl Jenna. Even T.J, who rarely says shit, brings up his girl at least twice a day. But you, you never mention the guy, and whenever I bring him up, you shut down like I've crossed into forbidden territory or something."

Rinsing my glass under the water, I then stuck it in the drying rack while avoiding Tanner's gaze. "We've been together forever, I guess I don't have much to say anymore."

"Maybe not, but when his name gets mentioned, it always induces a frown and negative comments from you. I've never heard you say anything positive."

Pushing past where he blocked the doorway, I headed to the front door and slid my wallet and keys in my pocket. "Look, there are all kinds of good things to say. I'm just not one to share my life like that I guess."

Tanner joined me in the front hall, but wouldn't let the subject drop. He held his hand on the door, keeping me from opening it and frowned. "Why is it you only want to hang out with me when he's out of town?"

"Tanner. Stop. Let's go."

"Answer the question first, and we can leave."

I studied his face and let out a frustrated huff. "You'll make it into a big deal, and it's not."

"Like him not letting you pick your own clothes, big deal?"

"Yes. Exactly like that."

"Angie said you just don't go out much and I shouldn't take it personally."

"Sure. Sounds right. Maybe you should listen to her. Can we go?"

"Why don't you go out much?"

"Why do you ask so many annoying questions?"

Seeing as we obviously weren't leaving any time soon, I moved back into the living room and flopped on the couch.

"Zander, I'm just trying to understand you better. Last time Paul was out of town we had a great weekend together. Every attempt I've made at getting together to hang out after that, you've shot down. Now he's gone again, and here we are going out."

"He hates me having friends. There. Are you happy? He wants me home immediately after work every night and thinks I shouldn't divide my time with anyone else. He tolerates my friendship with Angie, but we don't hang out. Ask her. You? I have barely mentioned our friendship to him because he'd probably fly off the handle."

"Why?"

"Because you're a guy and you're gay and good looking. He'd flip out, I know it. He'd make it into something it's not."

There. I'd said it and had successfully worked us into an awkward silence, ruining our evening. Laying my arm across my eyes, I leaned back on the couch, no longer feeling the desire to go out. My original plan of takeout in the living room and Netflix was sounding much more desirable again. The couch dipped beside me, and a hand peeled my arm away from my face.

"I'm sorry I pushed."

"No, you're not."

"I am. He sounds kinda like a control freak, and I didn't like hearing what you said about that shirt."

Control freak, ha, understatement of the year.

"It's not all bad if that's what you think."

"I didn't say it was, but you got pretty defensive."

I thought it best not to respond. He'd already pulled far more from me than I'd wished to share and it was officially weird between us.

"Look. I stuck my nose in where it didn't belong. I'm sorry. If you say there's good, I believe you."

"Like I said. It's not all bad. Can we go now?"

Tanner didn't move, he just continued to stare with a critical eye that made me want to run and hide. Masking my feelings wasn't my strong suit. I was completely transparent, and I knew it. I was certain he could see right through to the lies I was dishing out.

"We can go, but can you do something for me first? I don't want to have this clawing at me all night in the back of my mind."

Groaning on the inside, unsure what I was agreeing to, I nodded.

"Can you tell me one good thing?"

Replacing my arm over my eyes, I wished I could rewind time and take back all the inadvertent slipups that had gotten me into that tangled mess.

One good thing. It was a joke. I'd spent at least six years wallowing in the negatives because the positives had long ago slipped through my fingers. I wasn't even sure I'd recognize them if they slapped me in the face at that point. One good thing. I had nothing to share. When I didn't answer, he patted my leg and hopped off the couch.

"Never mind. Let's go out and have fun."

Hesitantly, I lowered my arm and peered to where he waited by the door. He didn't look at me, just busied himself with his helmet.

Silently, I followed him out the door and down the hall to the elevator as guilt snuck in. "Look, Tanner—"

"Never mind, Z." He turned to me while we waited for the elevator to arrive. "It's not my business."

I lowered my head to look at my feet. "Okay."

We rode down together, saying nothing, and out at the road where Tanner had parked his motorcycle, we stood and put on our helmets. The nervousness of riding was back, and I bounced on my feet as he got on first. Before I swung my foot over the back, Tanner turned to me, halting me with a hand on my arm.

"One last thing and I swear I won't bring it up again tonight. I promise."

My shoulders slumped wearily, and I fought the urge to roll my eyes while I waited for him to continue.

"Just something I want you to think about. For you and no one else. You should have no problem coming up with one good thing every day when it comes to you and Paul. It should be automatic. Relationships are built on moments you share together. If you can't come up with one thing a day. Or even, let's say, one every other day, one a week even, then maybe you need to ask yourself if you're really happy."

His words punched me in the gut. Seven years in a relationship and I knew I'd have trouble coming up with a list long enough to fill a post-it note, let alone one thing a day which would constitute filling pages in a notebook. I didn't need a list to tell me I wasn't happy; I knew I wasn't. In fact, I'd known for a long time. It was my prison sentence, and I was in for life. The prospects of getting out were nonexistent in my book. I gave Tanner a half-assed, acknowledging nod and slid on the bike behind him.

Chapter Twelve

Tanner-*Mid-August*

After a few hardcore hours of battling it out on Halo and having my ass well and truly handed to me, I flopped back on my bed.

"I can't do it anymore. You win. You are the master. I kneel before your awesomeness."

Zander laughed and tossed his controller beside him before flopping down and lying next to me.

Paul had been sent out of town again for an unanticipated conference, and Zander had jumped all over the idea of hanging out and gaming our faces off all weekend. That was twice in three weeks Paul had needed to leave, and Zander seemed to be enjoying his free time. That evening was a perfect guy's night because Stacey and Anna had gone to a cousin's overnight and wouldn't be home until morning. We had the place entirely to ourselves.

"I'm glad you recognize the skill."

The grin he sported could have lit up a room. I loved seeing him like that. Happy. Free. Relaxed. Shuffling to my side, I watched him gloat, not feeling the sore loser at all.

"Put Skyrim in," he said turning his beaming smile on me. "I know it's not two-player, but I like watching you play."

"You sure?" It felt weird having someone watch me. Being a spectator didn't sound enjoyable, but for some odd reason, Zander seemed to have fun with it. "We could set up the N64 and play some two-player Mario."

"Nah. Seriously. I'm tired of playing, I just wanna watch."

Zander jumped off the bed and flipped through my stack of games beside the console. Finding Skyrim, he then changed it out with Halo.

"Wanna order some food? I'm starving," I asked, shuffling to sit at the edge of the bed.

"Sure. Can we get sandwiches from that new deli down the street? I tried them when they opened last week, and they're amazing. The Grainery Bistro."

I whipped my phone out of my pocket and searched up their information. "On it. What do you want?"

"Steak and provolone on whole wheat with grilled onions and mushrooms."

After ordering our dinner and being told I could pick it up in twenty minutes—they sadly didn't deliver—I loaded my active character on Skyrim and we both sank back on the bed and leaned against the headboard, settled in for an evening of fun.

Regardless of it being a one-player game, Zander and I somehow found a way to make it equally enjoyable for both of us. Zander picked my questing direction and helped me navigate the world map—I had no sense of direction and managed to get lost all the time, despite the in-game mapping system pointing me exactly where I needed to go. Zander poked fun at me, encouraging attempts at crazy feats of strength that inevitably ended with me dead, but we both laughed as we passed the time.

My phone buzzed on the end table a little while later, and we both paused to stare at it. When I picked it up and saw who it was, I laughed.

"Shit. Our food. It's the deli. I forgot all about it."

Jumping up and tossing the controller at Zander, I answered and explained I was on my way having lost track of time.

"I'll be right back. Go ahead and play. Don't kill me."

"As if. Grab a few Cokes too," Zander yelled after me as I flew down the hall.

The deli was only two blocks away from my sister's house, so I walked fast, watching the dark clouds looming in the distance. The forecasted storm for that evening was moving in fast, the smell of rain already hung in the air and I wanted to get back home before it hit.

After grabbing our takeout, I popped into a convenience store on my return trip and bought us a few Cokes.

Once back, we paused the game and relaxed on the bed to enjoy our sandwiches. As was always the case, conversation flowed easily between us, and we laughed and shared stories of how we both became such hardcore gamers growing up.

It was during that segue I learned Zander didn't exactly have the kind of youth I'd expected. It shed a lot of light on what Angie had meant at his birthday dinner the previous month when she'd said he didn't really have any family. It was a passing remark that had stuck with me ever since.

"I grew up in the system. Bounced foster homes until I was thirteen, then I moved in with Ray and Georgina. They were the closest thing to home and family I knew, and they tried to give me the life most teenagers had without making me feel different than other kids. They're an older couple, and I ended up being their last foster kid. They bought me my first game system and computer when I landed there, and I was hooked ever since. I think it was their way of keeping me settled. They'd had a few kids in and out before me who were handfuls. I was the quiet one in comparison."

I nibbled at the crust of my sandwich, my heart aching as I listened to his story. "How'd you end up in the system?"

"Mom was an addict, and my dad was some high-as-fark, stoned out, bump in the night. I was taken away when I was a baby. I guess she ended up OD'ing when I was nine. I didn't really know her because I had never been allowed to go home. She was never clean, so I lived in foster care all my life."

I couldn't contain my momentary burst of inappropriate laughter and was rewarded with a hurt expression that made me instantly bury it. "Sorry, you said 'fark,' I love when you try to swear."

Rewarded with a shove, Zander tried not to smile. "Shut it."

"But really, that totally sucks. I can't imagine growing up like that."

"It's my life. Ray and Georgina keep in touch, but they moved to Calgary when I left for college, so I don't see them anymore."

"Do they know you're gay?"

"They do now. I didn't come out until after I moved away. I was afraid they'd reject me, and I'd bounce homes again. I liked it there. Turns out they were fine with it."

His story left me with a sour stomach, even though I could tell he didn't regret the way he'd grown up. He spoke humbly about his foster parents, and it was sad to hear they lived so far away. As a child who grew up in the typical, two parents, two children, one boy, and one girl home, it somehow felt sad.

Later, as we continued our Skyrim junk-out, the storm moved in. It hit with a sudden crash of thunder and downpour of rain that made us both jump. No lead-up or anything, just a really loud crack that broke through the sky, followed by a rumble that rattled the windows in their frames and vibrated through our bones.

We both laughed at our initial reactions, but Zander couldn't keep his gaze off the window after that. There was nervousness behind his hazel eyes, and I knew I didn't imagine it when he shimmied a little closer to me on the bed. He didn't have to admit it out loud, his apprehension was clear as day. It took some time, but eventually, he settled back in beside me, and we lost ourselves in the game again. The storm continued to rage outside as trolls and giants met their demise.

It wasn't long before another deafening, sky-splitting crack plunged the house and neighborhood into complete darkness. Apart from the fading rumble rolling away into the distance and the rain pattering on the roof, the night was dark and eerily silent.

The ordinarily unnoticed hum of the lights and running motors of the Xbox and appliances in the kitchen downstairs were gone. We both sat without speaking, waiting for the lights to come back on. As the minutes ticked by and nothing happened, Zander spoke.

"Well... You were probably gonna die on that dragon again anyway."

I gave him a hard shove while laughing, "You wish, he was as good as dead." I tossed the controller on the bed, and we waited some more.

"Don't you have a flashlight or something?" The hesitance and distress in his voice was back.

"Afraid of the dark, Z?"

"No," he denied a little too abruptly. "I was just asking."

"I think there are candles in a drawer in the kitchen. I'll be back. Stay here. I don't want to lose you."

I jumped over him on the bed and made my way through the familiar space in the dark and down the stairs to the kitchen where I pulled out half a dozen candles and a book of matches from a drawer. They were fancy, mulberry scented ones my sister had probably paid way too much money for at one of those candle parties she liked to go to. She'd probably kill me for using them because God knows there would be a special occasion, years in the future that would require the use of those specific candles.

Back in my room, I set them up all around us and lit them.

"They're fruity scented. Don't judge me," I said when I saw Zander sniffing the air. "They're Stacey's."

"Sure they are. So they aren't the ones you save for your weekly bubble bath nights?"

"You're an ass," I said without heat.

Zander laughed and rolled over to his stomach propping himself on his elbows at the end of the bed. "So what do you wanna do now?"

Lighting the last candle, I blew out the match and bounced down beside him. "We could tell ghost stories. It's all stormy and creepy."

Zander buried his face into the mattress as he laughed. "You're kidding, right? Tell me you're kidding. We aren't ten, and this isn't some birthday slumber party."

"I'm very serious." I nudged him in the ribs to make him glance over. The candlelight cast an orange glow over his perfect smile. Putting on my most serious face, I lowered my voice to an eerie whisper. "It was a dark and stormy night…"

Zander rolled onto his back, unable to hold back his fit of laughter anymore. "Here we go…"

"No, seriously. Listen." I cleared my throat and went back into my storytelling voice, which for some reason sounded a lot like Robert Stack from Unsolved Mysteries. "It was in this very house that the accident occurred. A young girl murdered at the hands of her father."

Zander whacked me as he continued to laugh. "Stop. You're killing me."

"No, no, listen," I said trying and failing to hold back my own laughter. "The father killed the girl and buried her in the basement under the concrete and on nights like this, the ones that are the very same as the night she was murdered…"

Zander rolled on top of me and clamped a hand over my mouth. "This is so terrible. You suck at ghost stories. For the love of God stop."

"You aren't scared?" I asked when I pried his hand off, still grinning so hard my face hurt.

"Oh, I'm scared. Scared you are going to keep going. Scared I'm gonna puke up my sandwich from laughing so hard." He rolled back off me, and I remorsefully missed his warmth.

"All right, all right. I'm done."

We lay side by side, calming down again.

"So no ghost stories?"

"Please no. Do you have any board games?"

"Nope. Not unless you want to play Candy Land. They're Anna's games, but I would think you get enough preschool shit at work," I teased.

"You know it. I'd kick your butt at Candy Land too. I can rock that game like a boss. Anyway, scratch the board game idea."

I watched as Zander continued to think. His eyes were downcast as he played with the comforter underneath us, his long lashes brushing his cheeks. The softness and fullness of his lips accentuated by the candlelight made every flowing curve all the more prominent and alluring. Not for the first time, I was drawn in by Zander's beauty. He was gorgeous, and I'd have to be blind not to notice.

It wasn't often he grew stubble on his chin. I tagged him as a ritualistic shaver, always with a smooth, razor clean face. That evening he had scruff. The low lighting didn't show the color well, but I knew it was just a shade darker than the blond hair on his head. It was seriously sexy, and I had to fight the urge to reach out and touch him. Fight to avoid drawing a thumb down his chiseled jawline and resist lifting his chin and bringing his eyes back up to my own.

A nagging little voice in my head wondered if the reason for the scruff was because Paul was away. I pushed it aside. The last thing I wanted was to feel anger and jealousy. Zander's asswipe of a boyfriend seemed to manage to drag that emotion out of me more times than I liked to admit.

What I wanted was to tell him it looked good on him, but I knew it wasn't really a friend-type thing to say. *Hey, by the way, that scruff you're sporting looks seriously sexy.* Yeah, not okay. In fact, all my thoughts had crossed that strict line I was supposed to stay behind, and I berated myself for being a bad friend.

Knowing I needed an immediate break from my inappropriate thoughts, I jumped off the bed. "I have an idea. Wait here."

Stumbling again through the darkness, I made my way down the hall to my niece's bedroom. She was an art fanatic, and I knew she'd have exactly what I was looking for. Rifling through her supplies, I grinned when I found what I wanted.

Back in the bedroom, I hopped up onto the bed, bouncing on my knees. "Okay, lay on your back and get comfy. You're gonna be there a while."

Zander raised a quizzical brow as he moved slowly to follow my directions, sliding down from a sit until he was flat out on his back. "Should I be worried?"

"Not at all. But before I start. Do you want a drink or something?"

"Start what exactly? And sure, a drink would be great."

Feeling a little like I had ADHD, I hopped off the bed again and flew down the dark staircase to the kitchen. When I couldn't find any beer in the fridge, I settled for an unopened bottle of wine my sister had on the counter. I was not a wine drinker, ordinarily. It was dry and bitter from experience, but that stuff she'd bought was sweet and fruity, tasting more like a wine cooler and was much more appealing. Grabbing two glasses, I then headed back upstairs.

I poured our drinks and put Zander's on the end table. "There was only wine. Hope that's okay?"

"I'm good with that, but again, fruity candles, wine. I suppose this is your sister's too, is it?"

"Yes," I said glaring at him in fun.

"Mmm hmm...so not from your bath collection?"

"Shut up and lay down."

"So defensive."

When Zander had settled on his back, I knelt beside him and took his arm in my hands, rolling his already short sleeve up over his shoulder.

"What are you doing?"

I shook the pencil case I'd brought from Anna's room. "I'm gonna give you a fake tattoo since you can't bring yourself to get a real one."

"Seriously?" His grin told me he was cool with the idea. "What are you using?"

I unzipped the pencil case and rooted around for the color I wanted. "Colored pens. Anna got this pack of twenty-four gel pens the other day at the toy store. They are pretty cool. And glittery."

Using the black pen, I freehanded a simpler version of the tattoo I'd designed and had framed for Zander's birthday. I used much of his upper arm, and Zander lay still and watched me. A soft curve of a smile crawled up one side of his face, and it thrilled me to my core when I saw how much he was enjoying my goofy idea.

When I was done with the outline, we took a break to enjoy a couple of glasses of wine. Coloring it in took over an hour, and by that point, the wine bottle was empty, and I had to rush back downstairs for the other one I'd seen stashed away.

The power stayed out, so we drank and talked as I filled in every part of the picture I'd drawn over his arm. When I was finished, even I had to admit, it looked pretty damn cool.

Zander couldn't stop grinning and staring. "You're really good, even when it's just a doodle on my arm with pens, it looks fantastic."

"I'm glad you like it. You don't know how awesome it would be to put that on you for real."

Zander's smile faltered momentarily before he caught himself. I didn't miss it, and it bugged me. I knew the truth he wasn't voicing. Why did he let that man have so much control?

Quick to manage the mood and prevent it from slipping, Zander grabbed the pencil case of colored pens and eyed me up, looking devilish. "Take off your shirt and lay down. I wanna do you now."

The fact that his words were innocent to his own ears made me both smile and groan internally. I couldn't pass up the opportunity to tease him. "I don't know. You didn't even buy me dinner. I don't usually put out on a first date."

The flicker of confusion that passed over his face was evident, even in the dim light and it made me laugh. "What? You're messing with me or something, aren't you?"

"God, you're innocent, Z. You want me to lay down so you can *do* me now?" I waited while realization sank in.

Zander punched my arm and flushed red before grabbing my shirt and ripping it over my head for me. "You're a douche. Take your stupid shirt off and quit giving me a hard time." With my shirt off, he shoved me down with two hands on my shoulders. Rough and demanding Zander was kind of fun. "I'm warning you. I couldn't draw a banana if my life depended on it, so I'm apologizing for the mess I'm going to make on you right now."

I rested my hands behind my head and grinned up at him. "Go ahead and *make a mess on me*. Do your worst." I wiggled my eyebrows for emphasis that time.

Rewarded with an eye roll and a scowl, Zander began.

Chewing his lip, he traced a hand over my chest sending shivers over my skin and making me fight a battle with my traitorous cock who so desperately wanted to join the party.

The ink on my chest was less dense than my arms, and there were still all kinds of spots for Zander to work. I had intended one day to fill in every space there was, but it took time, and I planned my tattoos meticulously. My sleeves alone took three years to complete to my liking.

My chest would probably take at least another three or four before it was done too.

Once he chose a spot, he popped a cap on a pen and bent his head to work, letting his blond hair fall forward covering his face.

Closing my eyes, I enjoyed the cool rolling pen and soft touches over my skin. I laughed a few times at Zander's failed attempts at cursing under his breath, which only made him curse more because my movements were apparently "messing him up." Peeking out on occasion, I'd watch him as he worked intently over my chest, scrunching up his face in concentration.

He had decided to draw over my right ribs, and by the feel of it, he was taking up a large bit of space. I resisted the urge to look until he was done, enjoying waiting for the surprise unveiling.

It didn't take Zander quite as long as it had taken me, but when he sat back, capped his pen with a click, and patted my leg, I opened my eyes, still not looking.

"I'm done." He grinned, looking pleased.

"And?"

"It's horrible," he said as he burst out laughing. "I'm so sorry."

Lifting my head, I peered upside down at the art he'd drawn over my ribs. "Is that a stick person? Seriously?"

"I told you I couldn't draw. It's your Skyrim toon fighting a dragon here." He pointed. "This is his bow and arrow, and these over here are the giants in the distance with the mammoths. But don't worry, I knew you couldn't take them all at once, so I made them oblivious to the fight. They're not engaged."

Ignoring his jab at my fighting skills, I let myself take it all in. It really and truly was a horrible drawing and we both laughed as I tried to make out the other details he had incorporated into the picture.

"Remember, I have a preschool level art ability. I'm not you."

"It's awesome, Z. I love it, even though it's the most horrendous thing I've ever seen."

"Shut it," he said as he flopped down beside me.

The power was still out, and we were becoming hard pressed for anything to do, so we just ended up drinking through the entire second bottle of wine as we talked long into the night—my sister was going to skin me alive when she found out.

Fake tattoos led into conversations about our chosen professions and Zander shared he wanted to go back to school and become an actual grade school teacher someday but wasn't sure if it would ever happen. He'd looked into night classes, but explained they were pricey and he'd have to save up if he wanted to make it happen.

The hours ticked by, and before we knew it, it was after two in the morning, and we were both well past drunk. The wine seemed to help Zander relax, and when that happened, I learned he became less reserved and opened up, sharing more about his home life; more about Paul. It was a double-edged sword. I wanted him to feel comfortable with me, trust me, and talk to me, but everything I learned cut me to my core. The man he lived with, the man who was supposed to love him and be there for him was nothing short of a monster in my books.

Zander's head lulled to the side as he looked at me, inebriation clear in his glassy eyes. "Can I tell you something?"

"Of course. Anything."

"He doesn't like tattoos," Zander said, as his gaze shifted to the new "ink" I'd put on him. He was stating the obvious, affirming what I'd already figured was true. "He thinks they defile the body and look ridiculous. Anyone who has tattoos is a farging idiot and under no circumstances am I to mar up my body with them. He strictly forbids it."

It sounded an awful lot like a direct quote, and I hated it. "It's your body, Z. What if you just did it? It's not like he can tell you to get rid of it once it's on there."

Zander's eyes widened, and his body went stiff as he looked into a memory in his mind. "I couldn't do that."

Silence echoed through the room, and I needed a minute before I could speak. I hated the fear I saw in Zander's face and the way he slunk around in his life with Paul, allowing the man to rule his world. It was wrong on so many levels, and he just couldn't see it.

"Why are you with him, Z?"

His eyes shifted to me briefly before he looked around the room again. "It's not all bad."

So you've claimed. I call bullshit.

"You've still never told me anything good."

Zander gaze seemed lost in the flickering of a candle flame, and I couldn't be sure if he was going to answer, so I just waited him out. I had nowhere to be.

"It was really good in the beginning. He treated me like something special. Took me out. Wined and dined me. Always made sure I was taken care of. He was my 'big old protector' when other guys would come up and hit on me at the bars. It was flattering at first. He was great like that for about eight or nine months. Once we moved in together, I started seeing a lot more things I'd never seen before. He always had a temper, I just didn't realize how bad it got. He'd have road rage something awful. If someone cut him off on the road, he'd literally drive on the guy's ass down the freeway for miles, yelling, laying on his horn. It scared me. I didn't say anything because I was afraid of his fury. It didn't happen a lot... But then it was more. The girl at the coffee shop would get his coffee wrong, and he didn't notice until we got home and he'd go off swearing, throwing his coffee at the wall and then other things went flying too. All I could do was avoid flying projectiles and stay away from him. He's a big guy, you've met him. He flips like a switch, no warning, and I don't want it turned at me, so I'm careful to leave him alone whenever it happens. It's become routine. I've started learning his cues and how to avoid setting him off. It's automatic for me to slink away when he gets all heated."

"In other words, you've learned to walk on eggshells around him." I didn't mean to interrupt, but that was exactly what it was, clear as day, and I didn't think Zander saw it.

"He can still be a sweetheart, Tanner... When he wants to be. He's not all bad. He's a great cook. We enjoy some of the same TV shows. He likes to get dressed up and go out to dinner."

"How often does he lose his temper?"

Zander chewed his bottom lip and glanced sidelong at me. "A lot. A few times a week."

"And how many times has the anger turned on you, Z?"

Zander peered into his empty wine glass. His face was drawn and sad, and I regretted sounding so harsh and pushing him. His full bottom lip stuck out a little in an unconscious pout that broke my heart.

"He takes care of me." The words were whispered into the air and came out with little conviction. They sounded rehearsed. I didn't believe them, and by the sound of it, neither did he. They were what had been drilled in his head time and time again. So many times, their meaning was lost.

Zander's eyes were heavy with drink and sleep as he lay beside me. He shuffled over on his side to face me. I took the glass from his hand, putting it aside on the end table. His lids drooped, every blink taking longer and longer until his eyes stayed closed.

"You're a good friend, Tanner. I'm happy we found each other." His words were thick with sleep, and soon after they were spoken, his breathing deepened, and soft gentle snores passed through his parted lips.

A good friend. With all the conflicting things going on inside my body, I didn't feel like a good friend at all. I felt like a traitor in a way. Zander saw me as a friend, and all I did was fight to keep it that way. Fighting every urge I had, wanting nothing more than to hold him and touch him, yet not cross boundaries. I cared for him so much, which was okay, I thought. I wanted to protect him from hurt and pain, which was also okay. Friends did that. But I also wanted to wrap him up in my arms and never let him go. Kiss away his troubles and show him what good looked like.

Watching him sleep on my bed beside me in the darkness of the room with only candlelight to see, I knew I was falling for Zander. It wasn't brotherly love or the love of a friend either. I was falling *in* love with him, and I hated myself for it even more because I wasn't supposed to feel that way—it wasn't supposed to happen.

I didn't want to be the man to break up someone else's relationship, no matter how fucked up said relationship was turning out to be. It was wrong, and I didn't want to be that person. I most certainly was not a cheater or one to condone it in others either. For that reason, I knew Zander could never know how I felt, and I needed to push those feelings away and try to make them stop. They were treacherous and wrong.

With a deep sigh, I moved cautiously to the edge of the bed with the intent on going downstairs to sleep on the couch. Zander shuffled and mumbled at my movements. His hand reached out and took mine, holding me in place. "You don't have to leave. I won't grope you in my sleep, I promise. Stay with me?"

I froze on the edge of the bed, unsure what to do. My head screamed with confusion, fighting to know what was right and what was wrong. All my life I'd never questioned what was and wasn't appropriate behavior between friends but lately I was never sure. I released his hand and curled it back against his body before I lay on my back beside him. My drunken haze suddenly cleared and sleep was nowhere to be found.

"Thank you," he mumbled from somewhere in unconsciousness.

Long into the night, I listened to my accelerated heart rate pounding in my chest, refusing to calm down as my mind jumped about unsettled and I wondered what the fuck I was going to do.

Chapter Thirteen

Zander

Sometime in the wee hours of the morning, the power came back on, and with it, the house came alive again. Lights shone brightly where we hadn't thought to switch them off. The appliances beeped and hummed, and Tanner and I startled awake with a jump.

Added to the confusion, me waking up in Tanner's bed, tucked up against his side, and not quite remembering how I got there, brought me pretty close to cardiac arrest.

My head pounded as I squinted against the bright lights, flew out of bed and stood in the middle of the room, trying to put the pieces of the puzzle together.

"Z, relax. The power came back on, that's all." Tanner yawned and rubbed a hand over his eyes. He hadn't moved from the bed, and a hint of humor crossed his face as he raised an eyebrow at my sudden attempt to flee.

"I know. But why the hell am I asleep in your bed with you?" Pressing a hand to my temple, I cringed at the pain lashing into my brain. "And damn my head hurts."

Tanner crawled out of bed and move past me into the hallway. "First of all, you wouldn't let me leave. Second, lay down, we pounded back two bottles of that shit wine my sister drinks. That stuff will give anyone a wretched hangover. I'll get you some Tylenol or something."

I didn't have the strength to argue. Flopping back onto his bed, I covered my head with a pillow to hide from the light. "Kill the lights when you come back."

When Tanner returned, the room fell into darkness once again. The bed dipped, and I turned my head as he stuck out a hand with two pills in his palm and a glass of water in the other. "Not much of a drinker I take it?"

"Not wine." I managed to sit and throw the pills back with a couple of gulps of water. "What time is it?"

"Almost five. Go back to sleep."

Without objection, I flopped back down and squirmed under the covers. Even though I was fully dressed, I was chilled.

Tanner placed the water on the bedside table and stood before making his way to the door.

"Where are you going?"

"I'm gonna crash on the couch."

Before I could open my mouth to argue, I remembered waking up snuggled into his side. I wasn't sure how it had happened, but I knew I couldn't have a repeat, so I let him go.

Too much wine had made my tongue loose, and I lay awake after Tanner left, remembering and regretting all I'd said to him. I'd never opened up about my relationship with Paul to anyone before, not to that extent anyway, and it felt weird. Would Tanner judge me or try to interfere and fix it? Even Angie didn't know anything concrete, although I was sure she speculated all the time. As much as I tried to cover up the crap that went on at home, there were days it seeped through to the surface.

While replaying my night with Tanner over in my head, the pain meds kicked in and sleep took me back under its veil. When I opened my eyes again, it was late morning. The sound of voices and the smell of coffee came from downstairs.

After a quick trip to the bathroom to empty my bladder and finger comb some semblance of order back into my hair, I headed down to the kitchen.

Stacey was home again. She and Tanner were chatting at the small table in the kitchen, hands wrapped around mugs of coffee. Anna was on her knees in another chair, picking Fruit Loops out of a bowl of milk and shoving them in her mouth with sticky fingers.

Anna saw me first, and her eyes lit up. "Zander, why you at my house, silly?"

"Hey, princess. Good morning," I said to the other two, who smiled back. "Zander fell asleep last night after Uncle Tanner plied me with too much wine."

"Hey now, it's not like I forced it down your gullet. I seem to remember you drinking it quite willingly."

"Did you drink my wine?" Stacey fixed Tanner with an evil eye.

"Z helped. It wasn't all me." Tanner sipped his coffee playing the innocent card.

"You're buying me new wine."

I quirked a brow at Tanner. "Should I tell her about her candles?"

"What about my candles? What the hell were you guys doing last night?"

"Nothing!" We both stated a little too defensively.

"God, Stacey, the power was out half the night. It was dark, we needed to be able to see, and we were bored. Wine was required to kill the boredom." He turned to me. "Would you go pour yourself a coffee and quit getting me in trouble."

I laughed and worked my way over to the counter, shimmying around the table and chairs to fill a mug for myself.

When I sat down at the table opposite Anna, Stacey stared at me with a funny look on her face. Self-consciously, I averted my eyes and drank from my mug.

"Umm...Zander. What the hell is all over your arm?"

My eyes shot over to the fake tattoo Tanner had doodled on me last night where it was peeking out from under my sleeve. I'd forgotten all about it and smiled at the memory.

"Pens are for paper," Anna reminded me.

"Yeah, I know, princess. Tell Uncle Tanner that."

"We. Were. Bored," Tanner emphasized, reiterating his original point.

"This will come off, right?" Licking a finger, I started to rub vigorously over a small part at the base of the picture and was rewarded by only a slight smearing of ink.

Oh no! No, no, no!

"It should in a couple days. Just scrub it a few times. Most of it will come right off, the rest will wear away."

Frowning, leaving my coffee on the table, I excused myself and ran back upstairs to the bathroom. I hung my t-shirt on the towel rack and turned on warm water, wetting my arm over the inked-up surface. Using the soap I found beside the sink and a cloth I pulled from a drawer, I lathered it up and worked a good sudsy mess over my skin. I pressed into the cloth, making my skin burn as I scrubbed at it. Wiping the soap away, I examined my arm and found far too much ink left behind.

"Will he give you shit for that too?" Tanner's sudden appearance made me jump, and I shot him a dirty look.

Don't go judging my life. You have no idea. "I-I don't know. I'm not about to find out though."

"When does he fly in?"

"Tonight." I continued to scrub, making my skin red, yet not eliminating enough ink to satisfy myself. The turmoil built in my gut as I rubbed harder and more frantically.

"Shit, Z, stop. You'll take your skin off." Tanner covered a hand over mine and tried to remove the cloth.

I jerked away and snapped it from his grip. "You don't get it. I have to take it off. Leave me alone. I can do it."

"Zander. Just wait before you rub yourself bloody. Let me Google it." Tanner pulled his phone from his pocket as I hovered over him, looking upside down at his phone while he typed, "How to remove pen from skin" into the search engine. Holding the phone where we could both see it, we scanned the results.

"Alcohol. Do you have alcohol?" I asked, pointing to the number one way listed in a group of "Ten ways to remove pen using solvents."

"Here." Tanner opened a medicine cabinet above the sink and fished inside until he pulled out a bottle with a clear liquid inside. "Isopropyl alcohol. I bought it when I got my piercing."

"You have a piercing?" I'd never seen a piercing on his body, and I'd seen the man without a shirt the previous night. Unless it was somewhere below the belt. The thought made me cringe as my eyes dropped to his package encased in his jeans.

Tanner shoved my shoulder. "As if. I had my eyebrow pierced for all of three days. Hated it and took it out. I have no other holes in my body, I assure you."

"Oh." I took the alcohol from him as Tanner found another cloth in the drawer. I poured it on and wiped it over my skin. It took a few passes, but eventually, the ink became a lot less noticeable.

"There you go. See. Gone."

"It's not gone, gone. You can still see it."

"Wear a long-sleeved shirt. It will be gone by tomorrow."

"It's August, I'll cook."

Tanner took the cloth and helped me work over the rest of my arm until the picture was nothing more than a barely visible, faded resemblance of the original.

"Sorry I freaked out." It was shameful and embarrassing.

"No big deal. It's taken care of. Are you okay?"

"Yeah."

He watched me for many minutes before sighing that sigh I was waiting for, and I knew what was coming. "Z—"

"Can we not? Please."

He studied me closely, set his jaw and nodded.

"Come on. I'll make you a new coffee. I'm sure yours is cold by now."

I headed home just before the lunch hour. I'd never intended on spending the night, but after the storm rolled in and the wine was opened, any thoughts of leaving went out the window. It had been a lot of fun, despite my mini freak out session that morning. Tanner was fun to hang out with, and I was taking a lot of joy in having a friend again. I never realized how much I missed such small things. All my college friends had dropped me years before when I'd gotten together with Paul and started making excuses every time they wanted to do anything together. Tanner wasn't like them though. He seemed to understand things I'd never been able to explain to other people, even if he didn't agree with them.

After cleaning up the apartment and having a shower—making another pass over the remaining ghost of a picture on my arm—I settled in bed with my laptop on my knee and logged into Warcraft.

The instant my character was online, a chime indicated a private message.

Ceronys: Ahoy, oh great one. Tell me you've come to alleviate my pain by bringing your powerful, magical ass over here to help me kill this big nasty elite who keeps owning my ass.

Wormz: I swear you only want me for my shadow bolt.

Ceronys: I'll keep you around longer if you agree to grind me through dungeons too. Pwetty Pwease?

I sent him a group invite and relaxed back against my pillow. That was exactly what I needed; some downtime before Paul came home.

Ceronys: So is Paul home yet?

Wormz: Not yet. An hour still.

Ceronys: Your arm ink free?

Wormz: Pretty much. Long sleeves on just in case. I'm dying of heat stroke. Had to crank the AC.

That was all that was said outside game talk. For the following hour, I dragged his baby toon through a few dungeons and helped him kill his big bad elite in one shot.

When I heard the front door unlock, I dropped Tanner a quick message letting him know I had to go. Closing my laptop, I then went to greet Paul at the door.

"Hey, how was the conference?"

"Dry. But the food was decent, and they kept the drinks flowing afterward so I'll forgive it."

I watched as he unloaded his briefcase and jacket and unbuttoned the top two buttons of his dress shirt.

"It's freezing in here. Did you turn up the air?"

"Just a bit. I was hot."

Paul stomped to the thermostat and squinted at it. "Jesus, fuck. You have it set to arctic, do you have any idea what kind of fucking bill we'll have now? You could put a damn t-shirt on if you're hot and not wear your fucking winter wardrobe."

I'd only turned it down about two extra degrees from normal and less than two hours before. I doubted it was going to make even a noticeable difference on the bill, but I knowingly kept my opinions to myself. Especially when engaging in one fight to avoid another wasn't really what I had in mind.

"Sorry."

Paul rolled his eyes and went down the hall to the bathroom. "I'm showering. Make some food or something, I'm starving."

After the bathroom door clicked, I released the breath I'd been holding, blowing it out slowly from my lungs, trying to let go of my tension with it.

My weekend was great. Thanks for asking.

Tanner's challenge from a month before stuck in my mind. *Look for one good thing every day. If you can't find even one good thing a day, then ask yourself what you're doing with him. Are you really happy?* I'd been looking ever since, but as each day passed and I saw myself twisting moments around to make them "good" even when they weren't, I knew Tanner was right. I couldn't do it. Maybe I could find one good thing a week or even every couple of days, but what did it mean when I truly couldn't find anything most of the time. Was I happy?

No, I'm miserable.

Chapter Fourteen

Tanner-September

"I've got a touch up at four, so we only have a couple of hours. I still don't know why the fuck I'm apartment hunting with you, but whatever."

"Because Stacey is anti me moving out and Zander... He can't. I'm short on the friends list, and I hate doing this shit alone. Quit whining."

Ricky fastened his seatbelt and flipped through the radio stations until he found some horrible, new age country music and turned it up.

Crinkling a nose at his selection, I glared. "What the fuck is this shit? Seriously?"

"Hey, you want my company? Deal with it. I like it. So where to first?"

I pulled out into traffic and steered the truck toward Bloor Street. "There are a few off Jarvis I wanted to look at. Same general neighborhood so Stacey shouldn't be too pissed. I need to be able to help her out still."

We drove down the busy street in silence for a while, listening to some Carrie Underwood song that was making my ears bleed. I was pretty versatile with my music, but I figured I must have some weird, chemical imbalance in my brain that prevented me from stomaching country of any kind. All I could do was put up with it since Ricky had been kind enough to offer to come along.

"So, what's up with your boy, Zander? He never comes and joins us when we all hang, yet he's all you talk about at the shop. Is he closeted or something and doesn't want us knowing you two are fucking?"

Nearly driving off the road, I hit him with a heated scowl that could melt iron. "We're not fucking. He's a friend, Ricky. He has a boyfriend."

"Okay, relax." He held up his hands in defense. "I didn't know. I haven't seen you out with anyone. You don't club it. I figured maybe there was something there."

I wish.

"There's not." Staring ahead at the road, I ground my teeth. So I'd been completely celibate since I'd moved there and met Zander. Big deal. It hadn't even crossed my mind until Ricky brought it up.

"So, no boyfriend for you I take it?"

"No."

Pulling into a parking space at the complex on Jarvis, I then cut the engine and glanced up at the high rise. "Come on, let's check it out."

Thankfully, Ricky dropped the subject while we went through the place. It was a decent size and well kept. I was surprised. Initially, I'd expected it to be a dive with the price being so reasonably low. Money wasn't much of a concern. I had a decent cushion from selling my half of the shop back in Thunder Bay along with the little bit leftover from what my grandparents had left me, helped me live relatively comfortably.

"Why do you need two bedrooms?"

"I don't know. Gaming room, office. I like the bigger living space. The one bedrooms typically have smaller everything. Kitchen, living room, you know? Too cramped."

After viewing three more apartments in the area—each consecutively rattier than the one before—I decided the first was the diamond in the ruff, even if I had to wait nearly two months to move in. I called the superintendent and told him I'd take it, arranging to swing back around later to put down a deposit and sign the papers. November was going to feel like a long wait.

While driving Ricky back to the shop for his four o'clock, I took back the control over my radio, finding a classic rock station playing some good old Van Halen.

"So," Ricky said cracking his window and lighting a cigarette. "You interested in being set up with someone maybe?"

"Seriously? Ah, no."

"Come on, don't bash the idea just yet. Jenna's got a cousin who she's wanted to set you up with since she met you a few months back." Even though I was shaking my head, he kept plowing along. "He's twenty-two, taking some technology thing at Brown. Jenna says he's a cutie and you'd love him."

"No."

"Dinner with Jenna and me. A double date. Come on, you need a good sweet ass to make you less miserable."

"I'm not miserable, and are you trying to set me up on a date or get me laid?"

"Both. I'm not asking you to commit to him, just dinner, maybe a good fucking to chill you out."

Sighing, I turned the corner onto Spadina. "I don't know."

It was true, I hadn't been involved with anyone since Thunder Bay; since Greg. It would be nice to get over the damn obsession I'd developed with Zander because I knew it was only self-torturous and would amount to nothing. Besides, a warm mouth to suck my dick would sure be a nice change from the relationship I'd developed with my right hand lately.

"All right. One date and we'll see how it goes."

"Awesome. Jenna will be thrilled. I'll text you and let you know when she sets it up."

Pulling up to the curb, Ricky jumped out and gave a wave before disappearing into the shop.

* * *

The following Saturday was "date night." I should have been more excited, but I somehow couldn't manage to find any enthusiasm.

I had to Google the location of the restaurant, and once I was dressed in a dark pair of chinos and a red and black button up shirt, I walked through the busy streets with my stomach growling—it wasn't far enough to be bothered driving. It was warm still for September, but a nice breeze blew, keeping me cool enough I wouldn't sweat and turn up looking a mess.

It was a cute little Vietnamese restaurant that Ricky had claimed made the best Pad Thai he'd ever had. A beautiful young Asian woman with her dark hair pulled back into a high ponytail brought me to the table where I was the last to arrive.

"Hey, Tanner." Jenna greeted me with a smile and wave.

"T." Ricky stood and whacked me on the shoulder. "This is Ryan, Jenna's cousin." He gestured.

The guy seated across from Jenna stood and regarded me awkwardly. He was shorter than me by a few inches and had chestnut brown hair, cut short and spiked into a faux hawk. His eyes were crescent-shaped, a few shades darker blue than my own. All I could think when I saw them was how much more remarkable Zander's eyes were than his. There was nothing exceptionally stunning about him. He was attractive in an average sort of way; lithe with just a tiny detail of muscle, clean shaven, and had dazzling, perfect teeth.

I shook his hand in greeting and put on my most winning smile, hoping the guy wouldn't see that I wasn't really into the date at all.

As a group, we ordered a few platters to share and a round of Pho for everyone. It turned out Ricky was right; it was the best Pad Thai I'd ever eaten.

As for my date, he was chatty and talked more than he ate. By the end of the meal, he leaned in close to me, elbow propped on the table, and head rested in his hand as he went on about how much he enjoyed the great outdoors. His leg brushed mine under the table too many times to be considered an accident.

"You ever been camping?" he asked.

"Not since I was a kid and my parents rented a trailer so we could spend a summer on the lake."

"That's not camping. I mean in a tent, in the woods. Just you and the bears."

"Can't say I have." *Can't say that's appealing.*

After our meal, we all hung around the restaurant and enjoyed a few drinks. I may have indulged in more than was necessary. Not feeling the date thing, I needed something to help ease me into it a little more. Maybe I hadn't given the guy a chance. My brain seemed to insist I compare him to Zander and he just didn't measure up in any way. His smile didn't light up his face and shine through his eyes, he was too confident and lacked the sweet, innocent shyness Zander had. His lips were too thin, and he didn't worry at the bottom one in the same way I'd learned to love in Zander.

As the conversations continued around me, I realized that my obsession had reached unhealthy proportions, and I really needed to take a step back and examine my life. I'd spent all night sabotaging my date because the guy couldn't live up to the unavailable man I desired.

Fuck me!

It needed to turn around, and I needed to be the one to make it happen. When everyone stood to put on their jackets, and we paid our tabs, I made the decision to force myself on a different path. Leaning into Ryan's side, I whispered in his ear.

"Wanna hit a club?" They weren't my thing, but I was far too sober for anything to progress otherwise. I needed more drinks.

I was glad to see I hadn't totally ruined the evening when Ryan's smile split his face and he brushed his body to mine in a quite obvious manner. "Hell ya, sexy, lead the way."

We ended up at a club a few blocks down the road from the restaurant. It was still early, and the dance floor was relatively empty, so we sat at the bar and ordered a few drinks.

"I love your ink."

I was pretty sure it was an excuse to rub his hands all over me, but I didn't mind. The beer was starting to have its effect, and I'd decided that my night was going to end on a happy note if I had anything to say about it.

"Thanks. You have any?"

"Maybe." He winked with a sly expression. "It's hidden under these clothes, you'll have to see for yourself. Later."

"Challenge accepted."

By the time I developed a more than hefty alcohol buzz, there were a lot more people filling the once empty spaces in the club. The dance floor was cramping up with sweaty bodies while the smell of cigarette smoke and cologne filled the air. I swore they turned the music up even louder. The pounding bass riveted through my entire body and the flashing lights were nearly seizure inducing.

"You dance?" Ryan pressed himself at length against my body, his moist, alcohol tinted breath grazed my chin before his tongue licked its way up around my ear. His hands roamed over far more than my arms at that point.

"Sure."

We squeeze through the compression of bodies until we found a small bit of unoccupied space to dance. Ryan wasted no time pulling me in and grinding his body to mine along with the beat. We danced through a few songs before Ryan spun around and wrapped my arms around him, encouraging me to climb my hands up his shirt front, over his sweat-slicked abs. He rocked his ass back against me, probably hoping for some friction, but my dick was not cooperating and was lying dormant in my pants. What should have been kind of erotic, was doing absolutely nothing for me.

"Come on, sexy, I thought you wanted this ass." He tilted his head back and pulled my face down to his, thrusting his tongue down my throat.

I kissed him back, trying to work myself up to even a semi, but wasn't having any luck. I turned him back around in my arms, feeling embarrassed, and continued to kiss him, forcefully. He was stiff against my thigh and made it known by humping and rutting against my leg. The harder I tried, the more impossible it became until I pushed him off and shoved my way through the crush of bodies toward the bar.

Ordering a double Jack and Coke, I rested my head in my hands, elbows on the sticky bar and waited.

"You okay?"

I peeked out to see Ryan beside me. Grimacing, I buried my head again. "You should just take off, man. Find someone else, this ain't gonna happen tonight."

"Seriously? Maybe we just need some privacy. Let's go back to yours or something."

The bartender delivered my drink, and I slammed it back in one gulp. "Nope. I'm done. Sorry."

Not waiting to see his reaction, I made my way out the doors and flagged down the first cab I saw to take me home. I no longer felt like walking.

The entire time in the club, I couldn't wash my brain clean of thoughts of Zander, and it'd botched what should have been a great night. All I could think of as we'd danced was the night I'd gone clubbing with Z. I remembered the way he'd looked and smelled. Then I remembered the asshole that had tried to pick him up and the way it had shaken Zander enough for him to want to leave. Subsequently, I remembered the quiet night of movies we'd enjoyed instead.

Letting myself in the front door, I slunk to the bathroom. It was after one in the morning, and Stacey and Anna were fast asleep in their rooms, so I didn't want to wake them.

Stripped out of my clothes—that smelled strongly of Ryan's sweat and cologne—I started the shower. When the temperature was just right, I stepped under the water and let it rain over me, willing it to wash away the pitiful night I'd just had.

I didn't know what I was doing to myself. Never in my life had I become so worked up over one person. Not even my last boyfriend had had that effect on me.

Memories of past weeks replayed in my head. Particularly, the night the power had gone out. How Zander had drifted off to sleep and refused to let me leave. During that night, he'd inadvertently shuffled closer and slept snuggled up against my side. I wasn't awake when he'd put himself there, but when I'd woken up later on and found him beside me, I'd been unable to move. The guilt at staying put and letting it happen had been overwhelming. I knew it was wrong, but the look of him so relaxed while he'd slept and the way he'd felt warm against me, I'd been unable to pull away. I still remembered the way he smelled.

As I recaptured the moment with my eyes closed, standing under the spray of water, my cock decided that was the perfect time to wake up. *Fucker. You would betray me.* I tried to ignore him, but he refused to be overlooked.

In my mind's eye, I saw Zander's soft features as he slept. The curve of his mouth, slightly frowning and a little pouty. His barely-visible-in-the-candlelight blond eyelashes where they brushed against his cheeks. The rosy flush from having drunk too much wine.

My cock wept, and I bit into my lip as I took him in my hand, giving him the tug he was craving. Between my thoughts and my traitorous dick, I was quickly working past the point of no return. It wasn't the first time I'd jerked off with Zander's face in mind, and I was sure it wouldn't be the last. Every time the guilt mounted higher and higher, and I was starting to feel like a horrible person inside and out.

Torn between shutting off the water, along with my wayward thoughts or giving in to the pleasure and accompanying guilt, I chose the latter. Letting my mind run free, I increased my jerking and leaned my head against the wall.

Zander had such an amazing mouth, and it was easy to envision his lips wrapped around my thick head while I slid in and out of it, letting his tongue tease me. To have him kneeling before me, my fingers holding a firm grip in his hair while he worked me deep into the back of his throat, swallowing me down was a sight to behold. And in my head, I could see it clearly.

My cock pulsed as I increased my thrusts into my fist. I reached my other down to tug my balls as I bit back a moan in an effort to stay quiet. Beyond control, precum dripped over my hand, the slickness coated my fingers before the water washed it away. As I moved my hand faster, firming my grip a little more, I let my imagination steer to the one place that always tipped me over the edge.

I thought of being balls deep, buried in Zander's tight ass. Pounding into him, ripping pleasured sounds from his mouth and hearing my name roll off his lips as he shot all over. That did it. With a deep grunt, I was shooting all down the wall of the shower, and my legs wobbled beneath me with the force of my orgasm. It left me boneless and panting.

And within an instant…the guilt swept its way in.

I rinsed quickly and turned off the shower. Some fucking friend I was. Not only had I somehow fallen for the guy, but I randomly liked to jerk off to images of him in my mind as well. I thought I was a better person than that, but clearly, I'd been wrong.

Feeling pathetic and sorry for myself, I crawled under my covers and willed my drunken mind to sleep.

Chapter Fifteen

Zander-Early October

"Thomas, look at your hands. There's still paint on them. Go back to the washroom and try again."

Thomas stomped away in a huff, around the half-wall to the sink. The number of times I sent children on a return trip to the soap dispenser made me wonder why they didn't work harder at washing up the first time.

Angie was plating sixteen lunches by the counter while I monitored and refereed the commotion that was lunch hour in a preschool room.

"Find a different chair, Lou, I don't think I want you beside Carrie today, not after yesterday's nightmare."

"I'm so glad I have you, Zander. Have I ever told you I love you?" Angie set down plates loaded up with drumsticks, mashed potatoes, and peas in front of the few children who were already sitting.

"You only love my ability to round up rowdy animals and get them in line at the trough for lunch in an orderly fashion."

"Ha! Something like that. So, did Tanner get an apartment? I heard he was on the hunt."

"Yeah, on Jarvis I guess."

"That's not too far from you."

"Couple blocks. Hey, Dylan. Sit down in your seat, buddy. It's not playtime right now. Try your chicken."

Redirecting Dylan to his chair, I then pulled up a seat beside him to encourage him to stay put. Dylan was a runner and sometimes needed to be convinced to stay still and eat or else he would forgo lunch altogether for more playtime.

"I'm going to lay out the cots for naptime. Are you okay here while I do that?"

All the children were busy with their food. Even though it was one of the busier parts of the day, I had a knack for keeping control. I often tried to give Angie a break by letting her set up the room for the next transition of our day; naptime. Most of the children were still sleepers, some rested quietly with a book, while others fought the quiet-time routine entirely.

All in all, it was our favorite time of day because it meant we could relax as well from all the chaos that surrounded it.

"Tanner is picking Anna up just after lunch, so she won't need her bed."

"Alrighty."

Angie dimmed the lights, which helped bring the volume down a few notches before she proceeded to organize the cots into some semblance of order throughout the room. We clumped sleepers into one area while non-sleepers were given quiet activities to keep them occupied during the hour and a half rest period; books, puzzles, coloring pages, and crayons. Whatever worked to keep them busy and silent.

As the children finished their meals, I instructed them to go scrape their plates into the garbage one at a time and sent them to the washroom to wash up and use the toilet before bed.

Angie relocated to help with the bathroom routine and freshen up any children who weren't quite at the toilet using stage. We had a system, and it worked well for us; smooth and effortless—mostly effortless—some days the system failed, and it was more like, someone-let-Godzilla-loose-in-Manhattan kind of crazy. Thankfully, it wasn't one of those days.

Just as the last few children were moving to their cots, Tanner came into the room.

"Uncle Tanner." Anna ran and jumped into his waiting arms, clearly pleased to see him.

"Go get your stuff together, pea, I gotta talk to Zander before we go."

Anna ran to her cubby and worked at packing up the hundred and one pictures she'd made at the art table into her backpack.

Kneeling between two cots, encouraging two very wiggly bums to quit bopping around, I gave Tanner a wave.

He came over and squatted, lowering his voice out of respect, even though not a single worming body was asleep yet.

"Hey, T-man," Angie said as she squeezed by him, stepping over cots to get to a spot where more kiddos needed encouragement to lay still.

"Hey, baby doll." He winked at her.

"Please don't encourage her."

He chuckled quietly and turned back to me. "Hey, my landlord said I could repaint my apartment if I didn't like the colors before I moved in next month. I know it's not a glamorous job or anything, but I was wondering if you wanted to give me a hand. I'd get us dinner and beers or whatnot."

Shifting my gaze to readjust the body hanging off the end of the cot, I tried to come up with a conceivable excuse. Tanner was persistent. He hadn't given up like most other people who'd tried to friend me over the years.

The truth was, I'd have loved to hang out and paint an apartment. There was nothing fun sounding about it, except the hanging out and being buddies part. I enjoyed Tanner's company. The more time we spent together, the more I craved. However, he was starting to see through my excuses. But it didn't stop him from shining a spotlight on me and making me feel bad every time I ditched him.

"I'm not much of a painter."

"Neither am I, that wasn't the point."

I know.

Inadvertently, I sucked my bottom lip into my teeth and chewed it. It was a telltale sign of my discomfort with the situation, and I wasn't fooling him.

"Z, I just thought it'd be fun to hang out. I was giving you an excuse. Tell Paul you're gonna help me paint. It's reasonable."

I shrugged and turned back to tuck a blanket around the little girl beside me. "I'm gonna pass I think."

"You aren't even going to try?"

"Tanner, let it go. You know I can't. I don't know why you do this."

"I won't let it go. I'm your friend, and I want to hang out with you. Why is that not allowed?" When I didn't answer right away, he pushed on. "Okay, how about this. Ricky is having a poker night with a bunch of his buddies on Saturday night, there will be about ten of us, come with me. Just a bunch of guys hanging out."

I blew out a frustrated breath. "I have plans Saturday." If he wanted to play games, fine.

"Really, what plans?" His voice was inching past its original whisper, and I could hear the frustration behind it mounting.

"None of your business plans."

"Tell you what, how about I go tell Paul you and I are going to a poker party Saturday. He can talk to me if he has an issue with it."

"Tanner, you wouldn't." My panic must have read through loud and clear because it earned me an exaggerated eye roll.

"Oh good grief, relax. I should the way you're so fuc—" he scanned the room, "farging scared of him."

I almost laughed at his use of my fake swear word, but I was too pissed off to give him the pleasure.

"You should go. Anna's waiting for you." I needed him to leave. His determination was making me uncomfortable. He didn't get it. No one got it. Paul wasn't so easily satiated when it came to me going out. No matter who it was with. I got an earful, even when it was Angie. I couldn't imagine trying to make him see reason when it was Tanner who I wanted to hang out with. I saw the way he'd watched us together at my birthday celebration months before. If he knew we'd become friends outside of him picking up and dropping off Anna, I wasn't sure what would happen. I wasn't about to find out either.

Tanner let out an indignant noise and rose to his feet. Without another word, he took Anna's hand and led her out of the classroom. I felt like a tool. I didn't want him thinking I didn't want to be his friend, but I couldn't explain the whole truth to him either. That always happened. People tried with me, saw it was impossible, and then gave up.

Closing my eyes, I leaned back against the wall and rested a hand on the back of the two children at my sides, calming them and encouraging them to rest.

I might have dozed; it wouldn't have been the first time. After long mornings of running after little kids, breaking up fights, and running a daily program, naptime always hit hard. Sometimes harder for me than the kids. A short while later, Angie kicked my shoe, nudging me awake.

"You'd better not get caught sleeping. Moe will have a fit."

"I'm not sleeping," I mumbled. "I'm resting my eyes."

Noticing the two children beside me were out cold, I rose from the floor with creaking joints and aching muscles. I felt decades older than my years. I grabbed my packed lunch from the coat closet where Angie and I shared space and joined her at the child-sized table to eat.

"So, what were you and Tanner fighting about?"

"We weren't fighting," I said around a mouthful of sandwich.

"There was an awful lot of huffing and eye-rolling for not fighting."

"You're too nosey."

"Yes, I am. Tell me." Angie unpacked a container of salad from her lunch bag and a smaller jar of dressing.

"It's nothing. He wanted me to help him paint his new place. I said no."

"Why?"

Chewing slowly, I wished everyone would stop badgering me with questions that revolved around my personal life. Sometimes, I wished I was better at lying.

"I don't want to."

"Bullshit."

I guffawed.

"Come on, you won't help because you don't want to get into it with Paul. I'm not stupid, Zander. I've known you long enough to see through your shit."

I really needed to build bigger walls, the ones I currently had were clearly not tall enough to keep people out of my business.

"What if it was me?" she asked.

"What if it was you, what?"

Angie drizzled dressing over her salad and pulled a fork from her bag. "What if I'd asked you to help me paint?"

I shrugged, biting another, larger than was necessary bite off my lunch.

"You'd have helped me."

"Probably not," I said with my mouthful. "Paul doesn't like us hanging out either, he'd probably have bitched just as much."

"See, it does have to do with Paul."

Swallowing my bite, I sighed. "I don't want to cause a riff. What's wrong with that?"

"Why does you wanting to have friends cause a riff?"

"It just does. Can we talk about something else not me related?"

"Are you going to poker night?"

"How the hell do you know about that?"

Angie poked at her lettuce until her fork was loaded. "Tanner may have mentioned he was going to ask you." She shoved it in her mouth, shrugging.

"Tanner has a big mouth."

We ate in silence for a while until Angie pushed the lid back on her half-empty container. "Don't you enjoy hanging out with Tanner? You guys seem to get along really well. You nerd out on that game all the time; World of whatever it's called."

"Warcraft. We play all the time, almost every night. We *are* friends. Why can't that be enough? Why do we have to go out and play poker or paint?"

"Because friends hang out, Zander. I go out with my girlfriends all the time, and Brad doesn't give two shits about it. Don't you want to get out of the house sometimes? It's not healthy being stuck inside so much."

My anger sizzled inside me. Of course, I wanted to go out. Break free, have fun and do all the things normal people did without a second thought. But that wasn't *my* life.

I crumpled up my sandwich bag and stood from the table. "I'm done talking about this. Everyone needs to mind their own business."

The encounter with Tanner and Angie set my mood for the rest of the day. I was a complete bitch from that point on. Short tempered with the kids, and I even managed to snap at my boss, which was not like me at all.

Paul picked me up from work, and our ride home was more quiet than usual. I was afraid to even try a passive conversation because I didn't trust what might come out of my mouth. Paul picked up on my mood right away and called me on it.

"What the fuck's your problem?"

"Nothing. Bad day."

"Well don't bring your pissy-ass mood home with you if it's work shit. I don't need your extra drama."

Biting back a retort, I kept my head down the rest of the drive.

As we rode the elevator, I could feel Paul's eyes watching me. I didn't look up.

"What do you want for dinner?" he snapped.

"I don't know. I can heat us some leftovers from last night if you want."

"I don't want leftovers."

The elevator dinged, and Paul stepped out the minute the door slid open.

"Do you want me to make something? I could do up pasta? Maybe soup and sandwiches, you know, keep it simple?" I offered.

"I don't want that shit either."

I followed him into the apartment and closed the door behind me. "Well, what did you have in mind?"

"How about a burger from down the road with a side of cheer the fuck up."

My chest burned with the urge to snip back, and I knew my face was giving away all the rage I was feeling inside, but I breathed through it and tried to keep my voice level. "I'm trying. I'm sorry. Do you want me to go get burgers?"

"I thought you were going to make soup and sandwiches?"

Oh my God! Make up your mind!

I wanted to scream. He could be so infuriating sometimes. Without answering, I shoved past him a little too hard to go make us some dinner. Before I managed three steps, I was grabbed by the upper arm and spun back around.

"You better curb the fucking attitude you're pulling. Do you hear me?"

Loud and clear buddy! "Yes."

His fingers dug painfully into my arm. Hard enough to bruise, but I tried not to flinch or react, knowing it would only make it worse. I needed to shed my funk and quickly because it was digging me into a hole that I was going to be hard pressed to get out of unharmed.

Paul shoved me toward the kitchen, making me stumble before I caught myself. With shaky hands, I worked to put together sandwiches and heated a couple of cans of soup.

We ate in silence. I wasn't even hungry and the food curdled in my belly, but I plugged on. I wouldn't dare say anything, so I fought through every bite until I was finished.

Paul settled in to watch TV while I cleaned up the kitchen. He made no mention of me joining him so I took that as a hint to leave him alone.

Thank, God.

In our room with the door closed, I drew my laptop into my lap and logged into Warcraft. I needed to escape. Needed to wash away the remnants of my day and just lose myself in Azeroth for a few hours.

Mindless questing in a new zone helped calm my nerves to the point where I could breathe again without the tight constriction around my lungs. It was the only me time I got for the most part, and I soaked it up as much as I could. Starting another quest, staring zombie-like at my screen, moving robotically through killing mobs, knowing my character well enough I could play while half-asleep, I almost missed the chime indicating a private message. I glanced down to the bottom left corner of my screen.

Ceronys: You busy?

Tanner.

I considered ignoring him. The way he'd pushed me earlier had left me in a rotten mood, and I wasn't sure I wanted to rehash it all again since it was finally starting to clear. Paul had managed to piss further on my already pissy mood and I really just wanted to be alone.

Killing my way through another few mobs, I finally relented and sent him a short reply.

Wormz: Yup.
Ceronys: What are you busy doing?
Wormz: Questing.
Ceronys: You're top level. Why? Are you doing rep grind?
Wormz: No.
Ceronys: Are you still pissed at me?
Wormz: No.
Ceronys: Your one-word replies are saying different. I didn't mean to upset you today. I'm sorry if I did.

Sighing, I stopped fighting my way through mobs and found myself a safe place to stand while I satiated him with a longer answer because he clearly wasn't getting it.

Wormz: Look. I'm trying to clear my head right now. I'm not pissed at you. I'm pissed at me because I'm the one who has to live this stupid crap every day. Paul railroaded me with attitude the second I got off work, and now I just need to deflate before I get myself in a situation I don't want to be in. I need to be alone.

I waited for a reply, and when I didn't get one right away, I figured he'd taken the hint to leave me be. Returning to my random slaughtering, glad my mobs had respawned, I lost myself in the game again. My peace lasted about three minutes when a lengthy message came through from Tanner.

Ceronys: I'm worried about you. You've confided a lot of shit in me that I don't like and now I can't pretend I don't know it. I know I'm intruding and I know you want space, but I'm terrified you'll end up on my doorstep again because of that guy, and it will be worse than last time. Please tell me you're safe so I can at least sleep tonight. If you need me to, I can come right now and get you.

Wormz: I'm fine. Really.
Ceronys: Okay. I'm logging off. You have my number, do not hesitate to use it.

I didn't respond, and after another two minutes of silence, I saw the message go across my screen that Tanner had gone offline. The knot in my stomach tightened. I wanted Tanner as a friend, but I didn't know how much longer he'd put up with my on again off again personality. I'd told him more than I'd ever told anyone else. Some by accident, but most of it on purpose. There was something different about him that made me trust him, reach out to him. Scaring him away at that point would wreck me. I just didn't know how to maintain friendships with all the crap in my life the way it was. It didn't seem possible. No one could understand.

Chapter Sixteen

Tanner*-End of October*

The barista handed Ricky his mocha caramela while I stirred milk into my dark roast grande.

"How can you drink all that sugary shit?" I asked as he licked at the extra whipped cream and caramel syrup that ran down the side of his cup. Like a freak, he'd asked the girl to put extra on the top.

"It's good. Shut up. You drink old man coffee, you don't see me knocking it."

As if it wasn't bad enough, Ricky opened three packages of raw sugar and dumped them in his paper cup as well using a wooden stir stick to move the granulated sludge around. It was enough to trigger my gag reflex.

"You'll put yourself into a diabetic coma with that."

"Whatever." As though purposefully looking to put me over the edge, he added two more sugar packets. "So, what happened with Ryan last month, huh? I never heard nothin'. You guys get on okay? Jenna's been bugging the shit out of me to ask you."

Turning away from watching Ricky destroy his drink, I shrugged. "Not my type I guess. We went out dancing. It was okay."

"So nothing happened?"

The last thing I wanted was a reminder of my inability to become aroused when a perfectly good dick was being swung in my face. "Nope. Like I said, not my type."

"Shit, man. What is your type? Jenna will hook you up. She loves playing matchmaker."

Yeah, Zander's my type only he's not available.

"Please don't. I'm good. I don't need set up."

"Fine. If you change your mind, you know where we're at."

We walked swiftly down the road toward the shop. It was cold for the end of October; nearly cold enough to snow and we could see our breath puffing into the air as we breathed. Cold enough, people lost respect for each other and only showed concern for themselves as they rushed from one warm location to the next, heads ducked down and moving so fast they didn't care who they collided into.

Just before we turned the corner onto Spadina, I saw somebody familiar up ahead—or at least I thought it was someone I recognized. Slowing my step, I watched the person puffing on a cigarette outside the drugstore on the corner.

He was tall, even hunched over against the cold it was obvious he cleared six feet without a challenge. Under his jacket was a massive frame which was the dead giveaway for me and clicked all the pieces into place. It was Paul. I'd only met the guy once, at Zander's birthday celebration, but he was hard to forget. His size alone made him distinguishable, even at that distance.

"What the hell man. Why we stopping? It's fucking freezing out here."

"That guy. See him?" I nodded my head in Paul's direction.

"Who? The big fucker?"

"Yeah. That's Zander's boyfriend."

"No shit. The asswipe one?"

I may have let a few comments slip inadvertently over the past month, but not enough that Ricky knew how much that statement rang true. "That'd be the one."

"Okay. So that's nice. There he is. Can we go now? I'm cold."

"Go ahead. I need to do something."

Ricky seemed torn between finding warmth inside the shop and asking what I was up to. In the end, he bounced on his toes for warmth, shoulders hunched up to his ears and tilted his head. "What you gonna do?"

"Have a word with him."

I started forward, but Ricky pulled me back a step. "You're not getting your nose in Zander's business, are you? That's never wise, man."

Frowning, not really sure what I planned to say, I shoved my coffee into his hands, unlatched myself from Ricky's grasp and marched forward, ignoring his comment. Whether Ricky stayed or left didn't concern me, I needed to get some things off my chest that had been eating at me for far too long.

Paul was chatting it up with some woman with wavy, shoulder-length silver hair. She too was puffing on a cigarette, hugging herself against the cold. Not surprising, considering she only wore a knitted sweater over her white uniform. Apparently, she didn't get the message that it was minus a million degrees outside and maybe she should have put something more on. Paul had at least had the sensibility to wear a jacket.

When I was within proximity to be heard, I called out, "Hey, Paul."

He turned his head while he puffed a cloud of smoke passed his lips, scrutinizing me. "Do I know you?"

I hadn't slowed my advance and my body tensed with every step. That was the douche that shared Zander's bed every night. The one who thought it was okay to manhandle him and push him around. The one who yelled and threw shit, making Zander feel like his life wasn't worth anything. He was the guy who wouldn't so much as allow Zander to have friends.

The curdling rage in my belly roiled, ready to explode, and it was tinged an awful shade of green. My jealousy was so thick, I almost choked on it. Why him? What the fuck did that piece of shit have that made him worthy of a man like Zander? Nothing. I would never treat him that way, yet Paul was who he was with.

I didn't think. I didn't plan or consider anything beyond telling that asshole just what I thought of his manipulative, abusive behavior. The woman must have seen the burning vehemence behind my eyes because she snubbed out her cigarette and ducked inside before I came to a stop in front of Paul.

"You don't remember me? There's probably a reason for that, asshole. You'd know me if you weren't such a goddamn control freak over everything Zander did."

"Zander?" His quizzical look cleared and a smile that only fueled me more took over his face. "You're that guy from his birthday. Angie's friend. I remember you."

"Zander's friend," I corrected with emphasis. "And I'm getting really sick and tired of him having to make excuses to not hang out with me because he's too fucking scared of what you'll think. I'm not going to be a dirty fucking secret like that. Since when do you get to pick and choose who he hangs out with?"

Somewhere in my brain, I thought that was the perfect time to shove him in the chest. "He's a grown man, and I think he's capable of choosing his own friends without you lording over him telling him what's right and wrong."

"You're a mouthy little punk, aren't you? I'm gonna suggest you keep your fucking hands to yourself."

"Fuck you, buddy. You don't scare me."

The comment made him stand to his full height, and he squared his shoulders. "So you're telling me Zander's sneaking around behind my back, hiding shit? Is that what you're saying?"

"Wow, you really don't listen when people talk, do you? No, jackass, he's not sneaking around because you have him acting like a scared puppy hiding in the corner. He turns down every attempt Angie and I make at hanging out with him because of you. Maybe he won't stand up to you, but I sure as hell don't mind telling you how it is."

"So Zander's decided to friend your punk ass, has he?"

"Yes, douchebag." Was the guy slow or was I talking too fast for him to process? "Only he doesn't know how to go about having normal friendships with people because you won't let him. He wants to go out and do shit, but cowers at home instead, afraid you might get all pissed off. Well, I'm telling you right here and now, that shit is over. If Zander and I want to hang out, that's between him and me. If you have a problem with that speak up right now, buddy. Let's hear it. Do ya?"

He laughed in my face and flicked the butt of his cigarette to the ground, stomping it out. When he didn't answer, I pressed on, bursting with all the unsaid things I'd been holding onto for way too long. "This little power trip you're on is finished. If I hear of you doing anything to hurt Zander—"

"You'll what? What's he fucking told you?" I'd hit a cord and saw the change in his face instantly. He closed our gap, bringing his face less than an inch from mine, and the smell of cigarettes was so thick on his breath it choked out my argument. "I think I've heard enough out of you. I suggest you mind your own business and fuck the hell off right now."

My head spun with the urge to beat the living shit out of the guy right there on the street. Despite his obvious height and weight advantage, I was ready to go. Only, the sensible part of my brain—the one that had been in hiding over the last ten minutes—was screaming at me to stop because I'd said far too much already. My heart thudded painfully, and the rage pumping through my veins made me tremble with the urge to expel it. Paul wasn't backing down. His gaze never wavered, and I could see him ready to defend himself if I jumped on the crazy train and attacked him.

Neither of us moved. It was a silent standoff. One I wasn't sure was going to end well.

It wasn't until a hand pulled me backward that I tore my eyes away from Paul's. Ricky was glaring between us like he was ready for one of us to go off at any moment and he was preparing to jump in.

"Come on. He's not worth it. Let's go."

Ricky was right, Paul wasn't worth it, but Zander was, and all the emotions that had fueled the fire that ignited inside me was because of Zander. I wanted to do something. Had needed to for so long. I wanted to make his life better, but I didn't know how.

Watching Paul's retreating face as Ricky pulled me away, I got the feeling that I'd just made an even bigger mess, and it was the last thing I'd intended. The need to correct my mistake was huge, only I didn't know how to fix it, and with mine and Paul's tempers on edge, we'd probably end up in a bloodbath, fighting it out if I kept pushing.

Giving into defeat, I quit fighting against Ricky and allowed him to drag me back down the street. Paul didn't go inside, he watched me the entire time, sneering as I glared back at him until I turned the corner putting him out of sight.

My stomach turned, and I pulled out of Ricky's grasp to lean against the building beside us. That was bad. It was really, really bad. As clarity slowly made its way back into my brain and I thought of the ramifications of my actions, I bent over and threw up my breakfast. What had I just fucking done?

Chapter Seventeen

Tanner

"Go say goodnight to Uncle Tanner before Mommy puts you to bed, boo." Stacey shooed a bouncing Anna, clean from her bedtime bath, fresh in her fuzzy, one-piece doggy pajamas into the kitchen where I was unloading the dishwasher and putting dishes away.

"Night, Uncle Tanner," Anna said as she wrapped her arms around my leg. Swinging her up on my hip, I then planted a kiss on her cheek, her damp hair brushing against my face.

"Night, pea. I'll see you in the morning. I'm taking you to preschool tomorrow. Mommy is working early."

"Yay!"

When I put her down, Anna launched herself at her mother, and Stacey caught her in her arms midair to take her down to her bedroom.

Once I'd stacked the last plate into the cupboard, Stacey returned to the kitchen, arms stretched over her head while she let out a drawn-out yawn.

"You look whipped, and it's only Monday." I smiled over at her while shutting the dishwasher door.

"I am. I have some documents to read before my meeting tomorrow, then I think I'm going to call it a night."

Glancing around, noting that the kitchen looked about perfect, I headed to the fridge to grab a couple of beers.

"When can you move into your place?"

The question was asked tentatively. I knew Stacey wasn't looking forward to me leaving. No matter how many times I assured her I would still help with Anna, I got the feeling she rather enjoyed my living with her.

"End of next week. I took a few days off to move and get sorted out." The shop was closed Sundays, so I'd enlisted Ricky and T.J to help. "You know this won't change anything, right?"

"I know."

She took the beer I offered, and we headed into the living room. I sank into one corner of the sectional while Stacey made herself comfortable on the other side, stretching her legs out and tugging her laptop onto her knee.

Pulling up Netflix, I sat silently trying to find something interesting to watch while Stacey busied herself with work.

It amazed me how there could be hundreds of choices of shows, and nothing appealed to me. It wouldn't be the first time I spent hours flipping through options before eventually giving up, having watched nothing.

Twenty minutes into my unsuccessful perusing, my phone buzzed on the dining room table. I slugged off the couch—I needed a new beer anyhow—and headed to the kitchen, grabbing my phone on my way by. As I yanked the fridge door open, I swiped the screen and pulled up the new message. It was from Angie, which surprised me somewhat seeing as we didn't really communicate unless we were planning something.

Can u come over?

I put my new beer on the counter and closed the fridge with my foot, frowning at my phone.

Odd.

Leaning against the counter, I typed out a quick response, going for lighthearted and funny. A twisting in my gut made me uncomfortable, and I didn't want her text purpose to be bad—as though I could somehow change it.

Aww…baby doll, I love you, but I told you I'm gay, unless you grew a dick recently, it wouldn't work out.

Biting my lip, I waited. We always joked like that, and I crossed my fingers, hoping for a playful response.

"Tanner, can you grab me another beer while you're in there."

Absently picking up the one I'd placed on the counter, I wandered back into the living room, staring at my phone, willing Angie to answer me. I handed Stacey my beer and was about to slide back down onto the couch when my phone buzzed.

It's Zander. Please. I need your help.

"Shit!"

I flew off the couch again just as my ass hit the cushion, texting that I was on my way before dropping my phone in my pocket.

"Something wrong?" Stacey watched me from over her laptop, her beer halfway to her mouth. My sister knew me too well, and there was no point lying because she'd see right through it.

"I gotta go. It's Angie. Somethings up with Z."

Stacey's eyes followed me as I grabbed my leather jacket and pulled it on. I found my helmet and keys and was ripping the door open when she spoke again. She was right behind me. I hadn't even heard her approach.

"Tanner, drive safely, okay?"

The worry and concern in her eyes halted me. "I will," I assured her with a smile before flying out the door.

The drive to Angie's went by in a blur—a really cold blur. It was getting too late in the year to be riding, and I needed to pack my baby away soon.

As I pulled up in front of her house, I had a brief moment of panic not knowing how I'd even gotten there. I was ordinarily a cautious driver, but knowing something was wrong with Zander had made me tear across the city without thinking. The churning in my gut hadn't let up since Angie's first text. If anything, it had become worse, to the point I shook a little on the inside.

Zander had wedged himself into my life, and no matter how many times I tried to convince myself not to feel, it happened anyway. I was doing my best to push away the anger that was building inside. Somehow, I knew that whatever had happened had to do with that asshole of a boyfriend, Paul. The guy clearly didn't heed my warning from the other day. Maybe he and I would need to have another little heart to heart. Maybe he scared Zander, but he didn't scare me.

With a trembling fist, I banged on Angie's front door and waited while I bounced on my feet for her to answer.

Angie flung the door open with such force, I was surprised it didn't come off its hinges. I noticed Brad behind her.

"Thank God, Tanner." Her arms flew around me, and not understanding what was really going on, I hugged her back.

"What's going on?" I asked, trying not to sound desperate.

"Come in."

She ushered me inside where I acknowledged Brad with a handshake. I'd met the man a half a dozen times, but I didn't really feel like I knew him all that well.

When she'd closed and locked the door—I tried not to wonder why she felt it necessary to lock it—I asked again.

"What's going on, Angie? Where's Z?"

Angie peered over her shoulder, nodding in the direction of the hallway leading out of her living room to the other end of the house. She lowered her voice when she turned back to me. "He's in the bathroom. I convinced him to take a shower and relax, but..." Her face contorted and she glanced at Brad before continuing. "He doesn't talk to me, Tanner. I know something bad went down. He was so shaken when he showed up, and he was acting weird, but I don't know what happened. I know he's talked to you in the past so I don't get why he came to me." She shook her head in defeat.

"We thought he'd talk to you once he calmed a bit," Brad added when Angie couldn't continue.

I nodded, and without waiting for more explanation, I headed down the hall to where I presumed was the bathroom.

Outside the door, I heard the shower stop, so I stood for a few minutes to give him enough time to put himself together. When I figured enough time had passed, I knocked lightly and waited.

After a pause, a faint voice came through the door. Unless I imagined it, the voice shook and sounded forced. "I just need a minute."

He didn't know it was me. He didn't know Angie had called me and he might not be happy she had. Angie was right. I knew a lot more than she did. Zander had shared more than he probably thought he should. I knew what Paul was capable of and it was that knowledge which made it hard for me to keep my voice steady.

"Z, it's me. Can I come in?"

The silence that followed stretched out far longer than I liked and I shuffled on my feet, needing him to open the door. Needing to see him and know if he was all right.

"Zander. Let me in. I need to know you're okay."

Another short pause was quickly followed by a sharp, pointed response, "Why are you here?"

"Angie is worried about you, Z. We just want to know if you're okay."

"I don't need your help, Tanner. Go home and quit interfering in my life."

The anger laced around his words startled me, and I looked up to stare at the door separating us.

"What? Zander—"

"Go away. I'm fine."

Furrowing my brow, I stared at the wooden surface in confusion while I processed my next move. I peered down the hall to where Angie and Brad stood. Shrugging my shoulders, I held my hands up asking silently what I should do. Angie just pointed to the door and mouthed the words "go in."

Turning back, I sighed. She was right. Zander was not going to be happy, but if he didn't want help then he wouldn't be making small attempts at reaching out to his friends.

"Zander, I'm coming in." I gave him a beat before turning the knob and praying he didn't have it locked. He didn't. It turned, and I pushed it open.

Angie's bathroom was small. The toilet sat on the one wall with a vanity shelving unit built around it, cluttered with makeup and lotions. A pedestal sink sat across from it. The shower stall was a decent enough size with sliding frosted doors which stood open. Zander was perched on the edge of the tub, face in his hands. He had pulled on his pants and t-shirt, but his hair was soaking wet still and dripped onto a towel he had draped around his neck.

He didn't look up when I let myself in, so in respect for some privacy, I closed the door behind me. Watching him closely, I kneeled down in front of him. When I went to pull his hands from his face, he threw me off with surprising strength.

"I said go home." His words no longer held any punch, but I respected his desire to keep his face hidden and sat back on my heels to wait.

"I'll go home when I know you're okay."

"I'm okay. Go."

"Yeah, only I don't believe you."

He let out a sarcastic huff and drew his hand up on the towel, holding it around his neck and fiddling with it. With his head down, he raised his eyes briefly to meet mine and dropped them again.

No black eyes; that was a relief. I didn't get much more of a look.

"What are you gonna do, Tanner? Try and fix it again? Make it all better? I told you to let me handle my own life, and you didn't. You had to go and interfere."

"I'm only trying to help."

"Well stop it, okay? Stop. Trying. To help. Don't you get it? You make everything worse when you do that."

"What are you talking about?"

That nagging voice was back from the other day. The one that told me I'd made a huge mistake approaching Paul. My skin prickled at the implications he was tossing my way.

When he lifted his head, I could see his eyes more clearly. They were red, and I knew he'd been crying. He fiddled with the towel, drawing his hand up further, closing it around his neck, mopping at his face where more drips had fallen from his hair.

"You went and talked to him, didn't you?"

The venom in his words seeped into me, and I stared blankly.

"I did. I want to help you, Z."

"Stop. Trying. To help me. What part of this isn't clear to you?"

He shot up from the edge of the tub sending me off balance, and I nearly toppled backward. I stood, and he was right in my face. The hurt and defeat in his eyes crushed me.

"You have no idea what you did, do you? You've made it so much worse for me. You and your little act of bravado." A tear slid down his cheek, and his hand gripped the towel around his neck so hard his knuckles were white. What was he doing? My gaze fell to the towel then climbed back to the tortured look in his eyes. My skin heated and my heart thrummed painfully.

"What are you talking about, Z?"

"This." He whipped the towel off his neck and threw it to the floor. "This is what happens when you interfere, Tanner. I told you to let it be." His tears flowed down his face in waves. His lip quivered, and I couldn't look him in the eyes anymore for all the hurt he was sending my way. But, I didn't want to look at what I feared was down further so my eyes shifted everywhere but.

"Look at it, Tanner," he yelled. "Look! You see that?"

I looked. I saw.

There was no mistaking what I saw. The bruises around his neck were dark and defined. The horror of the incident pressed into his skin. It choked my next words, freezing them in my throat and it was me who couldn't breathe at that moment.

"You did this," he hollered. His pain spilled out of him and stabbed into me like a thousand little knives. All I could do was stare at his neck in disbelief. "This is your fault. I told you not to meddle, and you didn't listen."

What have I done?

"P-Paul did this to you?" I could barely stammer the words. I couldn't believe what I was seeing. My eyes stung and my vision blurred as I looked into his face again.

"Yes! Yes, he did this because *you* tried to fix things when I told you to stay out of it. He choked me until I nearly passed out. Held me to the wall by the throat until everything faded and I saw sparkles in my vision. I thought I was dead, Tanner. Because of you!"

Because of me? I didn't choke you.

I wanted to scream at him. Protest that no matter what I'd done, it was Paul who'd hurt him, not me. He needed to open his eyes. Go to the police and get out of that situation before it was too late. But he was beyond seeing reason. He opened the bathroom door and shoved me out. Yelling at me the entire time, blaming me for something Paul had done, and all I could do was stumble backward and catch myself on the wall before I fell.

The bathroom door slammed, and I sank down to sit on the floor. Angie was beside me, wiping at my face where I didn't even realize tears were falling unbidden in waves. I leaned against her and sobbed.

It was a few minutes before I was able to pull my shit together. Angie held my head up. Her eyes searched mine, begging for answers. What the fuck did I tell her? Zander was right. I'd done it. I'd gone to Paul and threatened that he back down. Warned him to leave Zander alone or I'd cause trouble. My actions had turned around and bit Zander in the ass and nearly cost him his life. I was in way over my head, and I'd failed my friend.

Shoving Angie's hands away, I scrambled to my feet and bolted for the front door, but Angie was hot on my heels and grabbed my shirt, spinning me around.

"What happened, Tanner?"

Brad loomed behind her, his expression drawn with worry.

"I-I..." What did I tell her? "Paul... He tried to kill him. He needs to go to the police. You need to convince him."

Pulling from her grasp, I sprinted out the door before she could stop me again.

I tore down the street on my bike at law-breaking speeds and took corners a little too fast. That time, I didn't even register the cold. I drove. I drove and drove and drove. Without a destination, knowing only that I needed to get away. All I could see were the finger-shaped bruises around Zander's neck and the anger behind his red-rimmed eyes. He blamed me. It was my fault. He was right. If I hadn't meddled, it would never have happened. I nearly got him killed.

Tears welled up in my eyes again, and I eventually had to pull over because it was too hard to drive. Somehow, I managed to take myself to the lake. I sat on my motorcycle looking out over the water to the lights shining off Centre Island in the near distance.

I'd fucked up. Huge. Zander was angry and would probably never forgive me. I'd promised him he could talk to me and I would listen without judgment, but that was easier said than done.

How could I listen, watch, and see him go through life in a seriously unhealthy relationship and not feel the urge to step in and help him? *Fuck!* It was more than unhealthy. That was abuse plain and simple. Domestic violence as it was read and written about every day come to life in my friend. How Zander sat by and took it day after day, I couldn't understand for the life of me. I'd just wanted to help. I'd never meant any harm. Never would I have purposefully set out to hurt him.

I got off my bike and wandered down to sit closer to the edge. The night was near freezing and the breeze blowing off the water made me shiver despite my leather jacket. Maybe it had nothing to do with the cold, maybe I was in shock.

It was getting late. I knew I had an early morning and needed to get home, but I sat regardless and let the wind and hum of people walking around lull me. Even as the moon peaked and began its descent in the sky, I was nowhere near calm. Eventually, I returned to my bike, numb to the bone, and made my way home.

I hoped Stacey was already in bed and hadn't waited up because I didn't want to have to explain anything. I'd kept her in the dark about most things Zander related. All she knew was that we were friends and it wasn't any more because Zander had a boyfriend. I was in no mood for deep revelations where Zander was concerned, and it would not bode well regardless, considering Stacey was starting to figure out how I truly felt about him. What I needed to do was go home and sleep my misery away. I'd ruined a friendship with a guy I'd inadvertently fallen for, all because I was trying to stand up for him and do what was right. Why hadn't I listened and minded my own business?

After sneaking back into the house, I stripped down to my boxer briefs and crawled into bed. Lying awake, I stared at the ceiling. So much for clearing my mind, it was still muddled and pounding with a headache. There was no way I was going to sleep. I snagged my phone from the bedside table and shot a quick text to Angie, hoping she was still up.

How is he? Did he tell you?

I chewed my nails as I waited for a response, staring at my phone like it was a grenade set to explode. Angie was quick to reply, and when my phone buzzed—even though I was expecting it—I nearly launched it across the room. My nerves were shot.

He told me what happened. He's asleep on the couch. He's really upset with u.

My heart ached all over again reading those words and guilt threatened to suffocate me. *I didn't mean any harm. I was only trying to help.* My phone buzzed again.

He may blame u right now, but this is NOT YOUR FAULT, Tanner. Stop blaming yourself like I know u r.

Ignoring her statement, not feeling like I should be absolved of anything at the moment, I typed out the question that had been eating at me all night.

Tell me he's reporting him to the police.

He doesn't want to. I tried convincing him. He's putting his foot down.

Dammit!

Why? Why? Why?

I'd have given anything to understand Zander's train of thought. Why on Earth he wouldn't take it to the police was beyond me. My phone buzzed again.

I'm going to keep pressing it. Get some sleep. We'll talk soon.

Thx Angie. I paused then added. *Take care of him, please xoxo*

I will xoxo

I tossed my phone aside and rolled over, pulling the blankets over my head. Somehow, I knew it wasn't going to be a restful night.

* * *

Zander wasn't at work Tuesday or Wednesday. Angie explained that against her better judgment he'd gone home to Paul. He was keeping contact with her through text, and she said he was doing all right considering. I texted him at least a dozen times, and he ignored every one.

On Thursday, he was back at work. I received a message from Angie at six-thirty that morning, and even though I was not needed to take Anna to daycare because Stacey worked later, I insisted because I needed to see him. He had yet to respond to any of my texts or calls, and he hadn't been online at all.

A lot of good it did, because the minute I pulled up, Angie explained he'd made excuses and took off to the storage room. I hung out in the classroom awhile, but when it became clear he was not returning until I was gone, I hung my head in defeat and left.

After another day of the exact same behavior, my desperation was turning to frustration and anger. He was acting like I'd been the one who'd pinned him to the wall and fucking strangled him. Yet he was back to playing house with Paul. Angie kept telling me he'd come around, but it was bullshit, and I was done trying to be the good guy. If Zander couldn't see I was just trying to help him, then fuck it. I couldn't sit around and watch him put himself through that any longer, and I certainly was not going to start taking the blame.

Another week passed. A full week of blatant ignoring. I stopped going unnecessarily to the daycare and quit texting him altogether. Completely heartbroken, I also worried myself sick. My sleep was messed up, and I was walking around like a zombie come the weekend, which sucked because it was the weekend I was moving into my apartment. I missed Zander like gaping-hole-in-my-heart missed him, and all I wanted was to make it better.

I spent the whole weekend moving my stuff into my new place with the help of T.J and Ricky for the low, low cost of a couple of extra-large pizzas and a case of beer. We got it done quickly, considering most of the things I'd put in the storage unit were still boxed and ready to go.

By late Sunday afternoon, I was mostly unpacked, and after a hot shower, I settled on my bed ready to crash for the night. I was exhausted. Before rolling over, I checked my phone and saw I had missed a call from Angie. She'd been keeping me up to date and felt bad for how things had played out with Zander and me. She'd left a voice mail that simply stated; "Call me." So I did.

As the phone rang, I settled back on my pillows and groaned at the ache in my muscles from having spent all weekend packing, lifting, and moving heavy boxes and furniture.

"Hey, sexy. All moved in?"

"Yeah." I sighed. "How's Zander?"

"You don't want to tell me about your new pad and how awesome it is?"

"No. I want to know how Z's doing."

"Come on, let him worry about his thing, and you tell me how you're liking living alone."

"I hate it so far. I'm lonely and worried about Z all the time. Cut the bullshit and tell me how he's doing."

She sighed on the other end of the line. "I don't know."

"What do you mean you don't know?"

"I pissed him off, and he's not talking to me now either."

I groaned and threw an arm across my eyes. "What did you do, Angie? You were my lifeline to him."

"Yesterday morning, I told him to quit being a dick and apologize to you because it wasn't your fault and he knew it. He got mad and stormed off. Now he won't answer my texts or calls either. Sorry, Tanner, but it's true, and I hate that he's doing this to you. It's not right."

"Hey, whatever. If that's the life he wants to live, then fine. Who am I to interfere? I should have kept my nose out of it."

"Tanner, it's not the life he wants. He's miserable."

"Then why does he stay?" I didn't mean to raise my voice, but for fuck's sake. *Why*, was the final jeopardy question that nobody seemed to know the answer to.

"He's afraid."

I could almost feel my blood pressure rising. "Afraid of what?" I barked. "He should be afraid to stay there, not leave."

Angie paused long enough I almost asked the question again. When she spoke, her voice was quiet and melancholy. "My sister's friend was in a violent relationship for years, and I remember my sister trying to help her get out. She researched all kinds of facilities and read the hell out of ways to help, because her friend, she wouldn't leave the guy for anything. My sister said a lot of it stemmed from fear. She was afraid if she left, the guy would come after her and force her back, and it would be worse. She feared that she couldn't truly get away with her life." There was a long pause, and Angie sighed again. "Zander probably doesn't think there is any way out."

Mulling it over, I tried to see the truth behind what Angie said. I recognized the fear in Zander's eyes sometimes. I'd seen it whenever I pressed him to hang out or questioned him about things he didn't want to talk about. Could she be right? Was that why he stayed?

It took me several seconds to find my voice, and when I did, it took me a minute longer to ensure it didn't break when I spoke. "You're killing me, Angie. I only want to help him. I don't know what to do."

"I know, Tanner. Me neither."

"I keep messing up."

"No. You were trying to help. His situation is what's messed up."

We sat in silence for a few minutes, both wallowing in our thoughts, when a knock on my door startled and confused me.

"Baby doll, someone is at my door, I gotta let you go."

"Sure. Take care, T-man. Keep in touch."

"Of course. Let me know if you hear anything. Kisses."

"Kisses."

I hung up and whipped on a pair of joggers before heading to answer the door. It was after eleven thirty, and I couldn't figure out who the hell would be calling that late. Ricky or T.J maybe? They'd probably left their smokes behind.

When I pulled the door open, I froze. The look on my face must have been pretty dumbstruck because the last person I was expecting to see was Zander.

Chapter Eighteen

Zander

I couldn't look at him. I knew if I did there would be hurt and possibly anger in his eyes, and I didn't know if I was ready to face it. I'd put it there. I'd caused it. Instead of placing blame where it was due, I'd lashed out at Tanner for being nothing more than a concerned friend. The repercussions of his actions were the result of my own weakness and cowardice at being unable to leave a truly horrible situation. They were *my* fault, not his.

When silence ensued, I chanced raising my head. With his arms crossed over his chest, I could tell he was trying to look pissed off, but the pain behind his eyes wasn't masked. It shone through like a beacon and caused an unexpected stab of pain in my heart.

"Can I come in?"

His nose curled and I thought he was considering slamming the door in my face. I braced myself for rejection, and when he stepped aside, granting me entrance, I breathed a sigh of relief. Wandering a few feet inside his new apartment, I looked around. I regretted not apartment hunting with him or helping him move, but he'd done well for himself.

The living room and dining room were an open-concept with tan colored walls and a large archway separating them. A door led into what I assumed was the kitchen, and a hallway ran down to another area, again I presumed to a bedroom and bathroom.

"Nice place." Shuffling, I tried again to hold his gaze.

He shrugged and turned, walking in farther.

"You want a beer or something? I don't think Ricky and T.J drank them all. There might be a couple left."

"Umm, sure." I pulled off my jacket and hung it over the doorknob, not finding a hook anywhere. There were still a number of boxes piled in the corners, but I was surprised at how much had already been unpacked.

An old-style boob-tube television sat on a chest by the wall—I presumed his flat screen was in the bedroom like before. Two empty bookshelves flanked either side with boxes sitting in front waiting to be unloaded. His couch was mustard yellow with chocolate brown cushions strewn over the top—very retro looking. I wandered over and sat, fingers dancing over his solid oak coffee table.

Tanner returned with two beers and handed me one.

"I didn't know you had furniture. I figured you'd be set up with lawn chairs and boxes for tables or something."

My attempt at humor fell flat. He shrugged, not looking my way. "I had a storage locker full of my shit from Thunder Bay. Odds and ends. Had it sent down with my bike in the spring."

I nodded and sipped at the beer. Tanner settled beside me, drinking in silence. The tension was thick, and I could tell he was biting back his words, waiting for me to explain why I'd come.

Fair enough.

Swigging another mouthful, I then placed my drink on the coffee table and turned to face him. "I-I'm sorry, Tanner." He stared at his hands, picking at the label on his beer, refusing to meet my eyes. "None of that stuff was your fault, and I was wrong to blame you."

Still nothing. Tanner's brow furrowed as he picked with more vigor, tearing off sections of the sticker, collecting them in a pile on his knee.

How could I make it better? Tanner was the closest thing I had to a friend, and I'd messed it all up. What if he couldn't forgive me? The jabbing pain was back, stinging inside my chest at the thought. The idea of losing our friendship physically hurt me in a way I couldn't understand. As much as I hated Tanner's interference, part of me clung to the fact that someone cared. Someone gave a shit about me.

"Tanner, I don't know what else to say. Talk to me, please."

His hand stilled; the picking stopped. He drank deep and deposited his drink beside mine. After swiping the bits of paper into his palm, he dropped them on the table as well and met my gaze. It was worse than just pain in his eyes. Their normal radiant blue had dimmed, and sadness had rooted itself there. He looked defeated. Lost. His lips moved around words he had yet to speak. As he scanned my face for a moment, I saw something more. Whatever it was, he hid it quickly and ducked his head.

"Why did you go back to him?" His words were soft, but they stung nonetheless.

It was the million dollar question. I huffed and slumped to cover my face with my hands, scrubbing and wishing I could cleanse away all the bullshit clinging to me.

"I wish I could explain it in a way you'd understand."

He pulled my hands back from my face and turned me to look at him again.

"Try me."

I rolled my eyes to the ceiling and stared at where flakes of paint were lifting. Running my tongue along my teeth, I contemplated how to put it into words. He waited patiently as I thought, watching me closely until I lowered my gaze and sighed wearily.

"I can't."

"Zander, the guy nearly killed you."

"But he didn't."

Tanner flinched and shook his head in disbelief. "Are you serious? Maybe not this time, but what about next time?"

I flopped back on the couch and pinched the bridge of my nose. "It wouldn't have happened if you hadn't gone and interfered. I know how to handle him. I know when to back down, and I know when to keep my mouth shut. I've been doing it for years."

"Do you hear yourself when you talk?"

Lowering my hand, I peered over to him. The look of disgust had returned. I'd seen that look before from friends I'd had in the past. The ones that were all gone, thanks to my damned life. Thanks to Paul.

I told you, you wouldn't understand. You think I want to live like this? You think I don't see how screwed up my life is?

"Tanner, I know how to slip under his radar and not piss him off for the most part. Until people put their noses in where they don't belong, I can handle him. Stuff like that doesn't happen normally. I know how to be careful."

"For the most part? My God. Listen to what you're saying. You've told me flat out he's hurt you before, so whose fault was it then, huh? Who are you going to blame for before?"

"Tanner. Don't."

"Me don't?" He pushed off the couch and started to pace. "I'm trying to help you see reason, but you're fucking blind. You've told me he yells, he breaks shit, throws things at you, and he's hurt you before. Fuck, Z, he tried to kill you. This isn't normal, don't you get it? You aren't supposed to song and dance around your fucking boyfriend. That's not how relationships work. Excuse me for being concerned for you and trying to help. I didn't mean for you to take a fucking beating because of me. If he'd have killed you, I'd...I'd never have been able to live with myself. I would never have forgiven myself."

I gripped both hands into my hair, fisting and pulling hard enough to make my head hurt before ripping them out and standing to match his height. "Tanner, I'm not looking for you to fix me. I know my relationship is a train wreck. I've known since the second I moved in with him it was a mistake. I can't just walk away. It's not as easy as you make it sound, and I don't expect you to understand."

Stopping his pacing, I spun him around to look me in the eye. "I need a friend. I need someone to talk to. I need someone to lean on and listen to me when I can't take it anymore. Because there are so many days I'm falling apart and I have no one. When everything inside me feels like it's going to explode or melt into a pool of sludge and I don't know what to do, I need someone to be there for me. I can't do this on my own anymore. I'm a mess. I'm falling apart."

Tears ran down my cheeks, and I cursed under my breath for letting them fall and showing weakness. "I may not know what the hell I'm doing most days, but instead of judging everything I'm doing wrong, can't you just be there? I need you, Tanner. I need a friend so badly right now I've come here to beg you not to give up on me. Begging you to try to understand the impossible and just be there."

My chest clenched and I knew I was about to unleash a flood more tears. I spun away and flopped back on the couch, burying my face in the cushion. I hated being so damn vulnerable. Hated my life even more for what it had become. I felt so trapped, I didn't know how to get free.

The silence deafening the room after my little rant was absolute like we'd been sucked into a vacuum where noise wasn't permitted. Less than a minute passed before he peeled me up from my nest in the pillow and wrapped arms around me, holding me tight. I leaned into Tanner's chest and clung like he was a single buoy in a vast ocean; the only thing keeping me from drowning.

"I'm sorry." Tanner stroked my hair from my face and continued to whisper assurances. "I'll be here for you no matter what, however you need me. I'm your friend, Zander. You can always talk to me."

Letting Tanner take some of my burdens was relieving. I'd spent so much time doing all of it on my own, telling nobody about the horrors behind the pulled curtain of my life. There was something about Tanner that induced trust. I wanted to trust him. I did trust him, it was why I'd reached out in the first place.

"You can hate what I'm doing by staying with him. You can hate Paul. But, please don't try to fix me. Please don't hate me for staying there."

"I couldn't hate you. I could never hate you. I only did it because I care."

"I know. Just let me deal with Paul, okay?"

Tanner exhaled and held me up to look him in the eyes. "I promise, I won't stick my nose where it doesn't belong anymore, and I'll try not to be too opinionated, but I care about you, Z. I hate seeing you like this."

I sat more upright and picked up my warming beer to take a swig. "It's not always this bad." Moving into defensive mode was reflexive. I didn't know why, but I always felt the need to defend Paul.

Tanner rolled his eyes. "Here we go."

"What?" I snapped. "It's not. He takes care of me. He does. You may not see it, but it's not always like this."

"One good thing, Z. Lay it on me. Tell me one, single good thing that's happened this week where Paul is concerned."

Drinking my beer down past halfway, my brain tripped over itself to answer his question.

"You can't do it, can you?"

"Give me a second to think."

"It shouldn't be that hard to answer."

"It's been a rough week. Give me a break."

"That's the third time I've asked you that question since we met and you have yet to give me one solid answer. Think about that."

That time, I drained my beer, slammed it on the coffee table and stood, making my way to the door and taking my coat from where it hung.

"I gotta go."

Tanner bounced up behind me and laid a hand on my shoulder. "Stop, Z."

"You just can't help yourself, can you? You have to be a jerk. You have to criticize everything."

"Forget I said anything. Don't leave angry. I'm an ass, but trust me it's only because I care."

As I pulled my coat on and zipped it under my chin, I tried to let my anger go. I really didn't want to leave like that.

"Are we good?" he asked.

My shoulders slumped, and I nodded. "We're good."

Tanner hugged me again, and I found I didn't want to let go. I deflated in his arms, leaned into him and nuzzled the crook of his neck, burying my face deeper into his warmth. I didn't want to go home to where the tension was so thick and heavy it made every muscle in my body hurt. Even with our disagreement, even when I hated Tanner for being right all the time, being with him made me feel safer and more at ease than I'd ever felt with Paul. It was affirmation that I couldn't lose our friendship, and I'd do anything to keep it intact. I needed it. I needed Tanner.

"Are you going to be okay going home?"

"Yeah. Paul was in a whiskey coma when I left, he shouldn't even know I was gone."

Releasing from our hug, I tugged my beanie over my ears. The air was cold, and I'd walked the four blocks to Tanner's new apartment. According to the weatherman, we were expecting snow, and it was certainly cold enough to do just that.

"Do you need a ride?"

"I'm gonna walk. I need the fresh air, but thanks."

Chapter Nineteen

Tanner-Mid-November

As I flew through the daycare's front doors, I glanced to the clock on the wall. Six-o-three. *Dammit!* I spun around the corner and barreled into the already tidied up preschool room. All the chairs had been stacked for the night, the tables were cleaned, the paints put away, and Anna was sitting on the carpet. She was fitting the pieces of a puzzle together with her bag packed at her side as Angie helped her along. I was late. Again.

"I'm so sorry. I had a seriously chatty client that wouldn't leave, even though I finished his session over an hour ago. Please don't slap me with a late charge or Stacey will kill me."

Zander was at the back coat closet, zipping up his jacket. "No worries, man. You always fly in by the skin of your teeth, we're getting used to it."

It wasn't far from the truth, and thank goodness Angie and Zander were friends or Stacey's late fees would have been stacked so high she'd have been throwing the daycare bill at me.

"Are you ready to go, Anna?" I asked, grabbing her coat off the floor from beside her. "Mama's going to be late tonight so Uncle T's cooking which means McDonalds. How does that sound?"

Anna's smile took over her entire face as she clapped fists full of puzzle pieces together. "Yay! I can finish my puzzle, Uncle Tanner?"

"Work on it tomorrow, pea. I'm sure Angie and Zander want to go home. It's late."

"She's okay, let her finish." Angie stood from where she'd been sitting. "I'm in no rush and Zander can go whenever. I can lock up."

"You have a ride, Z? I can drop you off if you want or you can join us for our Micky D's pig-out."

Zander slung his backpack over his shoulder and glanced out the window to the parking lot. "Paul's picking me up, but thanks."

Even the sound of his name made my muscles clench, and I tried to push it aside.

As Anna worked on her puzzle, I headed over to the window and propped myself on the edge of a table facing Zander.

"So, the guys from work are headed to the Convention Center this Saturday for a car show. They are bringing some buddies along, and we thought we'd head back to T.J's after to shoot some pool or play some darts. We're odd-numbered, I thought you might like to join us. Interested?"

Despite knowing the answer, I asked anyway. Zander never took me up on offers to hang out on weekends Paul was in town. I was starting to think Zander just didn't bother asking anymore. Since our problems a couple of weeks back, things had been okay between us. We played online together, and I continued my fruitless attempts to get Zander to go out and have fun while he continued to turn me down.

I could see Angie from the corner of my eye, studying Zander as she pulled her jacket and purse from the coat closet. As was the norm, Zander's eyes flicked around the room, refusing to look at me while he stumbled for an answer. Why he bothered making excuses anymore, I had no idea. We'd played that same game for seven months. I'd ask him to hang out, and ten times out of ten, he'd say no.

"Can I get back to you?"

In other words, no.

"You don't need to ask his permission, Z. You're a grown man. If you want to go out and have fun, just do it."

Zander tossed me a dirty look, and I screamed on the inside. "Don't go there. You know I can't," he said through gritted teeth, darting a panicked look at Angie who pretended not to notice.

"Can't or won't." I was so tired of the lies. I held his stare, unwilling to back down.

He ignored my question and held my unwavering gaze with his own. "Can. I. Get. Back. To. You?"

I tried to hide my brewing irritation. Everything Zander wanted to do needed to be run through the "acceptance board," aka Paul, first and it was getting downright annoying. Nothing had changed since we'd talked. He hadn't even tried to make things better for himself. I'd promised I would be his sounding board and not interfere, but I'd made no promises about voicing my objections loud and clear. At that moment, I wanted to scream, "I object!"

I'd never known someone to relinquish so much power to another human being before and call it a *loving* relationship. Zander didn't even know how to be his own person with his own mind to make his own choices. He was the puppet doing only what his master told him to do. It made me sick to watch.

Only when Paul was away, and I could get Zander out on his own, did I see glimpses of the man behind the controlling strings, and he was such a beautiful—albeit lost—man. It broke my heart to sit by and watch.

"Yeah," I said flatly. "T.J just needs to know numbers by Friday morning so he can grab tickets."

"Okay. I'll let you know."

Zander turned and stared back out the window to the parking lot where Paul's old rust box Ford Focus was pulling in. His tires barely came to a full stop when the man laid on the horn with the impatience of a starving infant. Before the noise finished piercing the air, Zander was halfway out the door.

"See you guys later."

I watched him go at an accelerated pace, head down with a deep frown on his face. He looked downright miserable, and I felt like a grade A twat for saying what I did. I seriously didn't know how to keep my mouth shut. Zander had enough bullshit without having me adding to it. I was being a terrible friend. Again. It bugged me to no end that he couldn't see what that guy was doing to him. However, it bugged me even more that I seemed to have a constant need to point it out.

As the car pulled away with a squeal of tires, I let out a frustrated grumble from deep inside; one laced with all the suppressed anger I'd been building up for the last few months.

"Fuck I hate that douchebag," I said to Angie who stood quietly at the closet doors, trying to be invisible. Sneaking a glance at Anna, I was glad to see she was oblivious to my temper and foul mouth as she continued with her puzzle. "What is Z doing with him?"

"I told you, I think he's afraid to leave. He thinks he's trapped."

"That's ridiculous. He needs to kick Paul to the curb is what he needs to do and move on with his life. Z's such a great guy, and Paul treats him like shit. He deserves so much better than that."

"He doesn't know how to get out, Tanner. He's afraid Paul won't let him leave, that he'll come after him. You've seen what the man's capable of."

"Then he needs to go to the police."

"He won't."

"Why?" I threaded fingers through my hair in frustration. "You've seen the bruises and marks. He has every reason to report him. I just don't get it. If he filed a restraining order, Paul couldn't go near him, at least not without getting his ass arrested."

"He knows. It's more than that, Tanner." Angie paused and pursed her lips.

"What then? What is it? Somebody please explain this to me because I'm seriously confused, and I don't know how much more I can take."

"I think he's also afraid of being alone. He's afraid of what's on the other side after he walks away. You know how he grew up. All he wants is to be loved, and he thinks Paul is the best he can do."

"Come on. That's bullshit. Even being alone would be better than him." I tossed my arm in the direction the vehicle had driven. "Besides he wouldn't be alone. I'd be there to—" I clamped my mouth shut before I could say more, but Angie's face softened as she watched me with sympathy. Glancing back out the window, I tried to ignore the fact that I was being studied like a term paper. After a long pause, Angie came up beside me and put her hand on my arm.

"Tell him, Tanner. Why are you holding back?"

A hot flush burned my cheeks as I turned back to Angie, prepared to completely deny whatever she was thinking. I'd fought it for months, and there was no way I was letting an almost slip up expose my secret. "I don't know what you're talking about? Tell him what?"

"Christ, Tanner." Angie turned me to face her. "You are so fucking in love with him. That's why you're so torn up and angry. Everyone knows it. Everyone sees it."

Shit, am I that obvious?

"E-everyone?"

"Except Zander. I'm pretty sure he's oblivious, but only because he's in denial too."

Denial?

"W-what do you mean?"

"Ugh…Men are so infuriating sometimes."

"Angie, I don't know—"

"Stop it, Tanner. Just stop. Why are you standing by watching him suffer? He needs you to help him break free of this…this...bullshit. He's terrified. He's been leaning on you for months. Begging you for help. Why do you think that is? He's shared things with you he's never shared with anyone. He trusts you. I don't honestly think even *he* knows what's happening between you two."

"Nothing is happening between us, Angie. Nothing." As much as I wanted it. As much as I dreamed about it. I'd kept it buried inside and not let it out. I'd respected our friendship. I hadn't crossed lines. "I will not interfere with someone else's relationship. I'm not that person. I did not set out to break them up. I—"

"Tanner. Stop." My heart pounded at the possibility that I'd failed at keeping my feelings hidden and that I was exactly the person I didn't want to be. "Tanner. Zander and Paul were a fucked-up mess long before you came into the picture. Seven years of fucked up. I know your intentions were good, but it didn't stop you falling in love with him—and seeing as you didn't deny it a second ago, I'm guessing I'm right."

Shit!

My shoulders fell. "I didn't mean for it to happen." The guilt I'd been holding onto for months seeped through my veins at the admission. I let it all out and turned a look of desperation and sorrow at Angie.

"I know." Angie stroked a hand down my cheek and pulled me into a hug. "You're such a good person, Tanner. Zander deserves someone like you. Tell him how you feel. Give him the push he needs to let go of this mess. Do it for both of you."

Angie's words tumbled around my head. She made it sound so simple, but a clenching, vice-like-grip tightened around my heart. The desire I'd been feeling for so long coursed over me. I wanted so badly to heed her suggestion and damn consequences.

"I can't." I shook my head, affirming my point before I could be swayed otherwise. "I can't. It's not right. He needs to make the decision on his own. If I tell him how I feel, then I'm that person, and even though I'd like nothing more than to knock Paul into next week for what he's doing to Zander, I-I can't be that person, Angie. I can't. I don't fuck with other people's relationships."

Angie let out a defeated sigh and released from our embrace. "Aww, sweetie, I understand. I just hate to sit on the sidelines and watch this all happening. It's not fair to either of you."

"Well, that's how it is." With a weak smile, I moved to where Anna was fitting the last few pieces of her puzzle together and collected her things off the floor. "Come on, Anna. I'm starving. Let's go grab some dinner."

Chapter Twenty

Zander

The tension between Paul and I mounted higher with each passing day. Whether it was Tanner's interference or my lack of will to keep going, I wasn't sure, but I was falling apart. It hadn't been that bad in all the years we'd been together. My nerves were shot, and it was starting to feel like no matter what I did, including breathing, was wrong and caused Paul to spaz.

For about thirty seconds I considered asking him if I could join Tanner and the guys at the Convention Center for the car show, but the words died on my lips before they were spoken. It was useless.

The weekend came, and I was moody and sulked around the house doing my best to avoid confrontation. I shut myself in the bedroom and junked out on Warcraft for hours while Paul watched some program by himself in the living room.

At one point, he sauntered into the bedroom, sat on the bed and stared at me. He was looking for a fight, so I edged myself up and made excuses that I was hungry, retreating to the kitchen.

While picking at a box of crackers, staring blankly out the kitchen window to the street below, Paul came up behind me. The dry cracker stuck in my throat as I shifted away again with my heart racing. I prayed he didn't stop me. It was glaringly obvious I was avoiding him. I feared slinking past him. Tensing when his shoulder brushed mine, I ran to the bathroom so I could put a door between us. I didn't even need to pee. I just needed to get away.

Since the night his hands had met my throat, I'd been all out panic-stricken in his presence. It'd been so easy for him. He was big; I was small. He could have ended it in an instant. Instead of fighting back, I'd shut down, seized up, and didn't react, even when it meant my life.

This was my life. I was a wounded, scared animal just waiting for the bigger, stronger beast to overtake me one day. My head spun as I sat down against the bathroom door and dropped my face into my hands. What was I going to do? I couldn't go on like that. The knowledge that if I didn't do something soon or I'd be dead rang through my brain every day, yet there I was *still* unable to get away. Still stuck.

A hard knock on the door made me jump and scramble to the opposite side of the room in terror. I was a basket of nerves.

"Is something wrong?"

He seemed calm… *For now.* I wasn't. I was a shaking, trembling mess and I couldn't seem to regain control no matter what I did.

"I-I just… Needed a Tylenol. I have a headache." My voice was weak and unconvincing.

"You're acting weird. You keep running away from me. Why?"

"I'm not. It's just a headache," I blurted out. Feeling the sting of tears wanting to fall, I blinked them back. Tears were weakness; Paul hated weakness, even though he brought it out in me.

Tearing open the medicine cabinet, I fished around for painkillers, knocking over other bottles in the process. I couldn't stop shaking. When I found them, I snatched them up and unlocked the bathroom door. I held out the bottle. "Found them. See."

He eyed me up and down. I hoped my panic wasn't as clear on my face as it felt. Even more, I hoped my eyes weren't red. Paul stepped aside, and I ran back to the kitchen to get a glass of water, popping pills I didn't even need.

"Maybe you shouldn't play that stupid game so much. You stare at that screen so long no wonder you have a headache."

"Probably."

"I'm gonna head to the store and get some smokes. You need anything?"

"Nah, I'm going to lie down."

He grunted something that sounded like an okay and headed to the door. Not waiting for him to leave, I went back to our bedroom and flopped down on the covers. I felt so trapped. The walls were closing in, getting closer every day. One day I'd be crushed. One day it would just be over.

Pulling my phone from my pocket, I flipped through my contacts and found Tanner's name. I needed to be grounded; slow my heart to a steadier pace. Hesitating, I finally shot him off a text.

How's the car show?

Waiting for a reply, I hugged my phone to my chest and stared at the ceiling. It would have been nice to get out of the house. I couldn't seem to keep my brain occupied. Feeling completely gamed out, I couldn't stay interested in anything, not even a book held my attention. All I could think about was the freedom I didn't have. My phone buzzed, and I lifted it to read.

It's okay. Cold out. Sucks you're not here.

I chewed my lip and thought of how to respond. I didn't want him to worry, and Tanner would flip if he thought I wasn't okay. Probably show up at my door.

Wish I was there too. Send me pics?

Lame, but I wanted to be included. For once, I wanted Tanner to see through my request for what it was; involve me, please, I need to be a part of it. After a few minutes, three texts came through showing pictures of some of my favorite muscle cars; a nineteen sixty-nine Chevy Camaro in LeMans blue, a nineteen sixty-nine Dodge Charger in metallic light green, and a nineteen seventy Plymouth Road Runner in frosted teal. For the first time in days, a smile beamed across my face. The text that accompanied it read simply,

I know what you like ;)

He did.

Is there a Shelby? Please, please, please. Need pic of a Shelby too.

I rolled onto my stomach and waited impatiently for a reply.

There is. Need a sec.

For the following twenty minutes, Tanner texted me picture after picture of the cars at the show. It went a long way in helping my feelings of isolation. When the front door slammed shut, I sent a quick text telling him thanks, and I had to go, knowing he'd understand. I dove my head under the pillow, and when Paul popped into the room, I pretended I was asleep.

I heard him mumble the word, "figures" as he closed it again.

That was the last time I talked to Tanner for the rest of the weekend. I lay in bed a long while just listening to the sounds of Paul moving around the house. Familiar with his noises and routine, I knew when he made himself food, and I knew when he cracked open the new bottle of rum he'd bought the other day. After years of sharpening my sense of hearing, I could pick up exactly what he was doing without even being in the room.

Gauging the amount he was drinking by how frequently I heard him get up, I figured by ten thirty that night he was probably half in the bag. Sneaking quietly out of bed and into the kitchen, I saw that I was right. He was passed out on the couch, full drink on the table in front of him, with the TV blaring. I didn't bother turning it off, not wanting to risk disturbing him. Grabbing a bottle of water and more crackers, I headed back to my room.

The air in the apartment smelled of stale cigarette smoke, and I curled my nose. There was supposed to be no smoking inside the building, we'd signed an agreement on our lease when we'd moved in, but Paul conveniently liked to forget that small detail whenever he drank. Apparently, the balcony was too far away.

One of those days a neighbor would complain, and we'd probably get evicted. I dreaded the thought of how that conversation might go over.

Returning to my room, I pulled out my laptop and loaded Warcraft. That was my life. No escaping it. Just suffer through day after day. Maybe someday it would change. Maybe Paul would have an epiphany, and everything would get better. That was a mighty big *maybe* to hold onto, and I knew it.

Chapter Twenty-One

Tanner-End of November

I stepped into my jeans as I made my way to the front door. Yanking them up my wet legs, I moved down the hall trying desperately not to trip and fall on my face. Whoever was knocking was becoming impatient and pounded without pause, using what must have been a closed fist and herculean strength on the other side.

"I'm coming. Hold your horses. Do you want me to answer naked, cuz that's what you'll get if you don't give me a second! My naked ass in your face. How about that?"

I'd just stepped out of the shower when I heard the first knock. I threw my clothes on as fast as I could without drying myself as I made my way down the hall to answer it. Swinging the door open with a huff, I found Angie on the other side looking frazzled.

A tingle of apprehension shot through me at the sight of her. Angie never came over to my house. I didn't even know she knew where my new apartment was because I couldn't remember having told her. Everything about her presence was wrong, and my body knew it. I tensed in the fraction of a second my brain had to process.

"What's wrong?" I asked, my heart skipping a beat.

"It's Zander. Put a shirt on we need to go. Now."

"Go where?" I yelled over my shoulder as I ran back down the hall to my bedroom to grab a shirt.

Angie didn't answer until I was in front of her again, searching her anxiety stricken face.

"Dammit, Angie. What the fuck happened? Where are we going?"

Don't say the hospital. Please, don't say the hospital.

She took my hand and pulled me closer, worry etched in her face. "He didn't want me to call you. So I'm here picking you up instead because that way he can't say I didn't listen—"

"Angie," I urged more forcefully.

"He's at the police station."

The air I was currently drawing into my lungs got stuck, and I choked on it, forgetting momentarily if I was inhaling or exhaling. Was he finally making a report? Was that why he went? Or…

"Did something happen? Is he okay?"

Angie grabbed my hand and pulled me through the door. I was in such a frantic hurry to follow, I almost forgot to lock up.

"I don't really know anything. He just texted and asked me to come… and don't call you."

That information stabbed right into my heart. Why didn't he want me there? I had tried to be supportive as best I could. I'd bit my tongue bloody holding back my opinions when I knew he didn't want to hear them—even though I failed miserably most days. I'd done everything I could to be the best damn friend, and he didn't want me there? That knowledge hurt, but I wouldn't dwell on it, because screw that, I was going to be there whether he liked it or not.

"Is he making a report or did something happen?" I asked as I pulled open the passenger side door to Angie's car.

"I don't know. I'm guessing something happened."

I rode with Angie to the police station. The cars and scenery passed by in a fog. All I could do was think about what could have happened to Zander that landed him at the police station. I knew what my brain was saying was probably right. Paul had done something, but what and how bad was it that he'd ended up there?

When Angie parked, I hopped out of the car and took off ahead of her at a run to the front doors. I could hear her running behind me, trying to catch up.

"Tanner, wait."

I couldn't. My heart pounded and the fear that had started out as tiny tendrils worming out of my stomach when I'd first opened the door to Angie were now strangling vines wrapped all around me, squeezing my chest so hard it hurt. An overwhelming need to look upon Zander with my own eyes overwhelmed me. I needed to know he was okay. My only solace was that he was at the police station and not a hospital—if that was solace.

Once inside, we had to wait our turn in line at the front desk. Waiting was not my strong suit, and I paced a hole in the floor while I listen to the couple in front of us trying to sort out criminal reference checks they needed to acquire for work. *Like I have time for this shit.* Angie pulled me to a stop and rubbed a hand up and down my back as we waited. I appreciated her attempt at comforting me, but it wasn't working.

"He'll be okay, Tanner."

"No, he won't," I snapped. "Unless he decides to leave that fucking prick he will never be okay. He will never be safe, and I will always worry about him."

She said nothing more because she knew I was right. Her soothing touches finally helped bring my breathing back to normal, but my heart wouldn't settle. It jumped frantically in my chest.

The couple finally finished, but before I could step forward, Angie halted me, giving me a look that told me she would handle it. That was probably wise considering I was over the top with emotions and would quite possibly get us in trouble.

"We are here about Zander Baker. We're his friends."

The stern-faced copper eyed us both before nodding for us to follow him.

I'd never had many dealings with police officers in my life, but for some reason, I had a huge aversion toward them. Something about their cocky, impenetrable attitudes was a complete turn-off. Was it a big fucking deal to smile once in a while? It wouldn't break their faces, and God knows, it wouldn't hurt to show a little humanity from time to time.

The sour-faced copper led us down a narrow hallway painted in that institutional looking pale blue that was practically coma-inducing. Steel, windowless doors ran down its length and only added to the whole claustrophobic feeling. At the last door on the right, officer grumpy face held it open for us.

Angie went in first, and Zander flew out of the chair into her arms before he even noticed me trailing behind. The minute our eyes met, his face fell, and he turned a look of venom at Angie.

"I said don't call him."

"I didn't," she said, giving him her best "no nonsense" glare. "I went and picked him up. No phone calls were exchanged. I promise you."

Zander sighed and closed his eyes. I took that moment to examine him head to toe and took inventory of what was wrong. His lip called my attention first. It was swollen and split wide open, his chin carrying traces of dried blood that had dripped down it earlier and had not been cleaned up. Bruising had started all around it, leaving the bottom half of his jaw a deep shade of purple. Seeing it caused a twinge in my belly, and I knew that as hard as I tried to steel my emotions, they reflected clear on my face.

The rest of him appeared unblemished so far as I could see and I let out a silent breath of relief. No violence was okay. Ever. But I had half-feared more marks on his neck, broken bones, or something far worse.

"What happened, Zander?" It was Angie who spoke first, her voice calm and gentle.

I remained silent, knowing I wasn't wanted, for reasons I still couldn't understand.

Zander stared at the floor and remained quiet and distant. I didn't think he was going to speak and was just about to excuse myself, feeling it was probably my presence holding him back when his soft voice broke through the stillness in the room.

"We went grocery shopping." The *we* being him and Paul, I knew. I balled my fists at my sides, digging my fingernails into my palms, bracing myself to hear the story. "We bought quite a bit and had a dozen plastic bags or so. I was helping carry them upstairs to the apartment." He paused and ran his tongue over his swollen lip. "But the lady at the store packed one of the bags pretty full with a lot of heavy things, and it broke in the lobby, sending the groceries to scatter all over the floor. Paul started losing it about this lady. Yelling and cursing her, saying how she didn't know how to do her job and how society has so many dumb f-fu— you know, in it." For the first time, Zander stumbling over curse words wasn't funny.

Sniffing and wiping at his nose, he continued. "Paul went on and on. It was stupid really, and there were people coming out of the elevator watching him. He didn't see them, but I did, and he was embarrassing and loud so I," again his tongue toyed with his lip and his eyes shifted between Angie and me, "I told him to relax, and it wasn't the lady's fault at the store. I was just trying to stop him from causing a scene, you know. But... he threw the bags he was carrying across the lobby, scattering the food and then b-backhanded me in the face. Really, really h-hard." His voice quivered. "Knocked me down... Asked me whose side I was on anyway standing up for that witch at the store. The ladies by the elevator gasped, and it drew Paul's attention. He yanked me up by the coat and dragged me upstairs. Literally dragged me. The ladies called the cops, and they came..." He trailed off and dropped his eyes again.

The vibrations through my body were uncontrollable, and I needed to work hard to contain my anger because I was seeing red at that moment.

Crimson. Fucking. Red. If Paul had been standing before me, I would have given him a taste of his own medicine. However, I knew doing that only put me at his level, and I wouldn't lower myself to that piece of shits level for anything.

Angie pulled Zander into her arms and held him while I worked through the internal rage that was making me want to combust. After a minute, Zander looked directly at me and approached, worry etched in his worn-out, battered face.

"I didn't want you to be mad. That's why I told Angie not to call you. You are always so worried. A-are you mad at me?"

His words cut into me and hurt with crippling pain. Why on Earth would I be mad at him? And why on Earth would he think for even a second that I would be? His fear of disappointing people was so deeply rooted it scared me. His insecurities ran deep, so deep he put everyone else above himself. Including Angie and me. Including Paul.

Including. Fucking. Paul.

I wanted to cry at the uncertainty in his eyes because he'd asked an honest question and truly wanted to know. I wanted to shake him and tell him to love himself because he was worth so much more. I wanted to scream at the unfairness of what I saw every day in his life.

But in the end, I didn't do any of those things. I didn't answer his question either, I simply reached out, drew him into my arms and held him. Wrapping myself all around him, I wanted nothing more than to protect him from all the injustices of the world that had landed on his shoulders. Squeezing him to me, I buried my face into his neck and didn't let him go. I didn't know how he would react, but when he was enclosed in my arms, he let go, sank into me and let me take the weight he carried for just that moment. Then, he cried. It was the first time I'd seen Zander pull down the wall he fought so hard to uphold. But right there in my arms, it crumbled apart, and he wept.

Angie ruffled my hair, leaned in and kissed my temple before whispering in my ear. "It's time, Tanner." Then she left us alone.

Time.

I knew exactly what she meant. Time for it to end. Time to call it quits and stop the tangled, fucked up game of Tom and Jerry that Zander and Paul were playing. Time to open my heart up and let it out. Time for Zander to know how I felt. Could I do it? Would telling him make me the person I'd been avoiding being? Was it right? Was it wrong? I was so confused, I didn't know anymore. The only thing I knew was I couldn't watch another day of his pain in silence. Maybe he would never talk to me again once he heard what I had to say, but it was a risk I had to take. Angie was right.

I rubbed Zander's back while he calmed in my arms, and I thought about what I wanted to say. Nothing sounded right, and I knew I'd be reduced to just blurting it out in the end which wasn't what I wanted. Lifting his head from my shoulder, I cradled his face gently in my hands, drying his tears with a soft brush of my thumbs across his cheeks.

"Z—"

"Please don't lecture me, Tanner. I can't take it right now."

"I'm not going to lecture you. I just have something I want to—"

The door banged open, interrupting us. A younger, softer faced officer walked into the room.

"Mr. Baker?" he said, referring to the chart he carried.

"Yes, that's me." Zander stepped out of my hold and faced the officer.

"We need to know if you are pressing charges."

"Oh… Umm… No."

"Wait." I bolted forward and snagged Zander's arm, halting him. "Can we have a minute, Officer?"

The man shifted his gaze between us and nodded. "I'll be back in a minute."

"Thank you."

Once he'd left, Zander turned to me, brow creased. "What are you doing, Tanner?"

"What are *you* doing?"

Zander let out a huff of air and ran a hand through his mess of blond hair. "This is another reason why I didn't want Angie to call you."

"Why? Because I care?"

"Because I see the way you look at me every time. I disappoint you."

I bit back my next words, not wanting to engage in an argument. It needed to end before the officer returned and Zander walked back into that apartment with Paul. Back into that life.

I pulled Zander toward me and held his face again like before, making him look me in the eyes. Fixing his ruffled hair and smoothing a thumb over his cheek, I smiled sadly. I'd never touched him like that before, and it felt so natural. So good. "I can't watch you do this to yourself anymore, Z."

"Tanner—"

"Hear me out. It's time to walk away. It's time to end this. You have the chance right now to do that. If you press charges and file a restraining order, then it's all over."

Zander's eyes brimmed with tears and he shook his head. "I can't."

"Why not, Z? Why can't you?"

"Where would I go? What would I do? H-he'd find me. He'd come looking for me, and h-he'd be so angry." His body shook, and my heart pounded as I pushed down the spiraling windstorm of emotions.

"No. You make it sound impossible. It's not. I know you're afraid, and it looks like you are stepping off the edge into the fucking Grand Canyon, but I'm telling you, when you let go, you'll see it's only a six-inch fall. It's a step. One step to begin a new life and free yourself from this monster. You can do this. Take the step."

"You don't get it. He's all I know. He… he takes care of me."

Those blasted words again, drilled so deep into his skull he believed them to be true.

"He doesn't take care of you, Zander. This," I grazed my finger over his split lip, "isn't taking care of you. This is abuse, and I'm not even sure you can see how bad it is."

"He loves me," he whispered as a tear slipped down his cheek.

"This isn't love. Someone who loves you doesn't try to control every aspect of your life. They don't humiliate you, and they most certainly don't hit you."

Another tear trickled down, followed by another and another after that. Soon they were free falling, wetting my hands where I continued to cradle his head.

"I don't want to be alone," he whimpered past his tears.

"You will not be alone. You have people in your life who really do care for you. Angie and Brad. Ray and Georgina. Me. Zander, you deserve so much more from life. You deserve someone who will treat you like a prince. Someone who can recognize all the wonderful things in you that make you a unique and beautiful person. You deserve someone who loves you for who you are and who will treasure every moment they spend with you. Someone who will show you what it means to be loved."

"I'll never find that. Things like that don't happen to me."

My breath hitched as I worked the next words out of my mouth. "*I* want to be that someone."

He stood frozen and looked at me, eyes searching while a mixture of both confusion and understanding crossed his face at the same time. "What?"

"I've wanted to be that person for a long time. I love you, Zander... I'm in love with you, and if you let me, I want to show you what it truly means to be someone's everything."

Of course, the stupid officer chose that exact moment to barge back into the room.

"I'm gonna need an answer, Mr. Baker. We're busy tonight."

"Give us a second," I snapped, as I waited for some kind of response from Zander.

"Z, if you press charges right now, you walk away for good. It'll be over. Angie, Brad and I will help you collect your things from the apartment, and you can come stay with me. I have a spare room. It doesn't have to be anything if you don't want it to be. You can ignore everything I just said and get your life back together. With a restraining order, Paul can't come near you again." I waited expectantly.

"You love me?"

I nodded. "For a long time. You are an amazing person, Zander. It was hard *not* to fall in love with you. Trust me, I tried." Having opened my heart, I felt lighter, freer.

Zander's hazel gaze was lost in mine.

Carefully, gently, reading his reaction and hoping I didn't scare him off, I leaned in and brushed our lips together in a soft, chaste kiss, being mindful of his swollen lip. A combination of fear and joy sang through me when they touched. Zander didn't pull away—in fact, he moved into it, pressing himself closer. I stayed there a minute, basking in their warmth, tasting the salty remains of shed tears, caressing his cheeks, and reveling in what couldn't have been more perfect. Butterflies played in my belly, and I didn't want it to end. When I pulled away, he took my hand in his and caressed his thumb over the top as he stared at me, deep in thought. I wish I knew if I'd done the right thing. Holding my breath, I waited.

"Mr. Baker?" The officer's tone was much softer, and I flushed slightly having forgotten he was standing right there through my entire speech. "I'll need an answer."

Zander looked to the officer and wiped at his damp cheeks with his sleeve before clearing his throat. "I'd like to press charges, Officer."

No words had ever rung so beautifully in my ears as those, and the pressure around my lungs loosened; I could breathe again.

"I'll go grab some paperwork. I'll need to take a statement. Would you like to file a restraining order?" The officer's eyes drifted to me and back to Zander.

"Yes, sir," Zander said.

With a nod, the man left us alone again.

Chapter Twenty-Two

Zander

    I walked through the few days following my trip to the police station as though I was in some kind of trance. It felt a little like an out of body type of experience where I could see myself doing everything, but felt detached and not really a part of it.

    Brad and Tanner both brought their trucks over to my apartment once I was done giving my statement and filling out the paperwork to file a restraining order. Then, they helped me clear out everything I owned. Between Brad and Tanner's trucks, I was grateful we only had to make one trip. I didn't own much.

    I couldn't stop shaking. My whole body vibrated with fear right down to my teeth chattering, and no matter what I did, I couldn't make it stop. Angie called it shock, but I thought that only happen to accident victims or something. I didn't have a reason to be in shock as far as I could see. It didn't make sense.

    I felt pretty useless because all the help I could manage was to indicate what stayed and what went. Tanner kept a close watch on me as they made several trips back and forth filling the trucks. Whenever he'd pass me by, he'd give my arm a squeeze and would gift me a soft smile. I couldn't make my face respond the way I wanted. In fact, I couldn't get my body to respond to anything I was telling it to do. It was in protest against my mind and moving on its own free will separate from the rest of me. Mostly, I hugged a wall and watched seven years of my life move out the door.

    At one point, a glass of water was shoved in my hand by Angie. She hugged me tight and kissed my cheek. "It'll be alright, Zander. You'll see."

    When I placed the glass to my lips for a drink, and the cold sting hit my tender flesh, I was reminded why we were all there in the first place. A flash of memories that had haunted me for years played on repeat through my mind. Harsh, screaming words rang in my ears, shattering glass and the loud cracking of furniture and dishes being smashed against walls. I squeezed my eyes closed to make it stop, but then, I saw him. His towering size launched across the room toward me, fists flying and fingers reaching out…

I was on the floor, gasping for air before I even knew what happened. Tanner flew to my side and peeled the glass of water from my fingers where I held it with a death grip.

"It's okay, Z. Come here." He folded me up in his arms and held me as I calmed.

When had I started crying? What was happening to me? Waves of grief flooded through me as I laid my head on his shoulder unable to control the tears any more than I was able to control the thoughts that had caused them.

"It's over, Z. You don't need to do this anymore. It's done." His voice calmed me like it might a frightened animal, and I clung to him and his words, too afraid to let go.

In the end, we left most of the furniture behind. The majority of it Paul and I had purchased together, but I didn't have an apartment to furnish or anywhere to store it. It was the least of my concerns. Like Angie said; it was just stuff. I could always buy more stuff.

At Tanner's apartment, he set me up in his spare room, doing his best to make it feel like home. He unpacked my clothes into a dresser, offered me a drawer in the bathroom, and gave the room as much of a personal feel as he could with what I owned. He put my Kindle on the end table by the bed with my laptop beside it, then he set my pictures on the dresser and even hung a few of the posters I'd said I didn't need around the room.

"You can't throw out Warcraft posters. I'm pretty sure there's a law against it."

Nothing more was said about our earlier conversation at the police station, but I sensed a shift in our friendship once we were alone. Tanner tried to hide his discomfort, but it played out all over his face. Did he feel bad for what he'd said? Maybe he didn't mean it and was using it as leverage to get me to leave.

"Well, everything is set up. Can I get you anything? Tea? Beer? A sandwich?" Apprehensive, he struggled to look me in the eye as he continued to shuffle things around the room unnecessarily.

"I'm okay. I might have a hot shower and try to sleep. I'm pretty tired."

"Sure. I'll…umm… I'll be down the hall if you need anything, okay?"

"Okay." Head down, he shifted to the door, slowly like he wanted to say more. "Tanner?"

He spun back and looked me straight in the eyes for the first time since we'd been alone. The trepidation was clear on his face. "Yeah."

"Thank you. I-I think you… I mean… You probably saved my life."

His eyes pooled, but he blinked back the tears before they could fall as he shifted his gaze around the room, nodding. "I didn't…ruin our friendship, did I? You know, saying what I did."

"No." No matter how overrun my brain was with so many thoughts colliding together at once, the answer came with certainty. "We're okay. I just have a lot going on in my head, and I need to sort it all out. Let me process."

He found my eyes again, relief sagging his body. "I understand. Try to get some sleep."

The following day was Sunday, and I lay in bed most of the day trying *not* to think. I'd spent all night with my brain in a knot, and a headache was forming.

Half-asleep during the night, I'd become filled with anxiety and was convinced Paul was hunting me down. Every unidentifiable noise, every unusual creak sent shivers up my spine, and I buried myself deeper in the blankets. It was obvious just how affected I was by that man. I wondered if I'd ever feel normal again.

Trying to divert my thoughts, I remembered the things Tanner had said to me and wondered how much of it he meant. Was he truly in love with me? Remembering back to all the times we'd spent together over the past eight months, the subtle flirtations I'd thought were meant as jokes, the looks we shared, and the concern he'd showed, somehow, I knew it was the truth.

With the exception of when we'd first met, and I'd noted just how good looking he was, I hadn't thought of him as anything more than a friend—or had I? I didn't think I had. We'd become close. So close, I told him almost everything. Before Tanner came along, no one knew how bad I had it living with Paul, not even Angie. For whatever reason, I felt comfortable with Tanner and had reached out to him. I'd leaned on him and used his strength to get me through as many bad days as I could. During all of it, I'd learned to trust him like I'd trusted nobody else in my life. Not even Ray and Georgina. There was something about Tanner that made me feel safe. Even when I tried to push him away and keep him at bay, it was only because what he'd tell me was the truth, and I hadn't wanted to hear it. Maybe, I hadn't been ready.

The sun crested the horizon, spilling soft morning light into the unfamiliar room. My thoughts turned to the soft brush of a kiss Tanner had pressed to my lips in the interview room the day before. My fingers involuntarily traveled to the swollen flesh on my face, tracing where his mouth had grazed mine. That kiss should have confused the hell out of me, but for some reason, it didn't. It had given me a sense of contentment, and my panic-stricken mind calmed when I closed my eyes and reenacted it again in my head. The pressure of his lips with mine had sent a jolt of electricity to fizzle through me, jump-starting my brain and waking me from a seven-year slumber. Like I was Sleeping Beauty, it showed me what needed to be done.

That kiss should have baffled me. Tanner's confession should have scrambled my brain to a pulp. Only, I'd never felt so calm and sure of anything in my whole life. And it was that sense of sureness and tranquility that *did* boggle my mind in the end.

Deciding I was a little too messed-up to lay in bed anymore, I padded down the hall to see if Tanner had anything resembling coffee in his cupboards.

After setting his pot to brew, I searched his half-empty fridge looking for some milk to add to my cup as I waited for it to be done.

"I'm not much of a cook. You won't find hardly anything in there."

I spun at the sound of him so close behind me and indicated to the coffee pot.

"Just looking for milk for coffee. I wasn't snooping or anything." I pushed the fridge closed behind me. "I'm sorry."

"There isn't any, but I'll run to the store and grab some. Why are you sorry? Because you looked in the fridge?"

Nodding, I dropped my gaze sheepishly to the ground to avoid making eye contact.

"Z." He came up in front of me, lifting my chin. "I invited you to live here. It's as much your home as it is mine now. You don't need to apologize for wanting to make coffee or food or whatever you need. Anything you find in that fridge is ours now."

"You're sharing a whole lot of nothing with me then. Have you looked in there?" My attempts at making light of my unease earned me a smile.

"Yeah. Like I said, not much of a cook. I'm going to run to the store. I'll just be a minute. I think there is some peanut butter and bread. We can have toast for breakfast, and I'll run for some real groceries later."

With mussed up bedhead, Tanner pulled on his shoes and coat before heading out. I watched him go and stared at the closed door long after he'd closed it. There was something incredibly simple about our exchange. It was easy and natural. There was no yelling, no accusing tones, and no pointing fingers, scolding me for using up the last of the milk. It was so right, my brain felt it was wrong. I guess I had a lot to get used to again.

A beeping from the coffee pot indicated it was done brewing and brought me out of my daze. I rooted through the cupboards in search of a couple of mugs and something resembling sugar. No luck. I skipped back to my room and found my phone on the end table. Hoping Tanner had his phone on him, I shot him off a quick text.

Sugar?
Sweetie?

"Ass." I smiled at my phone and jotted out another text, ignoring his remark.

Even honey would work, I'm easy. :P
I dunno. I'm partial to sweetie or maybe even babe.

I rolled my eyes, but couldn't help laughing at the ease at which he teased, even knowing I was in an awkward place.

U r a dork.
I know, but I made you smile, didn't I? I'll get your sugar. Be back in a few.

* * *

Monday, I returned to work. Getting to and from on the bus nearly sent me into a panic attack more than once. I'd suddenly developed an irrational fear of the outdoors. Certain Paul would pop up and drag me home at any moment by the scruff of my neck and punish me for pressing charges against him, I constantly checked over my shoulder. By the time I reached work, I was wound so tight I was ready to burst, and it took me half the day to calm down again.

Angie sensed my agitation and continually checked in on me making sure I was okay. I was certain she was texting back and forth with Tanner at one point, and it irritated me a little that I was being talked about behind my back, even if it was out of concern.

By the following week, I'd calmed significantly. I was still nervous leaving the house but forced myself to start doing things I'd always had to justify to Paul in the past. I wanted to regain control over my life and was taking baby steps to do so. Like detouring to the library or the café on my way home from work. Paul never allowed me to do that. Or, spending all weekend lounging around the house in my pajamas. You wouldn't have thought something like that was a big deal, but it drove Paul batshit crazy so I'd quit doing it years ago. It was liberating.

After a long, exhausting hump day of work, I lay on the couch, picking at a bag of potato chips, watching some documentary about ancient Egyptian pyramids as I waited for Tanner to get home.

A little after seven, I peeked my head up at the sound of keys rattling in the door. Tanner pushed through carrying a large bag of takeout. There were flakes of snow melting in his hair and on his jacket.

"Hey, I grabbed some Thai food from down the street, hope that's okay."

Jumping off the couch, I raced over to help unload his arms. "It smells amazing, I'm starving."

Tanner brushed off his coat and hung it up while I collected plates and utensils from the kitchen and brought them over to the coffee table. Yup, we ate in the living room.

"Is here okay?" I asked. "I thought we could watch a movie."

"Awesome. I'm so tired. Today felt like the longest day ever."

"I second that."

We ate through copious amounts of food as we flicked through the selections on Netflix deciding what to watch. We had the same taste in movies, which was a treat, so we never seemed to disagree over what to put on.

"How about something a little more classic?" Tanner suggested with a sly smirk.

"Like what?"

"Go back, you just passed one. There. *Princess Bride?*"

My head flipped around to stare at him, needing to assess his seriousness. Was he joking?

"What?" He looked at me with mock hurt on his face. "I like that movie."

"You're making that up, aren't you? Don't mess with me right now."

"I'm not. I swear. I really do like that movie. You don't?" His face fell, and his cheeks turned a slight shade of pink.

"Holy crap balls, you're for real. I love that movie too, but I've never told anyone before. Ever. It's like my secret guilty pleasure. I would only watch it when Paul would be away."

Tanner laughed and sank back into the couch. "Your secret is safe with me. Put it on."

Was it weird that we both liked that movie and decided to watch it together? No weirder than the comfort I felt being beside Tanner and sharing something I'd kept a secret for so long. He didn't mock me for it, he just rolled with it.

I knew the movie by heart and found myself watching Tanner more than the film itself. He was right into it and had curled up comfortably on his half of the couch. I curled up on mine, and our feet ended up tangled together in the middle. It wasn't something I would have noticed or cared about before, but recently I'd become hyper-aware of us touching.

Since that day at the police station, Tanner had made no more mention of what he'd said. He never pushed to see how I felt, just gave me space and let me muddle with it in my mind. The more I thought, the more I couldn't fight the way I was drawn to Tanner. We just clicked together so effortlessly with everything we did. It was like we'd known each other all our lives.

Could it be more?

I watched his face in the flicker of the television screen. His dark hair was tousled from a long day of running his fingers through it and flipping it out of his face. His profile showed off the beautiful curve of his jaw and slightly parted lips where he mouthed along with the dialog. They were damp from having been recently licked. He laughed at something that happened on the screen and turned to me smiling. I knew I was attracted to him. I'd known it for a long time, and his azure eyes roped me in just then, and I was stuck in a moment of uncertainty.

Our eyes locked when he found me watching him and I felt instant guilt and embarrassment at being caught. Breaking from his gaze, I turned back to the movie and feigned interest, not wanting him to know where my thoughts had strayed. I had been staring at his lips, remembering their softness as they'd come in contact with my own over a week and a half ago. My heart raced and a tingling that had started in my belly moved to my cock and made it swell slightly in my too thin sleep pants. I crammed my hand in my lap and prayed he didn't notice.

Tanner, ever the gentleman, turned his attention back to the movie, but I know I didn't imagine it when his foot made a gentle pass over mine in a way that assured me everything was okay.

Was it okay? What was I feeling? I couldn't identify or put my finger on where things were headed. There I was, living in his apartment, sharing his space, his time, everything like I belonged there. I felt like I belonged there. Whatever the path was that I'd been set on, wherever it led me, it didn't instill fear like so many things. It just felt right.

Chapter Twenty-Three

Tanner

I got home just after eight, later than I'd planned. My last client, a man whose sleeve I'd been working on steadily for the past two days, had only needed a few final touches for his tattoo to be finished. We'd decided to get it done that day instead of booking a whole other session to work on the bits that remained.

Hanging my jacket by the door, I glanced around the living room. There was no sign of Zander, and the apartment was quiet. Tossing my keys on the table, I headed to the kitchen to pour a glass of water. I was hungry. I hadn't eaten since before noon and was hoping Zander still needed dinner as well so we could order out. It was Friday night and the perfect evening for takeout, beers, and a movie. After finishing my glass of water, I headed down the hall and heard the shower running. I knocked and cracked the door.

"Hey, I'm home. Did you eat?"

"No. I was waiting for you. Thought we could order out."

"It's like you're in my head, Z. Any preferences?"

"Nah. Anything is fine. I'll be out in a few."

I headed back down the hall and pulled a stack of takeout menus from a drawer in the kitchen before settling in on the couch. Aside from eating out, we'd had nothing but an array of peanut butter and jelly sandwiches, Kraft Dinner, and frozen pizza since he'd moved in. Sooner or later, Zander was going to figure out I was shit in the kitchen. Who was I kidding? He'd been living there two weeks. That ship had sailed, he'd just had enough decency not to tease me about it yet.

I heard the shower turn off and frowned at the menus on my lap. Starving or not, I couldn't seem to make a decision.

"Did you order yet?" Zander called. I glanced down the hall where Zander poked his head out of the bathroom.

"No. Can't decide."

"Don't." He disappeared again behind the door. "I feel like cooking. Do you mind?"

Sighing, I chuckled. "You don't have to cook for me, Z. We can go out somewhere instead."

"I want to cook." I hadn't heard him come up behind me and spun to find him drying his hair with one of my navy towels. A second towel was wrapped around his waist and hung low on his hips.

I sucked in a breath at the sight. Beads of water dripped down the front of his chest, curving around the muscles of his abdomen, pooling and catching in his navel and the soft blond hairs that trailed below the towel.

Since that one kiss we'd shared at the police station two weeks before, I'd taken a step back and given all control over to Zander. He'd just left a seriously messed up relationship that had spanned over seven years, and the last thing he needed was for me to press myself on him. He knew how I felt, and he knew where I stood. The ball was in his court. If someday he wanted to pursue more, I'd be there. If not, then I would be happy at least knowing I'd helped him regain control over his life.

But, I couldn't take my eyes off of him. Only when he paused in drying his hair and lowered the towel did I glance back up to meet his gaze. He'd caught my lingering stares and watched me silently. He froze, eyes searching mine, lips parted ever so slightly.

It wasn't the first time we'd ended up in this high intensity stare off with enough heat between us you could almost hear it sizzle and pop.

"I-I'm sorry," I stammered. "I wasn't staring." *Yeah, I was.* More like practically drooling. "It's just... You're so gorgeous."

Shit! Shut up. Don't say things like that.

My heart slammed as he drew his bottom lip into his teeth. I jumped off the couch and held up my hands. "I shouldn't have said that. We should have boundaries. I-I can do boundaries. God, I'm so sorry."

He released his lip. "Don't be." He dropped the towel he'd used to dry his hair over the back of the couch, then closed the distance between us, stopping less than a foot away. The heat from his recently showered body rolled off him, and I couldn't control the way my own automatically responded to his close proximity.

My cock shifted against the confines of my jeans, and I held my next breath of air in my lungs too afraid to breathe.

"I like you, Tanner...a lot. There's something here—between us—I know there is and I feel like I should be more afraid than I am. I feel like I should think about it, but..." His Adam's apple bobbed as he swallowed, and his eyes remained fixed on mine.

Blood pounded in my ears as we both locked on each other. It was taking every ounce of self-restraint not to move forward and kiss him. Oh, how I wanted to kiss him. The hold he had on my life was more than I'd ever experienced before and I ached to take him in my arms and hold him. "I love you so much, Zander. You have no idea. I would never do anything to hurt you. I don't ever want to push you into—"

"I know," he whispered.

"I want to give you space to work things out, but you have no idea how hard it is to keep my hands to myself and not touch you."

He reached out and grazed gentle fingers up my thigh then hooked a hand around my waist. "What I'm trying to say is, I've been thinking a lot about this. I don't need space, Tanner. I need you. I want this." He leaned in and pressed his lips to mine. The shock of it knocked the breath clean out of my lungs.

Shuddering desire vibrated through my whole body as I sank into the softness of his kiss. The warmth of him pressed up against me shattered my already weakened resolve, and I reached up and cupped his face in my hands.

It'd been only two weeks since I'd had a sample taste of him, but already it was far better than the memory I'd been carrying around. Catching a hint taste of cappuccino and cinnamon, I smiled into his mouth, knowing his new routine of stopping at the café on his way home for a hot drink and scone. A small piece of independence he'd taken back since becoming free to make his own choices again. My heart swelled as I deepened the kiss, feeling the soft brush of his tongue with mine for the first time. His mouth was heavenly, and I threaded my fingers through his damp hair, pulling him in even closer.

Zander withdrew from the kiss first but left his lips a mere hairsbreadth away from my own, leaning his forehead to mine. He took a steadying breath before lifting his eyes. Pulling back a little more, his hazel warmth enveloped me and the fire behind them made my dick achingly hard. His hands moved ever so delicately over my hips to the hem of my shirt. He lifted it up over my head, discarding it on top of the towel on the couch. I closed my eyes as he brought his fingers back to my skin, trailing them up my chest and over my shoulders and arms, tracing the contours of my tattoos.

"I love these." Opening my eyes again, I saw how mesmerized he was, studying my ink as he followed their lines with his fingertips. His lips were pink from our kiss and his tongue teased out to wet them as his gaze returned to mine and held. "Take me to bed, Tanner. Please."

The sudden foray of butterflies invading my body left me trembling, and his words nearly brought me to my knees.

"Are you sure?" I could barely croak out the words, but I needed to know. I couldn't jeopardize what we had. Wouldn't. Zander meant too much to me.

"I'm sure." Taking my hand, he led me down the hall, past his bedroom to my own.

It was like walking through a dream, one I'd had a million times in the past few months only it was real. Zander's hand in my own was real.

Once in my bedroom, Zander turned to me. His eyes roamed my body as a soft smile played across his lips. He slipped a finger into the top of my jeans and pulled me forward until we collided. His mouth was on me again the moment our bodies came together, bare chest to bare chest; skin touching skin. He was solid and warm. His confidence outweighing my own.

I encased him in my arms and held him close, teasing my tongue with his and taking everything he offered. The fresh scent of body wash invaded my nose, and I inhaled deeply catching a hint of Zander's own natural scent, hidden amongst it as well. Heavenly.

His fingers worked at the button of my jeans, releasing my rock-hard cock from the confines of my constricting pants. Taking me in his hand through my briefs, he stroked with achingly slow pulls, and I groaned into his mouth. I was leaking and throbbing in his hand. I could feel it. I was right there; so close already. The kiss alone had me on edge, and I wasn't sure how much more I could take before spilling in my underwear.

With his other hand, Zander released the towel from his hips and let it fall to the ground, leaving himself naked as his name day in front of me. He pressed his own rigid thickness against mine, and our kiss stuttered as I forgot how to think. Gasping for air, I pulled off his mouth and clamped a hand over his wrist, stilling his persistent stroking.

"Shit, Z. I'm so close, let me breathe a sec, or I'll embarrass myself. I've waited a long time for this, you have me all worked up here. You feel fucking incredible."

Without pause, he moved both his hands to my chest as he licked at my neck, sucking the soft skin at its base behind my ear. God, he would be the death of me. I felt like a horny fucking teenager, ready to come in my pants at his touch. Peeling him off once again, I stepped back and looked at him for the first time; bare and delicious. My breathing was rapid, and my heart thundered as he devoured me with his eyes.

"On the bed." It came out of me as a growl and Zander's lips twitched into a devilish grin as he backed up the foot and a half to the bed and sat down. Shimmying back so he was in the middle, he rested on his elbows and stared up at me, invitation in his eyes as he parted his legs showing off everything. His full nakedness was on display without shame.

I shucked my briefs in one fluid motion and gripped my cock, stroking it as I look down at him, biting into my bottom lip. "Fuck, you are so beautiful."

I stepped until my shins hit the edge of the bed, continuing with long, full tugs as I watched him where he was sprawled out before me. Zander reached a hand up, and when I took it, he pulled me down on top of him, spreading his legs even wider and fitting me between his thighs. He lay back, and I held myself up reveling in the moment; a moment I never thought I'd have.

"You are a dream come true, Zander. I can't believe this is happening." It sounded sappy, but I didn't care. It was the truth.

"Neither can I."

"Tell me what you want, Z. I don't want to presume or overwhelm you. This has been a rollercoaster ride for you, and I've been craving you for a long time. I don't want to mess this up and do something you don't want."

Zander's hands slid up my sides and around my shoulders, pulling me down so our lips brushed together. "I want everything, Tanner. Two weeks ago, you offered me your heart. You told me you loved me and had for a long time. Show me. I want you, Tanner. Show me what you feel."

"Oh God, Z." I covered his mouth with my own, kissing up his words and pouring my heart into him, wanting to do exactly that; show him. Love him. Bringing my body down to lay against his, I grounded our stiff lengths together, the slick precum aiding the glide. The friction sent zaps of electricity to zing through me, and an aching need monopolized my whole body. I never wanted it to end. Zander reached a hand between us and took both our lengths and stroked us together. It was mind-numbingly good.

"You feel amazing," he said against my mouth.

"So do you. Better than every single fantasy I've jacked off to, and let me tell you, there have been plenty."

He chuckled, and the deep rumble in his chest only enticed my dick to weep more.

I kissed up his jaw toward his neck where I sucked and bit at the soft skin, making him moan and lose his rhythm on our cocks. Taking his hand from between us, I rested it above his head and shuffled down as I dusted kisses over his beautiful body and took my time enjoying every inch of him.

I marked his skin, as I'd always wanted to do, leaving a deep purple mark just under his collarbone before continuing my journey. I kissed a trail down his chest to his navel. Zander shuffled his feet higher, opening his thighs wider, granting me access. Nestling in between his legs, I traced my tongue down the groove of his upper leg, feeling his hardness caress against my cheek. God, he tasted good, smelled good, and looked good; my senses were on overload.

Using one hand, I cradled his balls, rolling them while I peered up to watch. Zander's head fell back, gasping and moaning, begging for more. I smiled, knowing I was affecting him in much the same way he was affecting me. My heart soared. With my other hand, I gripped around his solid length—a most beautiful sight—and gave him a few lengthy pulls, watching him shudder with desire before wetting my lips and tracing them around his slick head. I dipped my tongue in his slit and moaned at the salty, delicious taste of his precum. It wasn't enough; I wanted more, and I wasn't the only one.

"Fuck, Tanner. Please." Zander thrust his hips, begging to be sucked and I didn't deny him. I couldn't, not with him pulling out the big boy words all of a sudden. Trying not to laugh, I continued, needing it as much as he did. My mouth pooled with saliva in anticipation.

Tracing one last circle around his head, I fit my mouth around him and sucked him all the way to the back reaches of my throat. He cried out and bucked involuntarily. I moaned at his enjoyment. Just hearing those sounds was enough to make me want to spend an eternity simply pleasing him.

Eager with lust, Zander fisted a hand through my hair and pulled me up again only to thrust hard, back into my mouth, choking off my chuckle at his impatience. Obliging him, I let him fuck my mouth mercilessly, knowing my throat would be sore the next day from the assault, but not caring in the least. He moved me up and down his shaft, driving into me with a purpose. I sucked him hard with each thrust and let my tongue lick around his tip when I could. When was the last time anyone had given him such pleasure?

He kept a steady rhythm, and his cock spilled more and more precum into my mouth as I sucked him down over and over. I knew he was close, and after another long pull, he stilled, gripping my head firmly in his hands, trying to pull me off.

"Holy fuck. You better stop unless you want me to come."

Babe, it was you doing all the work.

I lifted off only to encourage him to let go, "Do it, Z. I want to taste you."

With one hand massaging his balls and the other moving along in time with my mouth, up and down his shaft, it only took two more thrusts for him to come unglued. His fingers gripped my hair painfully hard as he arched his back yelling.

"Tanner...Fuuuck...Gawwddd!"

His hot saltiness hit the back of my throat as I swallowed him down, milking him for every last drop as he shuddered, releasing his death grip on my hair and falling back on the bed limp and spent.

I crawled up to him, lying alongside his body and took him into a deep kiss, letting him taste himself on my tongue. He groaned again and plunged his tongue further inside, licking, sucking, and sharing what he'd given me.

"Fuck." He released my mouth, panting, and flopped back on the bed. "I wasn't expecting that. I-I thought you were going to fuck me senseless, not suck my brains out through my dick." If I wasn't mistaken, he seemed a little embarrassed.

Smiling, I stroked a thumb along his flushed cheek, gazing deep into his hooded, sated eyes. "Oh, I'm not finished with you yet, babe. I've only just begun." His eyes widened as he studied me with a smile.

"Oh?"

"Catch your breath." I took his hand and wrapped it around my aching cock, encouraging him to stroke it. "I want to sink this deep inside you and fuck you into the bed until you come so hard you can't move until tomorrow."

Zander sucked in a breath between clenched teeth. "Shitballs, Tanner. I'm on board with that."

I couldn't contain my laughter. "So now I know how to get all those bad words out of you. Just turn you inside out with an earth-shattering orgasm, and they're unstoppable."

Zander blushed deep red, down his neck and to his ears. "Shut up and kiss me again."

We kissed lazily for a while, letting our hands explore what was new for both of us. We couldn't seem to get enough of each other's mouths, and if my lips were a reflection of his than they were red, swollen, and raw. Worth it.

"Tanner," his lips never parted from mine as he worked the words around our kiss, "I can't wait anymore. I'm ready. I want to feel you inside me."

He shuffled his body closer. He wasn't kidding. He was already semi-hard again after maybe only fifteen minutes, and he rutted himself against my leg, dry humping me as he worked my length in his hand. I reclaimed his mouth, urging him to lie back again. The kiss turned hungry and heavy, both of us needing more.

Breaking free from his lips, I grinned. "Give me a second."

Jumping off the bed, I ran to my dresser for supplies. I tossed them down beside Zander and lay alongside him again, kissing him and urging his thighs apart. I popped the lid on the bottle of lube and coated my fingers.

Staring into his flushed face, I nibbled his bottom lip as I worked my them inside him one at a time, stretching him and preparing him to take me. He wrapped his hands around my neck, holding me close as he pressed down on the invasion, encouraging and accepting me greedily. Watching him beg with his body was the most beautiful thing I'd ever seen.

"I need you, Tanner. Please."

"I don't want to hurt you."

"I'm ready. Give me your dick. Please."

Settling between his legs, I admired his beautiful form as I grabbed the condom wrapper and held it in my mouth for a second more while I pressed his knees back and exposed his beautiful hole.

Shifting my eyes to watch him, I took my length and ran it over the outside of his heated entrance, feeling his warmth against me. None of it felt real. Zander underneath me, opening up, waiting for me to take him had been nothing more than a dream up until then. I slicked my cock against his entrance, enjoying the sensation of sliding along his crack. He bucked his hips, pressing himself against me, but I stilled him, pulling away and shaking my head.

"Not yet, babe. I'm not ready. I just wanted to feel you like that. You feel good. Really good." I tore open the wrapper with my teeth and rolled the condom down my length before lubing it up.

"Please, Tanner. Hurry up."

I chuckled as I fell down on top of him, bracing myself with my elbows on either side. "You're more anxious than me. How is that possible?" He didn't answer, only fisted my hair again, pulling me into a deep throated kiss.

Breaking free, resting our foreheads together, I watched his kiss-swollen lips as I pressed against his tight hole, edging myself inside.

"God. Yes!" Zander took his bottom lip in his teeth and bit down, staring up with lust filled eyes. He was so breathtaking in that moment, so beautiful it took all of my self-control not to ram right into his ass in one good hard thrust.

I never wanted it to end. I wanted to have him like that, under me and around me forever. In fear of scaring him off, I didn't say anything and simply continued to press slowly inside him, past his tight ring and further until I bottomed out and my balls rested against his ass. We both sighed together while I watched him closely.

"You okay?" I asked.

He nodded and gripped his hands on my hips, urging me to move. So I did.

As our bodies move together, unhurried and languidly, pleasure mounted behind his eyes. His breathing became uneven, and his nails dug into my sides, encouraging me to move faster and harder.

"More," he begged, lifting his body up to meet my every thrust. "God, Tanner, like that. Right there."

I lifted off him and hooked his legs over my shoulders to give him what he needed. Finding that sweet spot, our sensual rhythm turned heavy and rough as I slammed savagely into his body over and over. His control slipped away, and his cock wept, begging to be touched, leaving strings of cum running down to his stomach.

"Let go, babe. Come for me, I'm right behind you."

Zander reached down and fisted himself, tugging along with my every deep thrust. It didn't take much before thick jets of cum shot out of him, covering his taut abs.

"Fuuuuuckk, Tanner."

I fell onto him, keeping pace as his muscles tightened around me, tipping me over the edge. With two more hard thrusts, I pressed deep inside him as my orgasm ripped through my body.

We both stared at each other in disbelief as the last trembling shudders rippled through us and our breathing slowly calmed. The moment was surreal.

"Fuck, I love you so much, Zander. I feel like my heart might explode." And it was the honest to God truth. I'd never felt that way in my entire life.

I kissed him hard and deep, thrusting my tongue around the contours of his mouth, loving and taking all that I could until my cock began to soften. I slid out and rolled to my side.

Removing the condom and disposing of it into the wastebasket beside the bed, I then snapped up the towel Zander had dropped earlier from the floor to clean us up.

I pulled Zander into my arms and held him tight to my body. His eyes were heavy with sleep as he snuggled into my side. Just as I was drifting off, he drew his head up from my chest, regarding me with a hazy, deeply satisfied smile.

"You okay?" I asked.

"More than okay. I just need you to know something."

"Mmm...What's that?"

He traced his fingers over my cheek and brushed a soft kiss on my lips. "I love you too. I think I might have loved you for a while now, only I was too afraid to see it until now."

His words rendered me speechless, and all I could do was take pleasure in the moment in front of me. I drew him back into my arms and held him. That was exactly where I wanted to be. Nothing could have been more perfect.

Chapter Twenty-Four

Zander

My stomach woke me with an audible groan before the sun the following morning, and it was then when I realized we'd forgone supper the previous night in exchange for better activities. I smiled at the memory and nudged my happily aching ass against the warm body at my back, reveling in Tanner's comforting arms surrounding me. He pulled me snug against his body and buried his face into my neck, still snoring softly.

I'd been conflicted all week over how I felt, but last night when Tanner stood from the couch and looked at me the way he had, the scrambled puzzle in my head became crystal clear. I knew what I wanted beyond a shadow of a doubt, and that morning, I harbored no guilt or regret for my decision. For once in my life, I was content to just be. Everything was aligned and right in my world and the burden of worry I'd carried for so long evaporated completely when I gave myself permission to trust Tanner.

Carefully peeling myself from under the comforting weight of his arm, I slid out of bed and headed to the bathroom. Once I cleaned up and brushed my teeth, I found something to wear and went to the kitchen to put together some breakfast. I'd promised to cook dinner the previous night, but since those plans had fallen by the wayside, I figured an awesome breakfast was a must.

Rooting around in the fridge, I found some eggs, a gnarly looking basket of mushrooms that curled my nose—I tossed them in the garbage—and an almost empty container of milk. We really needed to grocery shop. I scanned the counter and found a half a loaf of bread. Placing the eggs and milk on the counter beside the bread, I then fished in the cupboard for a frying pan. French toast it was going to be.

Before starting on the food, I set the coffee pot to brew so it would be ready by the time I was finished.

I was just dunking the bread in the egg mixture and placing it into the pan when I heard feet padding up behind me. Before I could turn around, arms linked around my waist and a wet mouth nuzzled into my neck, kissing me.

"Morning. I'm making French toast. Are you hungry?"

"Starving. I think we missed dinner."

"I was going to cook for you, but you distracted me."

He chuckled, tickling my ear. "I distracted you? I seem to remember it the other way around." He nudged his stiffening length against the crack of my ass. "Either way it was worth missing a meal."

With the egged bread sizzling gently in the pan, I turned in his arms and was rewarded with soft lips right away against my own. I was still amazed at how fantastic they felt. It was a shocking bonus last night when we'd started kissing, and I learned just how skilled Tanner was with his tongue. I'd never been kissed like that before. Between those memories and the kiss I was presently receiving, my own cock reawakened, and I pressed against him, earning me a groan.

"I sure as hell hope this isn't a dream, Z. I'll cry for a week, I swear it."

"Not a dream, but if you don't stop kissing me like this, we'll likely starve to death because I'll be taking you back to bed without breakfast."

"It'd be worth it." He reclaimed my mouth and kissed me until my knees threatened to buckle. The smell of burning made me spring away.

"Shit." I turned in haste to flip the French toast and grimaced at the overly darkened side that had been facing down. "Pour some coffee," I said over my shoulder, "while I try to salvage this."

Tanner slapped my ass, and I winced at the slight tenderness from the previous night's ministrations. What Tanner didn't know was just how long it'd been since I'd had sex like that. I'd quit letting Paul use me that way two years ago and kept him sated with blowjobs to shut him up. It wasn't often that he'd even reciprocate. Basically, I'd been so eager to have Tanner inside me, I'd hardly let him prep me properly. But thinking back brought a smile to my face. It was worth it.

I slid the French toast onto plates and brought them to the table where Tanner sat watching me as he sipped his coffee.

"I love seeing that smile on your face."

"What smile?" Sitting across from him, I could feel said smile growing.

"The new one you seem to have developed in the last two weeks. I haven't seen you look this happy since I met you."

"I blame you." I stabbed a few bites of food onto my fork and shoved them in my mouth as I watched him with a grin.

"I'd love to be the reason it's there every day."

There was that look again. Tanner looked at me like I hung the moon. No one had ever looked at me like that. In that moment, I was the center of his universe, and nothing else mattered. There was so much love in his eyes it made me frightened and exhilarated all at the same time because I knew whatever was between us held so much possibility that together we could do anything.

After we cleaned up breakfast, Tanner headed into work for a little while for a session with a client, so I decided to grab some groceries and replenish the empty fridge and cupboards. I also decided it might be nice to grab a few extra things and make us a nice dinner.

Using a post-it, I wrote a quick list of items I needed, found my backpack, and headed out to catch the bus to the store.

Being out of the house still brought on a sense of anxiety I couldn't quite shake. I was constantly looking over my shoulder and scanning the crowds for signs of Paul. If I let my mind get carried away, I could still put myself into an all-out panic attack just by thinking about running into him. It was getting better, but it wasn't gone, not by a longshot.

The grocery store was crowded, and I worked my way up and down the aisles, placing carefully selected items into the cart as I went. I wasn't much of a cook, but I thought I'd try to make beef barley stew and homemade biscuits for dinner that evening. It was a wintertime staple in Ray and Georgina's house when I'd lived there. I'd watched Georgina put it together enough times I figured I could probably pull it off or at least fake it.

With everything I needed for dinner, along with a new loaf of bread, eggs, bacon, milk, and some fruit, I checked out and waited to catch the bus home.

While riding the bus back to Tanner's, I shot him a quick text to see when he thought he'd be home and told him I was cooking and wanted to have it ready for him. He said he planned to be home by five.

After chopping the veggies, searing the beef chunks and setting everything to stew on the stove, I felt restless and worked to straighten the apartment. It was just past four when I flopped down on the couch, deciding what to do next.

The apartment smelled amazing, and my stomach growled. I hoped it tasted as good as it smelled. Figuring I was good on time, I decided to hop in a quick shower and then start the biscuits before Tanner got home.

In my bedroom, I rooted through my drawers to find clean clothes. The picture Tanner had drawn for my birthday sat balanced on top of the dresser. With my clothes in one hand, I picked it up and sat down on the bed to look at it. I'd spent hours just indulging in its beauty. No one had ever made me anything like that before, and looking at it always warmed my heart. That evening, it brought even more feelings to the surface. The previous night I'd told Tanner I loved him as well. It was the truth. I couldn't pinpoint the day it had happened, why, or how, but I knew it was true. When I'd decided to trust Tanner with everything that was going on in my life, and he'd stood beside me through thick and thin, I'd given him a piece of my heart even then.

I carefully replaced the picture on my dresser and looked around at my room. Seven years, and for the first time, I felt free. I could make my own choices and do my own thing. I didn't know how much I'd missed it until I truly got it back.

After a quick shower, I worked at making the biscuits for dinner. It was just after five when Tanner got home.

"Oh my God, it smells amazing in here. If you are some kind of secret chef I'm going to be really sad you didn't tell me sooner. I've been feeding you PB and J for weeks now."

"Not a chef, I assure you."

Tanner came into the kitchen and scooped me into his arms like it was the most natural thing and we'd been together forever.

"Is it okay to do this?" he asked holding my hips and pulling me against his body.

"I should hope so." I laughed. "You had your dick in my ass last night, so I think we aren't strangers."

"I know, but I didn't know if maybe you'd spent all day thinking about it and changed your mind."

Hooking my hands around his neck, I pulled him into a quick kiss. "Nope. Still on board."

"Thank God." Glancing at the pot on the stove he quirked a brow. "Seriously though, what smells so good?"

"Beef barley stew. It's ready to go when you are. It can wait if you want to shower."

"Ok. I'll be right back. God that sounds amazing."

Once Tanner was back, I had the table set, bowls filled, and a plate of warm biscuits ready to go. We sat across from one another and enjoyed our meal—which turned out to be pretty darn good.

"Do you have a lot of clients this week?" I asked after he told me about the session he'd finished that day on a guy's calf. He'd outlined the beginnings of what would eventually be Altair from Assassins Creed.

"Not many. A few, but I get a lot of walk-ins so you never know. I keep spots open in case any of them are big jobs that need more sitting time."

"Hmm." I glanced up from my meal and watched him as he dunked his biscuit in his soup and shoved another piece into his mouth. "I was wondering…" Chewing my lip, I waited for him to look up.

"Yeah, what's up?"

"Will you tattoo me?"

He stopped mid-chew and tilted his head as a smile broke across his face. "Really?"

"Yeah. I've been thinking about it, and I want that drawing you made for me on my arm. It's my body and my choice, right?"

"Fuck yeah it is, Z. Oh my God. Yes, I'll tattoo you."

It was great to see him share my enthusiasm. "Promise you won't hurt me. I'm kind of a wimp."

"Oh boy." He chuckled as he pushed his bowl aside, standing from the table. "I can't promise that. But I can promise to make it up to you afterward."

"Is that so?" I helped him gather the dishes, and we brought them into the kitchen. "And how did you plan to do that?"

Setting the dishes aside, he then backed me out of the kitchen to the living room, landing me on the couch. "Like this." Straddling my lap, his mouth came down on mine in a powerful, consuming kiss that turned me to jelly on the spot. Our tongues tangled together as our hands found their way to each other's bodies. His held my head and gripped my hair, while mine roamed under his shirt to follow the curves of his muscles around his torso to his back. I was hard in an instant and Tanner pressed himself to me, letting me know he was aware and was in a similar state.

"I could get used to this," he said into our kiss before biting down on my lower lip and sucking it into his mouth.

I moaned at the assault. "Me too."

With Tanner's mouth set on mine, exploring and tasting, I brought my hands down to his strained pants and gave him some room with the pop of a button. He lifted his body and worked with me to shimmy his pants down his legs, never releasing his hold on my lips. I loved every part of his kiss. His taste, his warmth, the way he was rough and gentle all at the same time. I never wanted it to end, but the idea of having his cock in my mouth and working him until he shot his cum down my throat was almost a stronger desire.

Reluctantly, I broke free of our kiss and cupped his bare ass, encouraging him to rise up higher while I slouched down from where I sat. When Tanner caught on, he moved higher and aligned his cock with my mouth. He was already slick and dripping, and I licked my lips in anticipation as I peered up at him.

"Is this what you want?" He ran his wet tip over my waiting lips, and I nodded. "It's all yours, Z."

I flicked my tongue and licked a trail over his leaking slit. The taste of him exploded on my tongue, and I needed more. I took his head in my mouth and played my tongue around, rolling it over the top before inching my way down in an agonizingly slow move to his base making him shudder.

"That feels incredible." His fingers laced through my hair and he held me tight while letting me control the pace.

I sucked in my cheeks and pulled up with the same teasing speed. Tanner couldn't keep still any longer, and he pressed me forward again encouraging me to take his length back down my throat where I worked his tip and sucked back up again. I increased my rhythm until he was moaning and whimpering above me.

"Jesus you're good at that." As if his words weren't reward enough, his cock dripped more into my mouth as though affirming what he'd said.

I continued to work his cock until he was fucking into my mouth without abandon. I knew he was close. Moving a hand to his balls, I rolled them, and they drew up at my touch. In the next instant, his sweet, salty juices poured down my throat, and I was not giving up a single drop as I drank him down.

When his orgasm subsided, he collapsed on the couch beside me, limp. "Holy Fuck, that was amazing."

I couldn't help the grin of satisfaction as I leaned over him and latched onto his neck, kissing my way to his lips. "Amazing for me too. Thank you."

He watched me through sated, hooded eyes. "Take your pants off and feed me your cock like you did last night. I'm so returning the favor."

"You," I kissed his grinning mouth as I unbuttoned my jeans, "are awfully demanding."

"Says the guy who took over all control of the blowjob last night."

A while later, after more than one satisfying orgasm, we lay naked under a blanket on the couch, limbs entwined and watched a movie on Netflix. My eyes were heavy, and I knew I wouldn't be awake come the end of it. For once, I didn't worry about it and allowed my body to drift off. I was happy. The man curled around me made me feel safe and cared for. It was a freeing feeling, one that wasn't familiar, but one I was certainly getting used to.

Chapter Twenty-Five

Tanner

With only three weeks until Christmas, I'd ended up too busy at the shop to fit in Zander's first sitting. I'd so badly wanted to get started on his tattoo, but had been forced to put it off until that day. The shop was relatively quiet, and Zander was meeting me after work to kick off his first session. We planned to get the outline drawn on and see how he tolerated the pain before moving forward. If he did well, I was hoping to start working in some of the colors as well.

I wasn't sure if his complaints about his pain threshold were real or exaggerated. If he was someone who needed a lot of sessions to get through it because he could only take it in small doses, then it would probably take a couple of weeks. The tattoo was a significant size. I'd seen it before. Some of the biggest, scariest guys I'd tattooed turned out to be the wimpiest customers. You never could tell.

Zander arrived just before six thirty, and by that time, T.J was the last person in the shop with me and was packing up to go.

"Hey, Z." T.J clapped him on the shoulder when he entered. "I saw the piece, man. She's a beauty and Tanner's game work is fucking brilliant. It's going to look amazing."

"Thanks. Yeah, I'm really excited."

Zander dropped his backpack on the floor just inside the door, hung his coat on the hook and wandered inside the shop with hands deep in his pockets—a telltale sign of anxiety which I'd learned to recognize in him.

"Anyhow. I'm out. Good luck. See you tomorrow, Tanner. Bye, Z."

"See ya," we both said as T.J left.

"So, how you holding up? You look nervous." That was an understatement. His feet hadn't stopped shuffling since he'd walked in and his forehead gleamed with sweat.

"I am." He blew out a breath and shook his head. "But I want to do this. I'll be okay."

"We can take it as slow as you need. Even if it takes a ridiculous amount of sessions. We'll get through it, okay?"

"Okay."

"Come on. Take your shirt off and have a seat in this fancy, cushy chair over here and try to relax." Indicating to my station, I gave him a wink. "I got everything ready to go before you got here."

Once he settled and I was washed and gloved up, we worked at fitting the transfer onto his arm in the exact spot he wanted it. The tattoo was going to be a decent size when it was done, taking up a good portion of his upper arm and traveling down to almost his elbow.

With the drawing in place, I filled my pot with black ink, opened my sterile package of needles and sat back, ready to work. Zander had his bottom lip firm between his teeth and was staring at his arm where the design lay. I leaned in, drawing his attention and kissed him softly.

"You ready?"

"Yes," he said lying back in his seat. "I'm going to close my eyes and try to think of something else while you work."

"Okay. Puppies and rainbows. If you need me to stop, let me know."

I watched as he tried desperately to look relaxed. He took each breath with measured, exaggerated effort. His determination made me smile as I grabbed my iron and moved my ink to have it close at hand. With a rag ready, I ran a hand over my empty canvas—Zander's arm.

"You ready? Here I go."

Lowering my iron to his skin, starting up top near his shoulder, I began. Barely having made a mark, Zander sucked in a breath as the needle pierced his skin.

"Jesus snapping duckturds, that hurts."

Pulling back again, I burst out laughing. "You can't make me laugh, potty mouth, or I'll fuck up."

"Sorry. Keep going, I'm okay." He sucked his bottom lip in his teeth and bit down, nodding for me to continue.

He was too adorable. What a contradiction he was going to be, walking around all tatted up and incapable of swearing unless he was being turned inside out in bed.

We worked for the following hour and put down the majority of the outline. Zander decided after about ten minutes that it wasn't as horrendous as he'd expected and he might manage to actually get the tattoo finished that year. After a while, he was even brave enough to watch me work.

"You stick your tongue out when you concentrate. Did you know that?"

"No, I don't." I issued him a dirty look before I kept going, suddenly conscious of my tongue placement. Damn if he wasn't right. The minute I forgot to be aware of it, I caught my stupid tongue lulling out of my mouth.

The outlining took a decent amount of time, and Zander decided we should stop for the night because he couldn't sit still any longer. Also, he was starving, and his stomach was making ungodly noises that kept making us laugh.

I packed up my station as he admired the beginnings of his ink with a wide grin on his face.

"You like it so far?"

"I love it. I can't wait until it's done. It's going to look amazing."

Joining him at the mirror where he was giving himself a three-hundred and sixty-degree view, I leaned in and kissed his cheek.

"I love seeing you so happy."

He met my eyes in the mirror and leaned in. "I like feeling this happy. Thank you, Tanner."

"You did this. Not me. It was your bravery that made the decision to take your life back."

"But it was trusting you when you said I deserved better that made me believe in myself enough so that I could do it."

"I'm proud of you nonetheless." Wrapping my arms around his waist, I kissed his neck, bringing my mouth to his ear. "Come on. Let's go get some dinner in that belly and go home."

* * *

Zander handled the rest of the tattoo like a boss, and we managed to finish it over the course of the week. Once it was healed, I planned to go over it and touch up anything that might need it.

It was one week before Christmas and Zander's daycare was closed for the holidays until January. I'd taken some time off as well, booking new clients into the New Year so we could spend some time together just him and me.

Mother Nature had gotten the memo about winter's arrival, and it had been snowing steadily over the past three days. After a lazy morning in bed, exchanging blow jobs and messing around on Halo—where I got my ass handed to me more times than I could count—we decided to have a late breakfast at the café down the road.

Bundled up in our winter gear, we headed through the bustling, busy street to our destination, being mindful of the Christmas shoppers who were everywhere and had little to no consideration for people outside their own bubbles.

We found a vacant table in the corner of the little coffee house and shed our coats, hanging them over the backs of our chairs. The fireplace in the little shop made it cozy and warm, and we were both pleasantly comfortable in just our t-shirts. We ordered a couple of coffees and breakfast wraps.

Leaning up against the counter as we waited for them to be made, Zander linked his fingers in mine and shifted his body close to lean up against me. We'd never discussed public affection but the gesture told me where Zander stood on the matter, and I didn't mind having him plastered to my side in the least. I brought his fingers up and kissed his knuckles as he smiled back. We were so lost in our own world that the thundering, angry voice booming across the small café made us both jump.

"You've got to be fucking kidding me."

Zander's whole body went rigid, his eyes became saucers, and his fingers fell from my grasp to his side. I knew who it was even before I turned around.

Spinning in place, I found Paul less than five feet away and closing in fast. Instinctively, I put my body in front of Zander's, in case the guy was stupid enough to try anything in public.

"Don't be an idiot, Paul."

He ignored my warning and tried to move around me. I shuffled and blocked him. Zander still hadn't moved. He was rooted and frozen in terror.

"Are you serious, Zander? Tell me you're not fucking this piece of shit now. Are you out of your mind? This asshole told you to press charges against me, didn't he? Why? So you could run to his bed? Jesus fuck!"

He tried again to get around me, and I stepped in his way.

"Paul, stop!" It was like I wasn't even there. His focus was all on Zander, and I was just an obstacle he continued to dodge. Suddenly, he stopped abruptly and narrowed his eyes, scanning over my shoulder.

"What the hell is that shit on your arm? Did you let him do that to you too? What the fuck were you thinking?" In the following moment, I was physically shoved out of the way.

"Paul!" I got my face right in front of him so he had no choice but to look at me. "Back down and leave him alone. You aren't even supposed to be near him."

For the first time since opening his mouth, he turned his attention on me. All his attention and all his rage. Not going to lie, I nearly pissed my pants. It was like facing off with King Kong.

Paul took note of my protective stance and straightened his body to his full height, pulling the intimidation degree up a few more notches. Well, it wasn't going to work, even if the guy could probably flatten me with one arm tied behind his back, and even though all my instincts told me to run screaming like a little girl. I refused to move.

"You'll need to go through me, asshole. Zander is not your fucking play toy anymore, and if you don't turn around and walk out that door, I'll call the cops. They will arrest your ass, and you know it so—Back. Off."

He fisted my shirt and got in my face. I gulped. "Get out of my way you son of a bitch."

I moved into his fist, hoping he didn't see the fear coursing through me—because I was trembling like a leaf. I got so close to his face, I breathed his air. "Zander, babe, call the cops." It shocked even me when my voice came out clear and confident sounding.

I couldn't look behind me to see if Zander was doing as I asked because my eyes were locked on Paul's and there was no way I was breaking our stare down. Fearing Zander wouldn't find enough courage to do it, I kept pressing.

"Zander. I need you to trust me. You said you could trust me, babe. Trust me now. Call the police."

I finally heard him come to life behind me and a shuffling told me he was doing as I asked. Paul glimpsed over my shoulder, and his fist fell from my shirt, shoving me backward.

"Fuck it. I'm leaving." He stepped back a few feet, and I turned to Zander who was holding his phone, ready to dial, glaring at Paul.

The fear was gone. His chest rose and fell with the effects of his rapid breathing, but he looked so brave and confident in that moment. Without saying a word, he was sending a message to Paul, letting him know he was no longer his to control.

When Paul stopped his retreat, Zander raised a finger to his phone and quirked a brow. "Go," he warned.

It was Paul's last chance, and he went. Once the door closed behind him and the people in the café—who'd stopped to watch the show—returned to their meals, Zander fell into my arms and hugged me with a ferocity I wasn't expecting.

"That was the scariest thing I've ever done," he admitted. I wasn't the only one trembling.

I returned his embrace, squeezing him back, whispering in his ear, "And the bravest. I'm really proud of you, Z."

After a somber breakfast, both of us mostly picking at our food, we wandered back toward the apartment.

"Are you okay?" I asked.

"Yeah. Just need something to take my mind off it all. I hate letting him consume my thoughts."

"We'll find something to do at home. Maybe game some more or watch a flick?"

"Sure."

Midway down the block, Zander spun, halting me in the middle of the street with two hands on my shoulders. His face lit up, and I could visibly see his mood shift as an idea struck him.

"I know. We need a Christmas tree. It's almost Christmas, and we don't have one. We should go get a tree and decorations."

"Seriously? I haven't had one since I lived at home."

"Oh my God. What is wrong with you? That is not okay. Come on, we need to go shopping."

And that was that, Zander clasped my hand and dragged me down the street. We went in and out of all kinds of stores until we had bags full of Christmas decorations hanging off our arms including a small, pre-lit Christmas tree—apparently, I was Tanner Mc. Grinchy Pants because I wouldn't agree to have a real one. We were loaded to the gills as we made our way back home. We spent the rest of the afternoon decorating the tree and making the apartment look more festive.

Zander put on Christmas music, danced around and sang in a way I'd never seen him before. I liked that Zander. He was free, fun, and completely uninhibited. The weight of the world no longer dragged him down, and his smile was brighter than any of the lights we hung.

Later that evening, we sipped hot chocolate while we curled up together watching stupid comedies on Netflix. During an *Austin Powers* marathon, Zander did his best to recite all the lines along with Mike Myers until he was laughing so hard he couldn't keep up and ended up tumbling off the couch.

"That's what you get for trying to keep up with so many characters at once."

"Hey, if Mike Myers can do it, why not me too." He snorted, still unable to stop laughing.

As he repositioned himself beside me, snuggled into my side, I wrapped my arms around him tighter to keep him securely in place. As his laughing fit calmed, he tilted his head around to meet my gaze. His cheeks were flushed from his fit of giggles, and he leaned up and kissed me on the nose.

"What was that for?"

"Because I love you."

Just like that. It was simple and from the heart. Nothing complicated, just like what we had between us. Perfect. I traced a hand over the scruff on his chin and pecked him on the nose in response. "My God I love you, Z."

Chapter Twenty-Six

Zander

Angie and Brad had a party on Christmas Eve. It wasn't a huge gathering, but enough people were there that it made for a festively, fun celebration. Tanner and I arrived a little late and flush-cheeked due to some pre-party celebrating of our own.

"You're late." Angie kissed my cheek and then Tanner's before turning a skeptical eye between us. "And you're guilty looking."

"Sorry...We were just—" I was terrible with excuses and fumbled to find a response.

"Z was reinventing the swear word," Tanner said with a chuckle, slapping my ass and moving us into the house. "I'll get us a drink."

I watched him as he moved away before turning a mortified glance back to Angie's all too knowing grin. "No I wasn't." It came out far too defensively. I knew I was flaming red and all Angie could do was laugh. She took my hand and led me into the house.

"You two make the cutest couple."

Couple. I liked the sound of that.

Tanner and I had only just officially titled each other as boyfriends, and the more the word rang in my ears, the more it made me smile.

He'd worried about us moving too fast and how I felt over the whole situation so he'd been hesitant to bring it up. Having just left a seven-year relationship made Tanner tiptoe around subjects like that and had caused our budding relationship to backtrack some days when it should have been moving forward.

After much talking, Tanner was finally starting to see my point. True, I may have only walked away from Paul a month before, but in reality, our relationship had died years before. Paul and I had barely coexisted together, let alone had anything worth titling as a partnership. Tanner and I both understood I'd only stayed out of fear, not from love. I'd fallen out of love so long ago that I wasn't even sure if I'd ever truly loved him to begin with.

Angie steered me to the center of the party where people were chatting, and drinks were flowing. Everyone was enjoying the Christmas spirit. Tanner soon returned with two glasses of rum and eggnog sprinkled with cinnamon. Placing one in my hand, he kissed my lips and linked his fingers with mine. We worked our way around the room, mingling with the guests. There were so many strangers, but it didn't matter. It was the most fun I'd had in a long time. I was out of the house, hanging with friends and there was no unwelcomed fear following me around.

As the night moved on, the partygoers became more festive. Brad cranked up the Christmas tunes, and people started dancing all over the house. It was fun and freeing to be surrounded by people who were having such a good time. When one song ended and a Michael Bublé rendition of "I wish every day could be like Christmas" started to play, I took Tanner's and my drinks and put them down.

"What are you doing?"

I pressed my body to his and smiled up at him. "Dance with me?"

"I thought you didn't dance."

"I don't do the seedy club, grinding kind of dancing, but this is Christmas, and I like this song. Please."

Tanner laughed softly and dipped his head down to brush our lips together. "I'd love to, but I'm starting to think I may have over spiked your drink."

"Shut up and dance." I wrapped my arms around him, and we swayed to the soft Christmas tune.

We weren't the only two dancing, and even if we were, I wouldn't have cared. Resting my head on Tanner's shoulder, I breathed him in and closed my eyes. The moment was perfect. I couldn't have asked for anything more.

When the song came to an end, I opened my eyes and realized we'd moved from where we'd started out. I turned around to grab our drinks, but Tanner halted me, clasping my hand and pulling me back in.

"I think there are very strict rules about these sorts of things."

"Huh?" What the heck was he talking about?

My confusion showed, and Tanner pointed a finger to the ceiling. I craned my neck to look above us. The sly bugger had drifted us underneath a hanging mistletoe.

"I see." I smiled knowingly. "Rules are rules."

He dipped his head and claimed my mouth in a kiss that was borderline X-rated. It was dominating and sexy, and after only a minute, I pulled away panting and held him back with a hand because it was causing things to stir. Things I didn't need a house full of strangers to notice. He licked his lips and smirked.

"Later," he breathed in my ear before retreating into the room to find our drinks.

As it neared midnight, people began to say their goodbyes. We were the last two guests to leave, and Angie took us both into a simultaneous bear hug.

"Merry Christmas, you guys. I'm so glad you came."

"Merry Christmas, Angie." I kissed her cheek and Tanner did the same.

"Now go home and be good or Santa won't come," she said as she shoved us to the door.

"Oh, Santa's coming tonight, rest assured."

Angie and I groaned while Brad high-fived Tanner for his remark as they cracked up laughing.

"Go," Angie said, pushing us out the door.

We walked the few blocks back to our apartment hand in hand. The cold December air couldn't touch me. The warmth I felt came from deep inside, and it was all because of the man at my side.

When we got home, and out of our winter gear, Tanner settled on the couch while I raced down the hall to the room I used to occupy—we'd turned it into a storage room since I'd moved into the bedroom with Tanner.

"Where are you going?" Tanner called after me.

I came back with a large box wrapped in Christmas paper and a red bow. "Here. Merry Christmas."

"Seriously? You got me a present? Where the hell have you been hiding this? I thought we said no presents."

"It was in the spare room. It wasn't exactly hiding unless sitting in the middle of the floor in plain view for the last week is considered concealed? You really never go in there, do you?"

"Nope. But I don't get it, we pinky swore, no presents."

"I haven't made a pinky swear since I was a ten-year-old girl, I don't know what you're talking about. Besides, I had my fingers crossed, so it canceled it out."

"Z, you didn't have to do this."

"I know. I wanted to. It's been on my mind for a long time."

I laid it in his lap and knelt in front of him since it took up the better part of his lap and the space beside him.

"Open it."

Tanner sighed and smiled as he made a display of picking one piece of tape off at a time, placing them on my shirt.

"You're an ass," I said.

"Language, potty mouth. I think I'm a bad influence on you."

I swatted his arm away when he tried to put another piece of tape on me, and we both laughed. He ripped the rest of the paper off with more enthusiasm than a toddler to reveal what was inside.

His mouth fell open at the sight. "Zander." It was a Fender Stratocaster Electric guitar. Nowhere near as epic as some of the ones I'd researched online, but the perfect learning guitar—or so the guy at the store had assured me.

"Open the envelope, there's more."

"More?" Tanner cast a glance at me before detaching the sealed envelope from the box. Inside were coupons for six months of guitar lessons. Tanner's mouth hung open, and he kept shaking his head. "I can't believe you did this. I don't know what to say."

"A while back you said it was a dream you had. I wanted to make your dream come true because you've done so much for me."

Putting the guitar aside, Tanner pulled me up into his arms to straddle his lap. "You are a dream come true, Z. Thank you. No one has ever done anything this thoughtful for me. How can I compete with this? I thought we agreed not to exchange presents."

"I know. I didn't want you to get me anything. You've given me more than anyone ever has already." He looked confused, so I added, "You gave me your friendship, Tanner, and you gave me your heart. As hard as it was for you, you never gave up on me."

"I do love you, Zander."

"And I love you, Tanner. Merry Christmas."

The end

About the Author

Nicky James lives in the small town of Petrolia, Ontario, Canada. She is a mother to a wonderful teenage boy and wife to a truly supportive and understanding husband who, thankfully, doesn't think her crazy.
Nicky has always had two profound dreams in life; to fall back hundreds of years in time and live in a simpler world and to write novels. Since only one of those dreams was a possibility, she decided to make the other come alive on paper.
Nicky writes MM romance books in a variety of styles including contemporary, medieval, fantasy, and historical.

Other Titles by Nicky James

Standalone Contemporary

Trusting Tanner

Twinkle Star

Love Me Whole

Rocky Mountain Refuge

The Christmas I Know

Trials of Fear

Owl's Slumber

Shades of Darkness

Touch of Love

Fearless (A companion novel)

Healing Hearts Series

No Regrets (available in audio)

New Beginnings: Abel's Journey (available in audio)

The Escape: Soren's Saga

Lost Soul: AJ's Burden

Taboo

Sinfully Mine

Historical

Until the End of Time

Steel My Heart

Tales from Edovia Series

Something from Nothing

Buried Truths

Secrets Best Untold

Made in the USA
Monee, IL
05 May 2022